THE INFINITE BLACKTOP

THE INFINITE BLACKTOP

A NOVEL

SARA GRAN

ATRIA BOOKS

New York   London   Toronto   Sydney   New Delhi

ATRIA
BOOKS

An Imprint of Simon & Schuster, Inc.
1230 Avenue of the Americas
New York, NY 10020

First Atria Books hardcover edition September 2018

ATRIA BOOKS and colophon are trademarks of Simon & Schuster, Inc.

For information about special discounts for bulk purchases, please contact Simon & Schuster Special Sales at 1-866-506-1949 or business@simonandschuster.com.

The Simon & Schuster Speakers Bureau can bring authors to your live event. For more information, or to book an event, contact the Simon & Schuster Speakers Bureau at 1-866-248-3049 or visit our website at www.simonspeakers.com.

Interior design by Dana Sloan

Manufactured in the United States of America

10 9 8 7 6 5 4 3 2 1

Library of Congress Cataloging-in-Publication Data

Names: Gran, Sara, author.
Title: The Infinite blacktop : a novel / Sara Gran.
Description: First Atria Books hardcover edition. | New York : Atria Books, 2018. | Includes bibliographical references and index.
Identifiers: LCCN 2018026234 (print) | LCCN 2018030598 (ebook) | ISBN 9781501165733 (eBook) | ISBN 9781501165719 (hardcover : alk. paper)
Subjects: LCSH: Women private investigators—Fiction. | Murder—Investigation—Fiction. | GSAFD: Mystery fiction.
Classification: LCC PS3607.R362 (ebook) | LCC PS3607.R362 I54 2018 (print) | DDC 813/.6—dc23
LC record available at https://lccn.loc.gov/2018026234

ISBN 978-1-5011-6571-9
ISBN 978-1-5011-6573-3 (ebook)

Kill all the wise men. Burn all the books. The kingdom of truth is your birthright, and the only thing standing in between you and the kingdom is your own monstrous, idiotic, self.

JACQUES SILETTE, *DÉTECTION*

THE INFINITE BLACKTOP

CHAPTER 1

THE CASE OF THE INFINITE BLACKTOP

Oakland, 2011

I fell into consciousness with a sudden, frightening, crash. My eyes popped open into a line of bright white-hot pain. I couldn't see anything except blinding light. I squeezed my eyes back shut.

I gasped for air—

Remember, remember.

I guess I screamed, because I heard someone scream and then I felt someone squeeze my hand and say, "You're OK. You're OK."

I stopped screaming.

Thoughts fell into my head. Accident. I'd been in a car accident.

I remembered something huge and metal cracking through the door of my car and started screaming again.

"OK, easy," the voice said. The voice was a man's, fairly young, probably white.

I heard more sounds around the voice and felt cool air on my face. I was outside.

I heard another scream. Not me.

"I'll be right back," the voice said. "You're OK, just don't try to move."

He let go of my hand and left.

I knew who I was, but I couldn't form the words to understand it. My name was somewhere in my throat, but couldn't reach my mouth.

I tried moving. Some parts moved and some didn't. I tried raising my hand. It took a few tries for my mind to connect with my brain, then with my nerves, muscles, and flesh, but it all started working, and I lifted my hand to my eyes and tried opening them again. I forced myself not to scream. Better, but still painful. My hand was red and black against violently bright light. Pain ripped through my left eye and my eyes squeezed shut again.

Slowly, like ripping off a bandage, I opened my eyes again, and acclimated them to the light and me to the pain.

I looked around. I was in Brooklyn. No. San Francisco. No. Oakland. Yes. Oakland.

Everything in me screamed. Adrenaline screamed the loudest.

Think, think.

Who was I?

Claire DeWitt. I am Claire DeWitt, and I am—

Another memory fell in with a *thump*:

I'd been on the highway. The 80 to the 880 to—

It was a Lincoln. 1982. That was the thing that came cracking through my door.

Who was driving it? And how did I know that?

The image of the Lincoln hitting me washed over me again, erasing everything else. Everything started to go black again.

Think, think.

I remembered: *I am Claire DeWitt.*

Didn't I want to be a detective?

Yes. I wanted to be a detective, and I was.

I was Claire DeWitt, and I was the best detective in the world.

Think, Claire, think.

Was I on a case?

I'd figured out I was on some kind of gurney or bed. I sat up. My left leg and most of my ribs howled in protest. I was in an ambulance. The bright light above me was coming from the roof. The doors were open. I looked out.

The sun had gone down and it was dark. The car I'd been driving was a pile of broken metal and glass. The other screams—the screaming that wasn't mine—were coming from a woman across the street, who was standing above what was either a pile of clothes or a badly injured person. After another moment I saw that the screaming woman had blood pouring out of her head. An EMT worker, maybe the same one who'd been holding my hand a minute before, was trying to look at the woman's bloody forehead.

Lights blinked and blared from cop cars and ambulances. The black road glittered with glass and metal scraps. Around the ring of official responders was a circle of a few dozen citizens watching. The air had the smoky, bloody, disorienting smell and haze of a bad accident.

Remember, remember.

I was Claire DeWitt, the best detective in the world, and someone had just tried to kill me.

I took a deep breath. The woman who was screaming and bleeding—I'd seen her before the accident. She'd been standing across the street when I was hit.

"Holy shit," she'd said. "He's gonna kill her."

He.

My first clue.

I tried to remember the Lincoln without letting the memory overwhelm me. It was a direct hit: the car had driven right toward me, aiming for the driver's seat.

Not an accident. An attempted murder.

My second clue.

I looked around. I was on a broad street near Fruitvale.

I felt around in my clothes. No gun. Why didn't I have a gun?

I remembered: It had been in my car, taped under the passenger seat. Safer for driving. No way to get it now.

Then I gasped again and looked around with a start and realized: the Lincoln that had hit me wasn't here.

That car was a fucking monster. A near-murder would barely ding the chrome on the bumper. Whoever had tried to kill me was probably not too far away, waiting for their next chance.

I jumped off the gurney, then collapsed into a crouch when my legs crumpled from under me.

Think, Claire, think.

I sent my attention down to my legs, which were unwilling to stand. The right seemed OK. It was the left that didn't want to go anywhere. I put my weight on my right leg and pushed myself up. That was all right.

I stood, and looked around the accident scene again. I could use a gun. I could also use the cop attached to one of them.

Eight patrol officers. I knew plenty of cops in Oakland but I didn't know any of these cops. Seven men, one woman.

Think, think.

I realized my breath was so fast and shallow I was almost panting. I forced it to slow down. My left eye burned and my left leg screamed. The adrenaline flooding me made the pain tolerable, kept its sharp edges pushing me up and out instead of down and in.

I wasn't sure exactly where I was, or why, but something smart and mean took over. Something without words. Something that I knew would keep me alive, if I let it.

I looked around for something that would help me walk. I didn't see anything. I tried to move without help.

Pain shot up my left leg into my hip and I stifled a scream. I stopped. I tried moving my arms a little and they seemed to work OK. I took another step. Almost as bad.

I wasn't sure I could do it.

Do you want to live? I asked myself. Or do you want to stay here and die?

Swallowing the pain, one eye squeezed shut, I looked around and forced myself to be smart. On the floor of the ambulance was a big blue windbreaker, probably one of the EMTs'.

I looked at the cops. The closest one was the woman. She was standing by the crime scene, making sure no one fucked with my broken rental Kia.

I looked around. Everyone else was busy, most of them with the screaming woman.

I moved my arms a few more times, shook out my legs, grinding my teeth against the pain.

It's this or die, I told myself. It was an old line, and I'd used it on myself too many times before. But it still worked, because it was true.

I sat back down on the gurney. I looked around, mind racing, and saw a flashlight in a holder on the side of the ambulance. I grabbed the flashlight.

The lights from one of the cop cars flashed against the ambulance, red and blue and white. I took off my jacket and dropped it on the floor behind me, half on top of the windbreaker. There was a thin white sheet on the gurney and I added that to the pile. From a distance it would work well enough.

I stared at the cop and willed her to look at me, silently screaming to her. *Here is your destiny*, I screamed. *Here is where your eyes were meant to fall.*

After a minute she looked at me. When she saw that I was up she opened her mouth to call her coworkers but I put a finger to my lips—*shh*—and looked terrified. Which was easy, because I was terrified.

I had her eyes now. Half the war was won.

I pointed over my right shoulder, down toward where I'd ditched the clothes and sheet on the ambulance floor. With the uneven lighting, she couldn't tell what was behind me—a pile of clothes or a person.

He's here, I mouthed. I kept her eyes locked on mine.

Using the same finger, I cut a clean line across my throat.

He's going to kill me, I mouthed.

She put her hand on her gun and came toward me, stepping carefully in the dark night. Her skin was smooth and dark, the red and blue lights flashing over her face, beating out their ancient code of *help me, help me, help me*—

She stepped up to the ambulance slowly. As she got closer she got scared, and drew her gun. She was five feet away, then four, then one.

I put my hand on the flashlight.

I still looked terrified. I still was terrified.

She got to the entrance to the ambulance, gun out in her right hand.

"Don't scream," I said. She looked at me, confused—

Using every single ounce of power I could pull from the universe, in one quick quiet motion, I brought the flashlight down on her wrist.

She dropped the gun. God smiled on me. The gun landed on the floor of the ambulance and I grabbed it, struggling against blackness as the pain shot through my leg and up through my ribs as I twisted.

I held up the gun and pointed it at her.

"Don't scream," I said. "Don't say anything at all."

She looked pissed and scared and I didn't blame her.

"I'm not going to hurt you," I said. "Unless I have to. And don't feel bad," I said. "No one beats Claire DeWitt."

I couldn't remember everything. But I remembered that.

Claire DeWitt always wins.

She didn't say anything but I saw that she was thinking *We'll see.* That was about what I was thinking too. *We'll see.*

There was a first time for everything, and maybe this was it. Maybe this was the time I would lose.

"Now give me your radio," I said.

"What?" she said.

"Your radio," I said. "You're going to give me your radio, then I'm going to give you your gun back, and then I'm going to leave. And unless you want everyone to know that I stole your gun, and you want to spend the rest of your life answering phones at a desk, you're not going to tell anyone about it. You're going to say you have no idea what happened to your radio. That you must've lost it somewhere. Sound good?"

She looked around. She had a look on her face like she wanted to hit me. Like—

A face came into my head. Young. Big liquid eyes. Was that who was trying to kill me? No. A name came with the face with liquid eyes: Andray. I was going to look for Andray when I was hit. Why? The lama had called and said Andray, an old friend, who wasn't exactly a friend, was in trouble. The lama was another old friend. The lama and Nick Chang and Claude and Tabitha all fell back into my mind. And everyone I'd lost: Constance and Kelly and Paul and—

No. I could think about that later. What was important now was that I'd been going to look for Andray. No one knew except Claude and the lama. Did I trust them?

Yes. I trusted them.

I was going to look for Andray. There would be a change of plans now.

Now, I was very focused on helping myself.

Focus, Claire.

I looked at the cop. She was as angry as she was scared. Maybe more.

"No one's coming," I said to her. "No one's coming and no one's going to help you because this is what this is. This is what it is and this is exactly what was always meant to be."

As I spoke my words sounded odd, even to me. My voice was raspy and uneven. A breeze picked up and cool air blew on my face and my hand and the gun in it. My left eye seared and twitched.

But I knew those words were true. This was how it always was and always will be, exactly as it was meant to be.

Meant by who? Or what? That was a question I didn't count on ever knowing the answer to. At least not tonight. But I could feel it all the same. Right here, with this cop, with this gun, at this scene with blood in the air—

Something was beginning. And even more was ending.

The cop handed over her radio. I stuck it in the waistband of my pants.

"You wanted real life," I said to her. "Well here it is."

"Fuck you," she said, before she could stop herself.

"Fuck you too," I said. "And now you're giving me your Taser, too, 'cause I just don't trust you anymore."

I made myself get off the gurney and then step down to the pavement.

She didn't move. I was holding the gun down low, by my side, so no one would see it. Now I pressed it against her femoral artery in her leg. A kill shot.

"Taser," I said.

This time she handed it over. Her face was red-hot rage under her pretty dark skin.

"Go over there," I said, and pointed to the side of the ambulance, a good four feet from me. She did it. I crouched down and tossed the gun under the ambulance. I stood up.

"Now it's up to you," I said. "You can stop me, and end your career 'cause you let a PI everyone hates get your weapon away from you. Or you can buy a new Taser, let me go, and forget this ever happened."

"You're gonna pay for this," she said.

"I bet you're right," I said. I thought, but didn't say, *I already have, and steeply.*

She dove for the gun and I ran, or came as close to running as I could—really a kind of fast limping with one straight leg—grinding my teeth against a scream, and didn't stop until I was four blocks away, in the bathroom of a bar called The Dew Drop Inn, washing blood and glass out of my eyes.

Man. White Lincoln. 1982-ish. Not much to go on.

More of my self, and all that had happened to it, had come back as I ran. I was a detective. I solved mysteries. I had enemies. The Case of the Bird with Broken Wings. The Clue of the Misplaced Penny.

Plenty of people wanted me dead. I'd been a detective since I was a child. I'd solved mysteries no one wanted to solve. I'd cracked cases that had ruined lives and saved others.

But today, I realized, would have been a particularly hard day to kill me. I'd crashed my car a few weeks ago and was driving a rented Kia. I wasn't on an official case, just a personal one, which made me harder to track. No clients. No clues.

So a lot of people wanted me dead.

The question was: Who wanted me dead today?

CHAPTER 2

THE CLUE OF THE CHARNEL HOUSE

Brooklyn, 1985

The Case of the Drowned Girl was closed.

I knew the girl in the water. She was a year younger than me. Her heart was burnt black and I couldn't help but think, after fourteen years of burning, she was likely better off where she was.

Kelly and Tracy and I had worked the case together. We were fifteen. We were detectives. It was a ninety-degree night in July when we found her in the warm water of the Gowanus Canal, Brooklyn's most shameful body of water, face-down, tiny frame floating in a cloud of fabric from a white dress, dark skin gleaming, black hair spread around her like seaweed.

We laid it all out for the NYPD detective who showed up hours after the beat cops and the coroner. We knew dawn would break, at

least, before anyone other than us cared about the girl in the canal.
But when the detective showed up and we spelled it out for her—the
stepfather, the mother, the suicide, the other kid still in the house—
we realized it would be many, many dawns before anyone cared
about the girl in the canal. It would be until the earth wilted, until
time stopped, until the sun burned itself to a handful of dust, until
Judgment Day came and we were raised from our coffins and canals
and back-alleys and bedrooms, until we were called up to heaven and
then maybe, someone would care about the fucking girl in the canal.

Or more likely, at the end of time, our points would be added up
and our time cards punched and tests given and we would all of us
be found to be just as disposable as we were right now.

Dawn came and went. Then noon. I went home and tried to sleep.
I couldn't sleep and soon I got up again, and started drinking. It was
late afternoon.

That girl was just like me. Just like me and no one missed her.

Eight hours later I was alone in the playground, lying on a bench
above a pile of broken bottles that maybe I had broken, so drunk I
couldn't remember how I'd gotten there. I couldn't stop crying and
shaking and bleeding. I'd cut myself, I saw, with the broken glass.
Now I remembered: Yes; that was why I had broken it. To be done.
No one would miss me, either.

But two people did miss me. And they saved me.

———

On the first day of fourth grade in PS 108 in Brooklyn I sat next to
Tracy Farrell. Was it the first time I'd sat next to her? Was it the first
time we'd spoken? I don't know. I think so; I think, at least, it was
the first time we said more than a few words.

Then I spotted Tracy's Official Cynthia Silverton Girl Detective
Decoder Ring. She wore it on the ring finger of her left hand, as if
she were married.

Cynthia Silverton, teen sleuth and girl detective, was the closest thing I had to a friend. The fact that she was a fictional character was all the better. My relationships with actual people, fleshy and demanding, were a source of pain and confusion. But Cynthia was perfect. Especially in her imperfections.

I knew Cynthia from her monthly adventures in the *Cynthia Silverton Mystery Digest,* a periodical that ran comics, short stories about Cynthia, and real mysteries you could solve at home. I picked them up in the bookmobile that lurked around our neighborhood in lieu of an actual library. Cynthia was the best detective in her oddly crime-ridden hometown of Rapid Falls. Her parents killed in a mysterious automobile crash, Cynthia lived with her loving pagan housekeeper Mrs. McShane and was an A student at Rapid Falls Community College, where she was studying criminology under the wise tutelage of Professor Gold. Cynthia's life in wealthy and bright suburban America was as alien to me as the lives of the Yanomami of Brazil.

But I knew Cynthia was a detective. And somehow I knew that I was, too.

"Behind every woman's broken heart," said Professor Gold, when Cynthia had her moment of despair on the Case of the Scorpion's Tale, "is someone with a sledgehammer."

Of course Cynthia solved the case. Cynthia always solved the case.

After I recognized the ring, and knew Tracy had likewise been initiated into the mysteries of Rapid Falls, we were bound. Friends forever. She introduced me to her other friend, Kelly, already an initiate. Cynthia Silverton pulled us together like magnets.

We lived in a neighborhood no one exactly moved to: it was a place you ended up, and then tried to escape. Tracy was Irish on her father's side and undefined Brooklyn-European on her mother's. She didn't remember her mother, who died when she was two. Tracy's father was a decent man and a bad alcoholic. They lived in the vast housing

projects across the street from our house. He'd rarely left New York.
When he worked, he worked on the docks near where we'd found
the girl with black hair. When he didn't work, he drank. When her
father did well, he made decent money and didn't mind spending it
on her: Dr. Martens boots, a new vintage dress, books. When he was
drunk, Tracy came over to my house or Kelly's to eat.

Kelly lived with her mother in a tenement-type apartment around
the corner. Like us, Kelly's mother had wanted to escape. But she
got pregnant young and got trapped in the apartment she grew up
in, never able to scrape together the money to leave and give up rent
control, never able to accept it as her real home. She never forgave
Kelly for trapping her.

Our house was a giant and crumbling half a city block from
1850-something that somehow had survived both Robert Moses and
the erosion of polite capitalism all around. It was an inheritance. Everything was inherited; *work* was a dirty word to the DeWitts. There
was an old Brooklyn line of the DeWitts, naval officers or whalers or
maybe slave traders—the stories changed depending on who was telling them, how much the storyteller had had to drink, and what they
wanted out of the listener. Although visiting DeWitts—my father's
family—were rare. Most of the DeWitts were regular, normal, rich
people who didn't want anything to do with us. But occasionally one
of my father's brothers or a poor cousin would come by with one of
his ever-rotating spouses and always-surly children, all much older
than me. Everyone would get drunk. At least two people would end
up fighting, sometimes physically, over a slice of arcana from the past,
usually involving money: of course Cousin Philip was *legally* entitled
to one thirty-second of the Gold Coast estate, but everyone knew,
they fucking knew, don't pretend you didn't know, that Uncle Hammond
had meant it to go to Josephina's kids, and just hadn't rewritten the
will in time. *Josephina's kids loved the beach like their own mother's milk,
and it was a fucking sin to rip them apart from it, a fucking sin.*

My parents had snatched the house through some complicated, shady legal twists I never understood. My European mother, from a different city, every time I asked, was skilled at the art of theft without violence. The lawyer who'd helped them steal it still called every once in a while asking to get paid. My mother laughed at him. My father pretended not to be interested in things like money and status and houses; he collected books and drank and charmed younger women and at night, alone in his library, raged against anyone who had more than him. Which was almost everyone.

But half the house was rotting away, anyway, and Brooklyn had changed since the older DeWitts had settled here. Our neighborhood was majority black and minority Puerto Rican and Dominican. Otherwise there was one Chinese American family in the projects, one Pakistani family down the street, Tracy, Kelly, and me. Everyone in my family was racist, which made the house easier for my parents to steal—my parents being just as racist, but more desperate.

It didn't seem as strange to me as it should have that Tracy had the Cynthia Silverton Decoder Ring on her finger that day in fourth grade. I didn't know then that only a few hundred copies of the comics had been printed, that even fewer had been distributed, and that in thirtyish years I would be able to find just one surviving copy. Back then I only knew that Cynthia, my best friend, had introduced me to everything good in life: mysteries, solutions, and two people who loved me enough not only to miss me when I was gone, but to come and find me and bring me back.

———

I didn't know how they found me. Later Tracy would tell me she'd been sleeping, and she'd had a dream about me. Tracy told me about her dream as she and Kelly washed the blood and the dirt off me in Tracy's bathtub. I couldn't stop crying.

"I had to find you," Tracy said. "In the dream. Someone was waiting for you in front of this house. It was pink. The house. I couldn't really see the woman but I knew she was waiting for you. She needed you. I knew I had to help you or you wouldn't get there. To the street with the pink houses. She pointed toward the park. I woke up, and we found you."

Nine years later, I would be on the street with pink houses. But Tracy was gone by then, and Kelly didn't want to talk to me.

"I want to die," I said in the bathtub.

"We're all going to die," Kelly said, always the practical one. "But not today."

"None of us are going to die," Tracy said, less practical, putting Band-Aids on my wrists. "Because we're going to save each other. We're going to save ourselves."

And in a way, we did. Tracy saved me. Kelly saved me. Every time I fell down, they picked me up. Every time I cut myself, they bandaged me up.

And then, when they needed me, I left, and let them fall down alone.

Just over a year after the night when she washed my cuts and bandaged my hesitation marks, Tracy vanished. The police looked and I looked and Kelly looked. Prior to this case—the only case that mattered—we had an unblemished and unbroken 100 percent solve rate.

But we never solved the case of how Tracy disappeared one night from the Brooklyn Bridge subway station. No one found a single clue. Not one witness. Not one rumor, one eyewitness, one fingerprint.

Tracy had us—until it wasn't convenient for me to have her anymore. Until I decided that seeing the world and becoming a great detective and fulfilling what I imagined to be some kind of clever little destiny were more important to me than the people who, against all reason, loved me.

I left Brooklyn and I never, ever looked back.

Kelly stopped speaking to me, except for a phone call every year or two to run some clue by me, a fingerprint or a subway token or a can of spray paint.

I became the best detective in the world, just like I'd dreamed of. I met kings and I met magicians. I solved people's mysteries and I dug up their secrets. I walked into people's lives and I ripped them open and gave them the one and only thing they needed to build a life up again. I met people who had everything on earth except the one thing they wanted the least but needed the most—the truth.

I solved every mystery I came across.

Except my own.

CHAPTER 3

THE CASE OF THE INFINITE BLACKTOP

Oakland, 2011

A man named Eric banged on the bathroom door.

"It's Eric," Eric said over and over, "Jen, just come out and talk to me. I think that's reasonable. I think that's fair. Just listen to me. Come on."

I looked in the mirror with one eye. There were maybe half a dozen small cuts on my face, and a larger one under my left eye that could probably do with a few stitches, but I'd live without them.

I looked at the rest of my body. Along my left hip was a giant bruise, which was probably connected to the pain, which I'd narrowed down to the left thigh. Bruised femur maybe, injured hamstring maybe. There was a big scrape along the front of the right thigh and knee that had left my jeans stained with blood, but that I hadn't even felt—the other, louder, pain had drowned it out. Other than that all the damage seemed internal or at least invisible—I felt cracked ribs, and my left eye still seared, although less so after washing it out. I figured a light scratch on my cornea.

I bent over and shook my hair. Blood rushed to my brain and I came close to fainting; everything went spotted and black, but I steadied myself and it passed. A little storm of glass and metal flakes came out of my hair and fell to the ground. I came up slowly.

I checked my pockets. No wallet. A hundred and eighty bucks in cash, plus my Taser and my radio.

No one had noticed me come in the bar. I waited for Eric to give up and then I opened the bathroom door and looked around, my eyes scanning for the right combination of race, age, and unattended purse.

In about eight seconds I spotted her by the door, sitting with friends, purse dangling from the back of her chair. A white lady with strawberry blond hair from a bottle, about my age in tight jeans and white high-heeled ankle boots and a tank top that was printed with sports insignias. Her face was lightly pockmarked, as mine would likely be from now on, and she looked hard around the edges—but her eyes, under her layered strawberry blond hair, looked open and undefended. She was trying against all reason to have fun in this dive bar in the darkest corner of Oakland with a group of friends, and looked like she was succeeding—like she, and they, were having the kind of plain and joyful moment that refutes all theories and is so rare you could cry when you think about it—at least, rare enough for me.

I am so sorry, I silently thought to the strawberry blonde. *I am so sorry that I am me and you are you, and I am so sorry that this is how we will intersect.*

But being sorry had never stopped me before and wouldn't now. I walked up to the bar and ordered a Coke. I kept my face down and in shadow and the bartender and I noticed each other as little as possible. It was too dark to see most of the cuts on my face, and it was a rough enough place that the ones that could be seen wouldn't bother anyone. I grabbed a handful of napkins and walked toward the chair that held the strawberry blonde's purse as if I were going to walk past. Her purse, like her shoes, was white leather and cheap and beautiful.

When I reached the chair, almost to the door, I stumbled, and dropped the Coke so it spilled on the strawberry blonde's feet, ruining her white boots.

I immediately crouched down with the napkins and started cleaning it up before she realized what was going on.

"Oh my God!" I said. "I am so sorry!"

"What?" she looked down, confused, and figured it out. "Oh, it's OK. Let me just—"

"No, I've got it," I said.

She bent down to help.

"I'll get more napkins," I said. "Just one sec—"

While she was still looking down, I stood up and, behind her back, grabbed her purse off the back of her chair, and stepped outside, the cool night air bringing me back to life even as I gritted my teeth against the pain and limped away from the bar before anyone knew I was gone.

I thought of her good night ruined, of the money she couldn't afford to lose now lost, and I knew that someday, when all had ascended to the higher realms, I would be left alone to pay for the shit and the pain I'd caused.

Until that day, I would win.

Another few blocks away, I stopped and checked the police radio. It sounded like they'd gotten a good description of the Lincoln from the woman with the bleeding forehead and had at least two patrol cars out looking for it. I didn't doubt the Lincoln could still be running. It was a motherfucker of a car.

I looked through the purse I'd stolen. A phone with no password protection. A wallet with no cash but two credit cards and one ATM card and one driver's license in the name of Letitia Parnell. I bet people called her Letty.

Also a bottle of pills. The prescription label wasn't in Letitia's name. They'd been measured out for someone named Catherine Farmer. I didn't recognize the name of the medication. Dexmethyl-phenidate. There was only one reason someone would steal a bottle of pills, so I guessed that Letitia Parnell had recognized the name.

Uppers or downers?

Dexmethylphenidate. I did some quick Latin translations in my head.

Uppers.

I popped two in my mouth, swallowed them without water, and went out to steal a car.

———

The first car I broke into was a late-model BMW and I couldn't get it started for the life of me. I hadn't stolen a car more than a couple of times in the past twenty years, and it showed. The second car I tried was an older Ford Taurus and I couldn't even get in without breaking a window. The third was a 1995 Honda and I got it up and started in about twelve minutes. In the future I'd brush up on new automotive technology: for now I was happy to be in the Honda. I drove back toward the accident scene. It was mostly cleaned up, just a little pile of broken glass and plastic and the disturbing smell of burnt rubber left to mark the spot.

I wasn't worried about the cops. I knew the lady cop hadn't talked, and the rest of the cops in Oakland had better things to worry about than an accident victim who didn't want their help. They wouldn't be looking for me.

A few people were still hanging out around the accident. Or maybe they always hung out here. I drove up to two of them and parked the Honda. I got out and left it running. It had probably been two or three hours since the accident. They were certainly getting their money's worth out of it.

"Hey," I said. They turned around and looked at me, they being two women somewhere between thirty and fifty, both African American. One woman wore worn-out athletic shorts, flip-flops, and a Raiders T-shirt. The other woman wore jeans and a matching Raiders T-shirt. They both smoked cigarettes. I figured them for a couple although I wasn't sure and it didn't matter.

Neither of them said anything. They both looked confused. I figured they recognized me from the crash and I figured right.

Finally the woman in jeans said, "Hey, are you OK? Weren't you just—"

"Yeah," I said. "I'm OK, thanks. Did you see what happened to the other woman? The woman who was screaming?"

"The ambulance took her," the woman in jeans said.

The woman in shorts hit her friend on the hip.

"I don't want to bother her," I said. "I just want a statement for insurance. Do you know her name?"

Now both women looked at me, each with her mouth in a straight line. They were bigger than me, and there were two of them. I could do something about one of those problems, and so I did: before they could figure it out and stop me I took the Taser from my back pocket and brought it up to the bare arm of the woman in shorts and pressed the obvious button. I heard a low electrical hum and the woman shook and shook and made a strange sound in her throat and fell down. All of this took two or three seconds. Before the woman in jeans could retaliate I quickly, and very painfully, raised my left leg and kicked her in the waistline, as high as I could reach. When my ankle hit her waist she fell down and I bit back a scream of pain. I felt bones in my leg I'd never felt before, and it didn't feel good.

She was down and doubled over in pain. I crouched down, feeling new and equally painful leg components howl and shriek as I did, both woken and numbed by the pills, and held the Taser up to her neck.

"That would hurt a lot," I said. "I really don't want to do it. You seem like a nice person. All I want is her name. The name of the woman who went in the ambulance. And I promise, I'm going to protect her, not hurt her."

The woman kept her mouth shut, pulling her lips tight, until her fear got the better of her and she said, "Fuck," and then she said, "Fuck," again and then she said, "Daisy Ramirez. Her name is Daisy Ramirez."

———

As I drove to the hospital the pills I'd taken started to effervesce up my spine; I felt like I was a dying phone and someone had plugged me in. Or maybe it was the shameful, but undeniable, adrenaline high that always came with violence.

Claude was my latest assistant and seemed like he might stick, unlike dozens before. If he was still with me after the Case of the Kali Yuga, likely nothing would scare him off.

I trusted him.

I texted Claude: *911. Call me here use disposable.*

———

I drove through dark Oakland and tried to remember the last few days.

The Case of the Miniature Horses was closed. No one was murdering anyone over dwarf equines. The Case of the Kali Yuga was exactly the kind of case that people murdered each other over, but there was no one left to want me dead. The victim was dead and the murderer was locked up. The Clue of the Hawk's Tears—no, that was last year. I was still confused. Had I hit my head in the accident? I didn't think so. It was just shock.

Think, Claire. Think. There was an accident—an accident before this one. I was in Santa Cruz with the lama. Nick Chang gave me a new prescription. I stole a book from Bix about—

My thoughts stuttered a little. I stole a book? Why?

Not a book. A comic.

A Cynthia Silverton comic. I remembered the rough paper in my hand, slipping it into my jacket pocket. A loft in downtown Oakland. A book dealer I knew.

I hadn't known how rare Cynthia Silverton was until last year. Kelly had called me. I'd never thought much about the comics, which had been such a big part of our childhoods that they were invisible. I didn't notice them unless they weren't there.

But on the internet, Cynthia Silverton didn't exist. There was one short entry in an online directory of printed comics—

Cynthia Silverton: limited-run comic privately printed in Las Vegas, Nevada, 1978–1989. The adventures of Cynthia Silverton, teen detective and junior college student. Extremely rare, but of limited value.

I found one complete set of the books. They were in the collection of a book dealer in Oakland. He didn't want to sell them. Book dealers are funny like that. Drug dealers are much happier to part with their wares. But he did let me look at them.

Each issue had a Cynthia Silverton Comic, or more than one. A True-Life Mystery Not Quite Solved. A story from Case File of Cynthia Silverton. And one advertisement—

BE A DETECTIVE!

Money! Excitement! Women and men admire detectives. Everyone looks up to someone with knowledge and education. Our home-study course offers the chance to earn your detective's badge from the comfort of your own home.

There was an address in Las Vegas, Nevada, if the reader wished to reply. I'd looked the magazine over and over. There was no publication information. No colophon or copyright page. No other advertisements. Just that ad.

"But now," Kelly had said, when I'd last spoken to her, our semi-annual call where we hissed clues and accusations at each other, "when you think about it, don't the Silverton books seem strange to you? Doesn't it seem like they were written just for us? Like they weren't normal comics at all? And didn't you ever think about how weird it all was?"

But somehow, I hadn't. I was the best detective in the world, and I hadn't noticed the greatest mystery of all: the odd and twisted trajectory of my own life.

"I mean," Kelly went on, "who the fuck are we? Did you ever think about that? Who the fuck are we?"

Driving through Oakland, wondering who had tried to kill me, I remembered something.

Five days ago, after stealing one of the books from Bix, I'd answered the ad. The ad in the Cynthia Silverton comic book.

BE A DETECTIVE!

Money! Excitement! Women and men admire detectives. Everyone looks up to someone with knowledge and education. Our home-study course offers the chance to earn your detective's badge from the comfort of your own home.

I'd written:

To Whom It May Concern:
I am already a professional detective, but I would like to improve my skills. Do you offer a continuing education course? Or may I enroll in

*the standard home-study course despite my age and experience? Please
reply at this address.*

Sincerely,
Claire DeWitt

I mailed it to the address in the ad.

I didn't know exactly what I was trying to do when I sent the
letter. Maybe get answers. Maybe prove to someone that I was paying attention.

And I remembered something else: the Lincoln that had tried to
kill me had Nevada plates.

CHAPTER 4

THE MYSTERY OF THE CBSIS

Los Angeles, 1999

I met Constance Darling, at the time the best detective in the world, on July 18, 1994. It was in Los Angeles. I was drifting around the country, working for other PIs and solving cases as they came to me. I didn't want a steady job and I didn't want a steady life and I didn't want to love anyone.

When Tracy disappeared I wasn't a child anymore, but I was nothing close to an adult. Kelly and I spent two years looking for her; we never found a single clue. Had I been an adult, maybe I would have seen that that was a clue itself: that absence could be as meaningful as presence; that silence could be louder than a scream. Two years into the search I gave up and left Brooklyn. At the time I told myself I was saving my life.

LA was where I ended up. Where something ended, at least. When I got there I didn't know that things were ending; I thought I was passing through, like I'd passed through Portland, like I'd passed through Chicago, through Nashville, through Miami, through a dozen other cities.

I slept in a motel on Sunset on good days and in Griffith Park on less good nights. Worked a few small cases and did some research for a detective named Sean Risling on the side. Sean was writing a book on orchid poisons. Still is. I planned to drive down to San Diego whenever I was done with LA—which would be when the money dried up or I got kicked out—and from there maybe Tijuana and from there maybe Texas or maybe across Mexico and from there to I didn't know where for I didn't know what reason.

All I'd ever wanted was to grow up and leave Brooklyn and be a detective. And here I was, in a maybe-literally-lousy, maybe-literally-flea-infested motel, overlooking the night prostitutes of Sunset Boulevard, weedless, limited in intoxication to a little pint of something I'd bought at one of LA's endless liquor stores, with no one to love and no one to love me, with nothing to live for and nowhere in particular to do it.

And then one day Sean Risling called me and said Constance Darling was in town, and needed help for a few days with the Happy-Burger Murder Case. Was I free?

The only thing I had in life was freedom—that and a couple of hundred bucks and my own skin and bones and my car. All I wanted was the opposite of that—something I'd never seen and didn't even know the words for, and wouldn't know who to ask for even if I did know what it was.

I'd known who Constance Darling was since I was a girl, starstruck by Jacques Silette and his first, and best, protégé, Constance.

Jacques Silette, the French genius and visionary detective, wrote one brilliant, maddening book: *Détection*. Brilliant, that was, according to me and maybe a few dozen others around the world (although a *few dozen* was probably hopeful, even then). *Détection* was not a book that told you to change or asked you to change. It changed you. You could call it a book, and that was certainly what it looked like: a little yellow paperback, part of an educational series that included a book called *The Life of the Bee* and another called, demandingly, *Understand Physics!* But no other book could do what *Détection* did. It was a spell; a virus; somehow Silette knew just the right proportion of ink to pulp; letters to space; black to white; to effect permanent change. And by the time you realized that you had been changed, it was too late: your defenses were already proven to be worthless; your resolve had revealed itself an embarrassment. You were someone else now.

Other books would give you ideas and words and things to defend and argue. *Détection* gave just one thing—the truth—and in its short 123 pages (US reprint edition, 1959) offered us 123 different doors to the same place: each door locked, each ready to be picked open if you worked hard enough.

"Your assumptions," Silette wrote, "are your worst enemies. Throw away your clever thoughts. Let the rest of the world drown in lies. Rest on the life raft of truth."

A whole new life of misery and truth could be yours for a mere couple of bucks and a few ounces of paper—if you finished the book, that is. Most people gave up after one line or one page or sometimes even one word. More than once I'd seen someone open the book, get through a page or two, and literally throw it across their desk or into the trash or back to the idiot who'd given it to them, the idiot who'd thought maybe they were ready for the only thing worth having—real life.

And what was this truth that would rebuild your bones, rewire your veins?

"The detective who thinks she's found the truth is as wrong as the detective who never managed to look for it at all," Silette wrote. "The truth can never be limited and therefore never found. This is what makes it the only thing worth finding."

If that wasn't clear enough, turn to page sixty-eight:

"For the detective whose eyes have truly been opened," Silette wrote, "the solution to every mystery is never more than a breath away."

I first read those lines at fourteen. Kelly and Tracy and I were already exploring vices and solving mysteries across New York City. But when we didn't have the money or the time to get away we sometimes still spent afternoons exploring the vast DeWitt house, which had plenty of mysteries and vice of its own.

We found the book in my attic. As Silette said, detectives aren't made, they're born; a detective only needs to somehow be shown his true nature. Tracy, a born detective if there ever was one, was the first to find the book, the first to crack it open, the first to read. The world was oddly silent when she picked it up; later we compared notes and realized each one of us had been struck by something different at that exact moment: Kelly by the dust swirling in the sunlight; me by the pigeons cooing from the eaves, amplifying how otherwise oddly quiet the room was; Tracy, by the dusty smell of the book.

"The mystery that can be solved," Tracy read, "is not the eternal mystery."

When I heard those words I felt something turn, shiver, and fall down. I couldn't tell if it was inside me or next to me. I was frightened. Later I would learn that feeling was the beginning of the end of lies. Nothing would ever taste the same; nothing would ever smell the same.

I never knew which DeWitt from the past had bought the book and, knowing my ancestors, tossed the book in the unused wing, unread, after the first bite that left marks. We were already good detectives. With Cynthia Silverton as our guide, Tracy had discovered the Clue of the Broken Light Bulb, which had cost a man his life. Kelly had closed the Case of the Blue Moth at Dawn, which had not ended well for anyone.

But after we read *Détection*, it all changed. We did everything Silette said and, unlike anything else we'd ever encountered, unlike religion or money or love, it worked. We solved every case we found. But we still couldn't seem to solve the biggest mystery we had: why no one cared about our cases, no one cared about our solutions, and no one else seemed to care about mysteries at all. Didn't the truth matter? Wasn't reality different from a lie? The answers from the world at large were *no* and *no one cares*.

It wasn't long after finding the book that I first saw a picture of the great and beautiful Constance Darling. It was in a book called *Criminology through the Ages* that I'd stolen from the NYU Law Library. The book was sliced into twelve chapters each named after the major criminological movements throughout time—Aristotelian, Vidocqian, Occult, etc.—and then a thirteenth chapter on Minor Traditions and Trends. One of the Minor Trends, in between the Anarchists and the Sufis, were the Silettians.

"It would be unfair to call this so-called esoteric school of detection discredited," the book spelled out for all of eternity, its own idiocy frozen in print, "because that would imply it had ever been credited at all." Alongside the text was a photo of Jacques Silette and Constance Darling. The caption read: *Flim-flam artists Jacques Silette and Constance Darling, Paris, 1963*. Silette was already fifty-something. Constance was in her thirties. I didn't know for sure, but I came to suspect over the years that the photo was from a department party in L'École de Criminologie in Paris, where Silette taught for much of his life.

I was fourteen when I first saw that picture. Constance's hair was already white in the photo; her eyes, already wise. She and Silette were talking to each other, two alone in a crowd, and their deep rapport was clear on the page—somehow, some secret essence of what they had together had, wordlessly, silently, been transposed from soul to life to photo to page to me, a confused child in Brooklyn. I knew, because the world let me know, that I was a stupid child, hateful and hated. But I knew that if it took the rest of my life, I would find out what could be so thrilling and fascinating, so worth the time of these exotic and rarefied humans.

In the black-and-white photo, Silette was facing slightly toward the camera, Constance's body facing a little away—but her head was turned back and looking just to the left of the camera, with a dry and slightly irritated look at the photographer—or someone next to them—as if to ask: *What foolish thing are you up to now?* Her white hair was tall and elegantly teased, and she wore a black Chanel suit with white trim and an ocean of white pearls, each one, I later would learn, hand-plucked from the China Seas just for her by an overeager admirer. Around them, in the background, other people in suits and hairdos did whatever dull mortals did around gods. Silette was on the short side, with a strong square face and short, neat white hair and black-framed glasses. Always in a suit. Always the smartest man in the room.

The electric thrill of recognition and longing that rushed through me when I saw that photo stayed with me that day, and never left. I'd read everything I could find about Constance Darling and the tiny trail she'd blazed as Silette's finest student. There wasn't much to read: the occasional mention in *Detective's Quarterly*, which I found archived at the St. Francis College library in downtown Brooklyn; a few references in the New Orleans *Times-Picayune* at the Brooklyn Public Library for cases she solved. In the main New York library on Forty-Second Street a bored librarian helped me find more in the periodical indexes, and it wasn't long before I realized that Constance had accomplished what no detective on earth—other than Silette— had achieved: she had solved every fucking case put in front of her.

And not only had she not cherry-picked the easy solutions and big paychecks, she had taken cases that ten other detectives had failed at before.

A 100 percent solve rate was unheard of in mid-to-late-twentieth-century private detection. Constance should have been the most feted and admired detective in the world. Instead, each report, every time, treated her success as a fluky, inexplicable, coincidence: "Eccentric private investigator Constance Darling presided over . . ."; "Marginal sleuth solves cold case . . ."

Worse were the passive headlines: "Missing heiress found . . ."; "Murderous doctor finally charged . . ."; "Long-dormant homicide cracked . . ." It was as if all those cases had just solved themselves.

Later I would learn that Constance didn't know, or care, what the larger world said or thought about her. I once heard her refer to the *Washington Post* as "the *Babylon Daily News*." Not that she ever read it. Her own reputation—impeccable and iron clad—was known to anyone she wanted it to be known to.

When Sean called to ask if I wanted to meet Constance, I had nothing and no one. Tracy was long gone, Kelly never forgave me for leaving Brooklyn and was maybe going crazy, my family didn't miss me, and I sometimes wondered if I was real. I bought little bags of cocaine and heroin and snorted them or jumped in the cold ocean or got tattoos or got in fights or slept with strangers to see if I was real. I still wasn't sure.

Was I free?

Yes. I was free.

I met Constance two days later in a private room in a restaurant in Little Tokyo, where we drank rare green tea that tasted like grass and rain. After we chatted about books and poisons she asked me where I was from.

"New York," I said. "Brooklyn."

She looked at me with her sharp eyes. Her hair had already been white for years, and she wore it in a bun on top of her head like a dancer. Her face was all angles and edges, few soft spots. Constance had been at Silette's first lectures. It was Constance who Silette had entrusted with his legacy—which she, in turn, would entrust to me.

Constance was from an ancient New Orleans family, most of them now gone. When she was younger she'd traveled the world: for fun, for mysteries, for love. In 1978 she'd solved the Case of the Wilted Rose in Buenos Aires. In 1985 she'd uncovered the Clue of the Ancient Sin in Port-au-Prince. But by the time I met her she wasn't young, was close to old, and liked to stay in New Orleans. In the back of her house she grew poisons and entheogens. She could be cruel. Usually it was for a good cause: the cause of the truth.

"Brooklyn," she said. "Were you one of those girl detectives?"

"I-I was," I stammered, shocked she'd heard of me.

But then she nodded, and the way she nodded made me think the fact that she'd heard of me before was not necessarily a good thing. But somehow, over the next few weeks, she let me help her solve the HappyBurger Murder Case. Six weeks later I moved to New Orleans to be her assistant and apprentice. One year later we stood together on Prytania Street, *Times-Picayune* flashbulbs popping as the police took away the killer in the Case of the Crimson Hibiscus. We were the best detectives in the world and no one could deny it. Even more than our cases, we had each other. I sometimes lived with her in her big Garden District house and sometimes in various apartments around New Orleans when I needed time alone or she needed my room for a visiting detective from Morocco or a shaman she'd flown in from Siberia to help on a case. With Constance, all things were possible; with her at my side, my teacher and guide, I could conquer any demon and slay any falsehood. Together, we would live our lives as a wonderful and crooked line that always took us to the only place worth going to: the truth.

That night on Prytania Street I was sure I felt my life settle into new and better patterns. I knew I was done with the worst of life now. All of that pain, it seemed now, red and blue lights flashing across the scene, sliding into the back seat of Constance's chauffeured Jaguar, had just been the prelude to this. And it seemed like a fair price, now that it was over. I could almost look back on the years before Constance with a kind of affection, now that they were so far away.

Back at Constance's house, her other assistant Mick was still awake, along with their friend Brother John, who'd come by to drop off some Solomon's seal he'd been growing for her. Mick made tea and John passed around a bottle of homebrew and we stayed up late laughing and talking and being in love with ourselves, with each other, with the little slice of the world we'd carved out for ourselves, cut by cut.

But out of all the things I learned from Constance, the most important was that happiness doesn't last. In 1998, less than four years after I met her, Constance was shot and killed in a hold-up in the French Quarter. There was no conspiracy. No big mystery. Two kids needed money and so they shot her for her purse. If they'd asked, she would have given them whatever they needed. Instead they shot her, and then a few days later someone else shot them. No mystery. No justice.

A few days later I left New Orleans and drove west. A few months and a few hard cases later I landed in San Francisco.

"Happiness is for idiots," Silette wrote. "But if we try, something much better than happiness is possible."

I'd lived by that rule for all my life. This was where it'd gotten me, a year after Constance's death: to a hotel room in San Francisco's Chinatown that I sometimes shared with a stray cat named Flea. Flea came with the room, along with a TV that got in three channels and a view of an alley below and the sound from a never-ending, heartbreaking erhu on the street outside.

I'd thought I knew what it was to be alone.

Before Constance died, I didn't have a fucking clue.

I was exactly where I'd started, but I had a little more money in the bank. I cared about as much for money as Constance had. If anyone missed me when I left New Orleans—or Brooklyn or anywhere else—they were doing a good job of making a fucking mystery out of it.

I was starting to think Silette was wrong. It wasn't happiness, and it wasn't better.

———

In the year since Constance had died I'd tried settling down in a couple of different cities—Portland, Detroit—and none of them stuck. I liked San Francisco. I'd been there for a few months and come to think I wanted to stay. I didn't know I would stay for fifteen years. But I knew it was just as good as anywhere else and had plenty of work to keep me in hotel rooms and cat food for as long as I wanted.

No one seemed to be particularly happy about this. San Francisco didn't throw open her arms and welcome me to her bosom. No place ever had. But the only unhappy residents whose opinions I had to care about were the police.

On my first case in San Francisco—the Case of the Emerald Peacock—I ran into trouble. The case was easy enough, barely a mystery at all, and a nice way to make five grand. After solving it, I was on my way back to my hotel room with a bottle of malt liquor in a paper bag when I saw two cops in front of the door to the hotel.

They didn't move to let me pass. They were both young and in uniform. A matched set: boy and girl.

"You Claire DeWitt?" the woman cop said.

"Yeah?" I said.

The woman slugged me in the gut, hard.

I fell down to the ground, head spinning. She kicked me.

"San Francisco doesn't need another PI," the woman said. "Go fuck yourself."

"And do it someplace else," the man said.

I crawled over to the gutter and vomited. The cops laughed.

Turned out those two weren't the only cops who were excited to meet the new PI in town.

"Listen," Officer Heather Fong said a few days later. Fong was a brand-new patrol cop in Hunters Point. We weren't friends, and we never would be, but I'd done her a good favor on one of her own cases, and lied to the right people about it when her job was at stake. She owed me. Back then that was the best I hoped for: being owed. I'd called her after the warm welcome to ask what the big fucking problem was.

Turned out the problem was, as it so often was, me.

"Pretty much everyone on the force has it out for you," Fong said. "Like they pretty much all hate you."

I'd kind of suspected that already, but it was always interesting to see these things spelled right out. These things being other people's dislike and sometimes hatred of you.

"I mean," Heather said, "they really, really don't—"

"I get it," I said.

"I heard some of the guys say that if they catch you doing anything like a PI again they're turning you in to the Bureau."

"Fuck," I said. "They would do that?"

"Not usually," Fong said. "But for you? Yeah, I think so. I think they would."

The Bureau, aka the CBSIS, properly known as the California Bureau of Security and Investigative Services, was the division of the California state government in charge of PI licenses, along with regulating security guards, locksmiths, and other occultists. Each American state had its own rules for operating as a PI; in some a PI card was easy to get as a candy bar and barely needed; in liberal, regulated California, we had the CBSIS. And if the CBSIS caught you stepping out without a license, you could consider yourself done: maybe fines, maybe jail, and zero chance of ever practicing again in the state. You so much as think of a mystery without a license in California and you're skating on thin ice.

The CBSIS was a shadowy organization, entirely autonomous, with no relation to any other governmental body. Their membership roster was strictly private, supposedly for the members' own safety. Their decisions were indecipherable, and there was never any appeal. There was a rumor they had it out for Silettians. Lilly Hodgkins, Eli Singer, and Wally Christopher, all decent detectives with Silettian leanings, were all denied licenses. I'd heard that they'd had Hodgkins defend her PI exam for over forty-eight hours under hot lights in an airless room. I'd heard they wouldn't even let Eli take the test. I'd heard that Wally had taken the test every year for nine years straight before he finally gave up and moved to Florida. Later I would find out these stories were varying degrees of true.

"So get a PI license," Heather said. "Seriously."

Getting a PI license in California required six thousand hours of work under the supervision of a licensed private eye—there were other ways you could do it but none I was likely to accomplish in this lifetime. I'd done far more PI work than that in my life, but most of it without any official type of supervision. In Louisiana, it took only forty hours of coursework to become a certified PI, but I wasn't sure Constance had ever bothered. She'd had a framed business-looking certificate hanging on the wall of her room but if you looked closely enough it was a certificate from a witch school in Mississippi.

Via phone and fax I got Mick Pendell, Constance's other employee in New Orleans, who was licensed and bonded, to sign off on as many hours as he'd actually witnessed, which came out to 4,351. Sean Risling, who'd introduced me to Constance and hired me for odd jobs over the years, signed off on another 1,252. Of course, there was no thought of anyone fudging the hours or cutting me a break. Even Mick, tattooed anarchist, leader of the someday-soon-to-berevolution, who didn't live in California and was scared of very little in life, knew enough to be scared of the CBSIS.

I got their statements witnessed and notarized, according to procedure. But I still needed four hundred hours. Four hundred hours of supervised PI work. I'd been a working PI since I was twelve, and an amateur since I was nine. But I needed their fucking four hundred hours.

No one in San Francisco would take me. I asked every licensed PI in the city. I called a man I found in the phone book who specialized in Missing Treasure and Lost Fortunes. The Lost Fortunes man said no. He'd heard about me. "I don't need the trouble!" he yelled, having already explained that he'd left his hearing aid at an Ethiopian restaurant. "I am very close to retiring and I don't need the trouble! But God bless, DeWitt."

Finally Hans Jacobson, the Dutch Silettian scholar—and investor, wine merchant, and art dealer—heard about my situation and made some calls.

I never knew who told him. Just that one day I picked up the phone in my fleabag hotel and it was Hans. It took a few minutes to figure out who it was.

"Claire," he said in his heavy Dutch accent. "You've got a work!"

"Sorry?" I said. "What?" Like half of Europe, he thought he spoke English better than he did.

"A work!" he said. "I made some talks and I found you the work. For the license."

An involuntary sigh of relief escaped me.

"Adam Dubinsky in the Angel City," Hans said. "He's expecting you, you know, some of these times now. You call him, you work it out."

I didn't know what to say. I'd never met Hans. I only knew who he was from Constance. Unless they were feuding, which was often enough, the few Silettians left kept in touch, at least a little. Christmas cards and congratulatory notes after big cases. When possible, we helped each other. Over the years the little community would fall apart; personal insults and ideological differences and a lack of interest and death would pull us apart. But back then, in the glory days of the semi-annual *Détection* newsletter and semi-regular Silettian conferences where a bountiful dozen or even twenty fans might show up, we Silettians kept an eye on each other. Almost like a family.

"Hey, thanks," I said. I sounded about eight years old. "Really. Thank you."

"Eh," he said, like it was nothing. "For Constance. Let me know. I will be happiness to see your progressings."

———

I didn't have much to tie up in San Francisco. I knew a lot of people, but that didn't mean they cared about me, or that I cared about them. Other than Nick Chang—my doctor who wasn't a friend yet, but would be in years to come—I had had no friends, no obligations, no houseplants. The cat was an acquaintance. The guy who managed the hotel, Billy, said he'd feed her while I was gone. I lingered for a few days to prove a point and then I packed some clothes and some books and a decent .45 and a silly little pocket-size .22 and drove down to Los Angeles in the 1982 Mercedes I'd accepted as payment for revealing the Clue of the Broken Glass, a case that ended with nothing but misery and death. And one very good car.

Ecclesiastes 1:2–5: "'Meaningless! Meaningless!' says the Teacher. 'Utterly meaningless!' What do people gain from all their labors at which they toil under the sun? Generations come and generations go, but the earth remains forever. The sun rises and the sun sets, and hurries back to where it rises."

I'd been reading Bible verses for months, trying to find the Clue of the Phoenix Strangler. He'd put together bits and pieces from psalms and proverbs and made his own book with its own numbers, pages of which he'd left at his crime scenes. The Book of Paradise Valley. The

Gospel of Biltmore. Now he was in jail waiting for his trial and the women of Phoenix were safe—at least from him—and I was banned from entering the city of Phoenix until the turn of the millennium.

Daniel 4:28: "All this happened to King Nebuchadnezzar."

———

Adam's office was on Wilshire Boulevard in a neighborhood called Miracle Mile. I didn't know what was miraculous about it, or exactly where the mile was. It seemed to me like a middling neighborhood of offices and stores on Wilshire and small houses on the side streets. The boulevards and the side streets were entirely out of proportion to each other, as if two different neighborhoods were duking out the rights to the scale of Los Angeles. Adam's office was in a small commercial building—neutral ground, maybe, in the war of scale—in between a business called SKJ Imports and another called Allied Natural Products. There was no receptionist at his office; instead the frosted glass door opened up into a kind of waiting area with a few leather chairs separated by a wall and a door from an inner office. Everything was gray and all the lights were fluorescent. Fifteen minutes after we were supposed to meet Adam opened the door and gestured that I should come in. In the office was a desk and a couple of chairs and three filing cabinets and a painting of a horse. It seemed like a particular horse; maybe a horse Adam knew. His desk was messy with pens and books and a seemingly infinite number of papers—typed, printed, scrawled-on, and blank.

Adam was a short man and his eyes were large and brown. He smoked Pall Malls, one after the other, like it was his religion. He had a long face that was perpetually sad and wise. You couldn't imagine his face ever being younger than forty, or ever having a heart that wasn't broken—but I wasn't sure anymore if anyone had a heart that hadn't been broken. Maybe everyone else just did a better job of hiding it than Adam.

He had no idea who I was.

"So you say you had some trouble with the police in San Francisco?"

"Um, well, yeah," I said. "I think Hans Jacobson called you? I'm a detective? Claire DeWitt? And—"

"Wait," Adam said. "Oh yes, yes." But then he frowned and said, "Hans said I'd do what, exactly?"

"Hours," I said. I looked around the office. Stacks of files looked like they hadn't been touched in years. A window was open to an alley where two pigeons cooed.

Sometimes since Constance died I wondered if people could see me. If maybe there was some kind of filter around me that made it impossible for people to know I was there if I wasn't holding a gun to their neck.

I didn't think that would accomplish anything here.

Adam looked at me. "What?" he said.

"Hours," I said again. "I need hours. For my license."

Adam's face lit up. "Oh, right! Constance Darling! Constance's girl! You need the hours. Well—"

I sat on the other side of Adam's desk and he smoked his Pall Malls and shuffled some papers on his desk until he found what he was looking for. It was a thin manila file folder and he handed it to me.

"The Merritt Underwood Case," he said. I took the file and opened it. Not much. "Unsolved. That should keep you busy for four hundred hours."

"OK," I said.

I waited for him to say something more about the case. He didn't.

He turned back to his fascinating eddy of papers and starting sifting through.

"So it's all here?" I asked. "All here in the file?"

"Yes," he said evenly, glancing up. "All there in the file."

"OK," I said again. "So I'll just dive in? And check in with you in a few days?"

"That sounds good," he said. "Let's do that."

He went back to his papers.

"And I'll keep track of my hours?" I said. "Should I make some kind of a chart or something?"

"Yes," he said. "Something, you know, workman-like. Something official."

"OK," I said. "Well, I guess I'll start."

"Good," he said. "That sounds good."

"OK," I said again. "Thank you. Thanks for doing this. I really do appreciate it. I'm really happy to be in LA."

"Great," he said. "And it's Los Angeles."

"Sorry?" I said.

"It isn't LA," Adam said, looking up again with a little disapproval. "It's Los Angeles."

"OK," I said. "Thanks."

He made a tight-lipped smile and I left.

He didn't look up again.

————

The first time I came to Los Angeles, in the early nineties, in the days before I met Constance Darling, the detectives' bar in Los Angeles had been the Velvet Turtle down in Chinatown. Back then every city had a detectives' bar, where PIs would meet and trade hope and bullshit and company when they passed through town. The Turtle had black leather booths and dark wood fixtures and good drinks. The men—they were all men then, the few female detectives shut out of the club, except for those of us who found secret doors in when no men were looking—back then in the early nineties the men talked about the heyday of the sixties and fifties, when the Spot, the detectives' bar of their era, was elbow-to-elbow with PIs in sharp suits with sharper wisecracks at the ready, trading information, starting feuds, breaking each other's hearts.

By the 1970s, the Spot in Bunker Hill was long demolished and forgotten, and you'd be lucky to find a dozen detectives at the Turtle on a Saturday night. Now, in 1999, you'd be lucky to find a half dozen in a month. All the traditions were dying out and there was just enough tradition left to make you ache for it. The few detectives left—those good enough to survive the coming decimation by search engines and public databases—would come to see each other more as petty rivals than as grand and worthy enemies. Or even, God forbid, friends.

Not that it mattered much to us Silettians, anyway. No one else wanted us around. Among ourselves, most of the Silettians were on a scale from dislike to loathe, and electronic communication didn't help us much. Now we could loathe and ignore each other on computerized bulletin boards and listservs instead of in person.

That night I thought about driving by the Turtle to see who was around but figured it would be more depressing than useful. Being around people I sort-of kind-of knew but didn't want to know better was, debatably, more lonely than being alone. The only person in Los Angeles I could convince myself cared about me was Sean Risling, the detective who had introduced me to Constance, but he was hunting down flowers in Siberia.

Instead I found a cheap hotel in Hollywood and bought some weed from a guy on Sunset. The guy I bought weed from had long blond hair and a sunburned face, and he was hanging out in front of the Rainbow. I didn't know how I knew he had weed. I just knew.

"Got any plans for the night?" he asked, after he took my money and gave me my drugs.

"Yeah," I said. "These are my plans," and we looked around at the wasteland of Sunset Boulevard, rising up and down toward the vast nothingness of the ocean, at the long road to nowhere, at the street that just went and went until there was nowhere left to go, and then I changed my mind and said, "Actually, I have no plans. I have nothing to do, and I have no plans."

"Yeah," the guy said, laughing a little. "Sounds good to me."

It did not sound good to me. But I kept that to myself, went back to my hotel room, shut the door, and smoked my weed alone.

CHAPTER 5

THE CASE OF THE INFINITE BLACKTOP

Oakland, 2011

Getting into the hospital was not hard. No one was looking for me. Apparently the lady cop I'd stolen the radio from had taken my advice and kept it to herself.

I went into the ER. The waiting room was the usual backlog of misery, thirty or forty people who'd moved from fear and pain to frustration and pain to the deadness of giving up and pain. First I found the vending machines—they always have vending machines—where I bought some peanut butter crackers and a bottle of water. Then I went to the swinging door to the ER and pushed and stepped through. I was almost in when a security guard, an African American man with gray hair who weighed about 125 and looked like an alcoholic going through withdrawal, stopped me.

"Hey," he said. "You check in with them?"

He nodded to the check-in counter.

"Yes!" I said, trying to sound like I'd been dealing with the ER all night. I'd done it enough times that my muscle memory jumped in and took over. I held up my peanut butter crackers. "My mother's in there! I just went to get her a snack!"

He waved me on. I knew no one else would stop me in the busy beehive of the ER. Patients were treated in little mini-rooms while doctors and nurses buzzed around, trying to figure out who to sting next. I stopped a nurse.

"Hey," I said, sounding as breathless and tired as I was. "I'm looking for my aunt. Daisy Ramirez?"

"In there." She pointed to a mini-room down the hall.

I went to Daisy Ramirez's room and opened the door. The wound on her head—a five-inch gash across her forehead and into her scalp—had been stitched up and I figured she was waiting for test results.

"You—" she began, but for the second time that night I put my finger to my lips and mouthed the sound *shhh*. I shut the folding papery door behind me.

"The cops were looking for you," she said.

"I know," I said. "But so is the person who hit me with the car. The thing is, they might be looking for you, too."

Daisy wasn't stupid, and I could tell the thought had crossed her mind. "Fuck," she said. My radio crackled with news of a shooting.

"You a cop?" she said.

"No," I said. "You got somewhere to go? People who can protect you?"

"I can protect myself," she said.

"Not in here, you can't. Get your stuff. Let's go."

Daisy looked at me.

"And I trust you why?" she said.

"Because," I said. "You've been in the hospital for three hours and you're still alone. So I'm guessing there's no one else you particularly trust more. Come on."

Leaving the hospital was as easy as getting in. The ER doesn't force its services on the unwilling. Daisy was OK other than cuts, bruises, and maybe a mild concussion, or so the doctor who'd seen her for ten minutes had said. She was waiting for tests. She would live without them, for now.

We went back to the parking lot where, just to be on the safe side, we stole another car.

"You gotta be kidding," Daisy said when I picked the lock on a Nissan from the early 2000s.

"There's worse things," I said.

"Yeah," she snorted. "I could be you."

"True enough," I said. "Thank your lucky fucking stars you're not."

I got the Nissan started and got out of the hospital lot and was on my way to the highway. I asked if she remembered the license plate on the Lincoln.

"I told the cop," she said. "I saw the last three digits—444. That's my lucky number, four. But that's it. I didn't catch the first part."

"How'd you get hurt?" I asked.

"After he hit you, I was scared. I got in my car, but he backed up into me. I hit my head on the windshield."

"What else did you see?" I asked.

"Nothing," she said.

"That's not true," I said. "Take a few deep breaths. Close your eyes. When did you first notice the car?"

She did what I asked and in a minute she said: "When it turned the corner. Because of the car, you know. I like old cars."

"Who was driving?" I asked.

"Some guy," she said.

"Some guy who looked like what?"

Daisy thought for a minute. "White guy. White hair. Like blond, not old. But really light blond. I couldn't really see any, like, detail or anything."

"Tell me something else about him," I said.

Daisy made a face. "I just said. I just told you. I couldn't really see."

"If you could see his hair color, you could see something else," I said. "His shape. Tell me about his shape."

"Narrow," Daisy said. "I mean, it might have been a shadow. I don't know what I was seeing, exactly. But that's what he looked like to me. Thin. Narrow."

———

In 1955, Jacques Silette had all of Paris—maybe all of the world—at his fingertips. He was the most renowned private investigator of the twentieth century. In the Case of the Melancholy Bibliophile, he'd solved the unsolvable. Using the Clue of the Forbidden Banknote, he'd proven the unprovable. *Le Monde* published no less than three full-length features on his dazzling exploits and modern tools.

He gave regular talks at L'École de Criminologie.

He fucked his willing students and clients with abandon and glee.

He was one of the highest-paid detectives in the world.

He was, by most accounts, a happy man.

And then everything changed.

Exactly how Silette got off the straight and narrow road of mediocrity and began to look for the truth is not known now and maybe never was, even to him. Was the path already there? Did Silette discover it, or only define it? How did he come to find himself in uncharted territory, and end up on the long, lost highway toward truth?

"There are no facts," Silette wrote, "only pebbles that may or may not be part of this path toward the truth."

The closest we have to a travelogue of how Silette found that road is an account by a man named Louis Fournier. Fournier was Silette's peer and acquaintance and maybe almost, not exactly, a friend. They knew each other from L'École de Criminologie. Fournier was a professor specializing in poisons and chemicals, but not without poetry in his soul; in 1974 he published a small and beautiful illustrated book of aphorisms inspired by his favorite venoms: "The rattlesnake might bite / but its rattle will sing you to sleep."

Which is maybe better in French.

Anyway. From an account Fournier gave to *Le Trimestriel des Détectives* in 1969:

> *Jacques was a man who knew how to enjoy life. When he wasn't working, he was eating, drinking, or off with a girl. But—oh, I don't know, maybe it was 1956 when that started to change. In the past, we would often go out for a drink or a meal. Now, never. It wasn't very sudden and it wasn't very gradual. I can tell you around holiday time in 1955, we went to some of the university parties—I remember very well because I was jealous of his ability to get along so well. I remember watching him across the room at a little party in Emile Jean-Baptiste's house—he was another professor, the fingerprints man—and I saw all the smart people around Jacques and I felt quite jealous. I was very lonely at the time; my wife had left me, my family was gone. And Jacques seemed to attract this life, this life filled with pleasure and company, without even trying.*
>
> *Now the next year, Emile had a party again. I went with my new wife, Christiane, and we were very happy. And Jacques—he wasn't there at all. He'd stopped going to parties.*

He'd stopped going to parties because he was home, alone, writing the book that would define his life and legacy: *Détection*.

Détection was a book about solving mysteries.

It was a book about crime.

It was a book about everything.

It was a book that seeped into your bones and changed you from the inside. It would pierce through the lifetime of armor you had built around your heart and show you how you had protected all the wrong things, hidden your best and, like a miser, given the world your worst. The fact that this was exactly what the world had asked of you could no longer be an excuse.

Now, you had the bricks of truth, and your only responsibility was to build your road.

"If life gave you answers outright," Silette wrote, "they would be meaningless. Each detective must take her clues and solve her mysteries for herself. No one can solve your mystery for you; a book cannot tell you the way."

Everyone knows what happened next: *Détection* was published, not to acclaim and celebration, but to derision, hostility and laughter. Those are the sounds of people running from reality. The high heels clacking on the pavement, the doors shutting as they leave: those are the sounds people make when they encounter the truth.

No one ever welcomes the truth. No one ever congratulates you for pointing it out and you will not be thanked.

And like all true things, *Détection* would change you forever if you weren't careful—if you didn't hold it at arm's length, reading with one eye on the page and the other on your friends, laughing a smug little laugh at the ridiculousness of it all. If you gave the book even a little bit of an honest shake, it would give you an entirely new life— and burn your old, better, safer life to the ground.

Now Silette was no longer the well-loved man with profiles in the paper and crowds around him at parties. Instead, he was the man people made blind-item cracks about in the paper and whispered about at parties: Did you hear about Jacques and his crazy book? What happened to him? And, unspoken: How can I make sure it doesn't happen to me?

But Silette still solved cases. More than ever before. His record before *Détection* was good; after *Détection*, perfect.

You'd think that would matter. It didn't.

Now, sixty-odd years later, the majority of people who'd heard of Jacques Silette knew him as a punch line, or maybe a cautionary tale. His followers were fewer and fewer every year. The first generation of intellectual offspring had mostly died off, and failed to reproduce. Jeanette Foster was already gone. Constance too. Hans Jacobson was facing old age without having converted a single detective to the Silettian path-of-no-path. Sean Risling, never particularly devout to begin with, only had biological offspring, not intellectual.

And then there was Jay Gleason, Jacques Silette's last student. And while the rest of us kept in touch somewhat over the years, emailing or calling or telegramming or messaging when we needed clues or money or confirmation—although less and less as the years crept on, and we each had less of those items to offer—Jay had never been part of our world, even as ill-defined and unsupported as that world was. He never connected with the other Silettians. Only with Silette himself.

Jay, the legend went, showed up on Silette's doorstep in Paris one day in 1970-something, young and beautiful and bright, overflowing with money and admiration and inspiration—all things in increasingly short supply for Silette, especially in his later years.

Long after Constance had moved to New Orleans and Hans had gone on to Amsterdam, Jay Gleason was there. What did they talk about? What did Jay learn?

By the time Jay came along, the world had largely passed Silette by, if it had ever paused for him at all. He'd gone from dull respect to a quick moment of notoriety to a long jag of ridicule and then been forgotten, like the Brownie camera or the IWW.

In the sixties, Silette was, I like to imagine, content in his own little world, comfortable with the ridicule of outsiders and inferiors. After a long affair with Constance and numerous shorter affairs with other women, he married one of his students, Marie, and they had a daughter, Belle. They were happy. They loved each other. Marie was intelligent and complicated. Silette was growing old and his rough edges were softening. They both had money. They had an apartment in Paris and had inherited a country house from Marie's family. There was an ancient little vineyard on the property: reportedly, before it all came crashing down, Silette was studying winemaking techniques. They weren't accepted by Silette's university colleagues or Marie's staid family, but they had their own circle of friends to keep them busy: artists, occultists, those few students and other detectives who chose to understand.

In 1971 their daughter Belle was born; both parents were delighted. You might imagine Jacques Silette to be a cold man, overly intellectual, judgmental of his child. By all accounts you would be wrong. Constance told me an offhand story one night about how, in his thank-you card for Belle's first-birthday gift (Constance sent a Chanel rattle), Silette went on a rapturous rant about the joy of changing diapers, about the bliss and depth of seeing material existence come full circle and the rare opportunity to spend so much time handling the *materia prima* the alchemists had spun into gold.

In 1973 Jacques and Marie took their first trip to America. There was a case to solve, but they also took a long trip across the country seeing friends and introducing their daughter. They visited Constance in New Orleans, of course. In Akron, Ohio, they spent a day with a visionary locksmith Silette had corresponded with since the 1950s. Next they spent a few days in New England visiting Marie's cousins at various universities: linguists; anthropologists; psychoanalysts. In Chicago, Silette gave a lecture to the Women's Society for Philosophy, where he apparently confused and dismayed the crowd of three who attended, although the night maid, listening from the hallway, afterward had dinner with Silette and Marie in their hotel, and they became fast friends. In Kansas City, he and Marie visited with an elderly detective named Horace Washington who, though solitary by nature and not given to discussing it much, was one of the first people in America to read and understand Silette's book.

Finally they landed in New York City. Silette had another lecture scheduled, this one at a small private library near Gramercy Park. He'd been asked to speak to a group of detective novel enthusiasts about something like "the eternal meaning of mysteries." He spent forty minutes talking about a rare kind of praying mantis that lived in a rose bush outside his house, and then another fifty minutes explaining the etymology of the word *clue*, yanking a thread out of a very expensive tapestry to illustrate. Most people left. A few fell asleep. Two became angry and tried to stop the lecture. One listened. That was enough for Silette.

Marie was tired. She stayed home to rest with Belle.

After the lecture Silette had dessert and cheese and coffee with the men in the book club. Most had left, but the two who stayed were by all accounts lively and appreciative. The desserts were excellent.

After midnight, Silette returned to their hotel to find Marie drugged and unconscious. Belle was gone.

There was a rumor, likely not true, that Silette—the man who solved the Case of the Bitten Apple without even getting out of his taxi, the man who found the Clue of the Watercolor Butterfly in forty-four minutes—strolled into the hotel, smiling and relaxed, took the elevator up to his room, walked in, saw Marie sleeping, and then looked for Belle. Only when he couldn't find her did he realize something was horribly wrong. The most brilliant mind of the twentieth century and he walked right into his own tragedy like any other stupid fucking sap.

There was another rumor, one I was more inclined to believe, that told the story differently. In this story, the men in the club had just put out dessert. Silette bit into a crisp sweet-bitter pignoli nut biscuit and said, "My life. Jesus Christ, my life," and dropped the cookie and ran back to the hotel, but he was too late. Belle was gone. Apparently the light from one of the men's cigarettes hit Silette's eye in a certain way that allowed him to put together the previously unrecognized clues—the unlocked door to the hotel staircase, the fingerprint on the elevator button—and let him see that his life, as he knew it, was now over.

The police came. Interpol came. The FBI. Every detective of any merit, real or imagined, wanted to solve the case, some to help one of their own, some to spite Silette.

No one ever found one clue. Not one hint, one word, one thread.

Ironically, the greatest detective the world ever knew never solved his own biggest mystery. Neither did anyone else. Belle was never found, dead or alive.

Silette and Marie were broken people. After they got back to France they were rarely seen in public again. Marie died two years later from a broken heart. Silette never wrote again, and died in 1981. He still worked a few cases over those years. Of course he solved them all. But fewer every year. Mostly he stayed in Marie's country house. He remained friendly with a few people he'd known in town—the butcher, his gardener, the man who owned the cigar store—but let most of his other relationships slide away.

But in the last years of his life, Silette made one new friend.

Jay Gleason.

Legend had it that Jay had shown up at Silette's door one night, leonine and lithe with long golden hair and bell-bottoms, empty inside from a louche childhood in the mansions of Newport and Cannes, lusted after but never loved, burning with an internal fire for the truth that brought him to Silette's door. The story was that he showed up, drunk on the thrill of mysteries, feverishly desperate to tell the great man his own little solution to the Case of the Murdered Madam. His solution was wrong. But for some reason—maybe loneliness—Silette invited Jay in, and let him stay. Maybe they were lovers. Maybe more like father and son. Either way, the two of them, by all accounts, formed their own little world, Jay alternately learning from the great man and protecting him from the sharp edges of life, which turn so much sharper as you age.

Sean Risling once told me a story about Jay. This was in Los Angeles, maybe 2005. Sean was still working the encyclopedia of flower poisons he'd been working on since I'd met him. I helped him out when I could—stopping by an herbarium in London if convenient or introducing him to a woman I'd met who'd lived through an accidental meal of *amaryllis belladonna* (she described the hallucinations to Sean as "being punished by witches who'd been sent by my father"). We'd have dinner once a year if he was in San Francisco (usually Cliff House; Sean liked the view) or if I was in Los Angeles (Musso & Frank's; we both liked the food).

We were at Musso's. I was in town for a funeral. We'd already eaten crab cakes and sand dabs and killed a bottle of wine. Now we were on to coffee and Diplomat Pudding. And somehow, as always on these nights, the topic came around to Silette.

"Did I ever tell you," Sean said, "about Chicago?"

"Chicago?" I said. I was a little drunk.

Sean raised his eyebrows a little, glad he hadn't told me about Chicago before so he could tell me now.

"Oh yeah," Sean said. "I never told you this?"

"I don't think so."

"So I'm in Chicago," Sean began. "I'm on a case for this investment firm. I used to do financial stuff. This was before you knew me. Long time ago. Whitley Cross. That was the client. Whitley Cross. A private bank. Horrible people. They've got me in Palmer House. I hated all of it, the finance people, the work, the math, everything—so I'm in the bar all the time. Amazing bar. They've got these olives stuffed with blue cheese in the martinis. They're like a meal. And of course the drinks.

"So I'm sitting at a table in the bar in Palmer House, going through this mountain of spreadsheets. Forensic accounting. It's incredibly boring. I'm drinking too much. I wish I was dead. And then someone sits at my table and I look up and it's Jay. Jay Gleason. He smiles and we shake hands."

"Wait," I said. "You knew Jay?"

Somehow I'd never realized this before. I'd met Jay once. I hadn't known it was him at the time.

"Kind of," Sean said. "I never met Silette, you know that, but we used to write sometimes. One time I was in France, I was hoping to meet him. We had a lunch scheduled in Paris, but he sent Jay to let me know he couldn't make it. We didn't talk much—I was waiting in this little café near the museum, Jay came by, introduced himself, sat down, explained that Silette wouldn't be making it, asked if I was getting around Paris OK, did I need anything. Just normal stuff. He bought me lunch and he left. I'd heard he was this vicious guy. He told me where to get my suit cleaned. Told me where to go for oysters.

"So here I am in Chicago, and Jay sits right down at my table. We shake hands, exchange small talk. He's very sketchy about why he's in town. I don't push it. This is 1989, maybe. 1988. I have no idea what he's been up to. I know the rumors.

"So I tell him about the work I'm doing. I guess it's obvious that I hate it. Not just that I hate the work, but that my life is just miserable at this point. I'm making a ton of money, I'm staying in the Palmer House, I'm at the top of my field, and I'm hating every day of it. My wife had left me like a year before. I hardly even noticed.

"So we sit, we have a few drinks, he's got nothing to do so we go to dinner. There's a steakhouse downstairs. Very civilized. We have a nice dinner, I try to pay, Jay won't let me. Pulls a roll of cash out of his pocket, a couple of thousand bucks, easy. In 1980-something. We talk about people we know, detectives, trade news. And then toward the end of dinner Jay says to me, 'Why are you doing this?'

"I don't even know what he means at first. Why am I doing what?

He looks around and makes this gesture with his hands. This gesture."

Sean tried to replicate it. It was kind of like a shrug, but with wide, expansive hands.

"This gesture," Sean went on. "This gesture, I can't do it right, but it was like—everything. Like this whole fucking life. Why are you doing this?

"We were both standing next to the table. And Jay looks at me and he does that gesture again, that thing with his hands, and he says, 'This is over for you, Sean. Starting right now. This is all over for you. You need money?' He takes that big fat roll of cash out of his pocket and holds it out to me. I didn't need money; I wouldn't take it. We shake hands; he leaves.

"That night, I have this crazy dream. I dream that I'm in the woods, and there's flowers all around me. They're incredibly beautiful, and they smell amazing. I never smelled anything like that in a dream before. Like roses just past their prime. Sweet, but almost too sweet. Somehow I knew not to touch them. I knew if I touched them, I would die. Not right away, not soon, but over the long run. These flowers would kill me. They were poison.

"The next morning I wake up and I have like five messages from Whitley Cross. I was fired. I never knew what happened. Never knew if Jay made it happen somehow or if it was all just a coincidence.

"But you know, after that dream I never took another financial job again. And a few days later, I started working on the *Encyclopedia of Poisonous Orchids*. And since then—"

Sean made another kind of gesture now—another shrug, another gesture with his hands. But this one said *All of this. I got all of this*.

I knew another story about Jay, too. The semi-annual *Détection* newsletter was published for eleven issues by a man named Lamar Livingston. Lamar was a criminology professor at UCLA. Most criminologists were sad and scarred people. Lamar was tall and excitable and optimistic. He never really understood Silette and never really understood Silettians; the newsletter was more of a gesture—a gesture of friendliness toward his fellow criminologists; of reconciliation toward rival schools of criminology; of his belief that all mysteries can be solved. He also ran a newsletter for forensic etymologists. He also did it, as he did everything, for the pure joy of doing things.

In issue 11, Summer 1991, Lamar had the idea to publish a directory of known Silettians, and their contact information. He meant well. He included Constance, of course, Sean, Janet Perth (a dull but serviceable Silettian detective in Australia), and Hans Jacobson.

And Jay. Somehow, I don't know through who, Lamar got an address for Jay Gleason in Las Vegas and, not knowing any better, published it.

The next day Lamar woke up to a bloody knife stuck into the door of his house in Westwood, and a note suggesting he refrain from publishing people's addresses in the future.

Lamar never published the Silettian newsletter again.

———

Some people said Jay was with Silette when he died. Some people said he'd absconded with the best of the Silette family silverware long before that. Some said Jay's rich family had cut him off altogether. Some said Jay had inherited a fortune.

The only concrete thing I knew about him was that he'd once lived in Las Vegas. I knew this because I'd seen him there.

After Sean Risling introduced me to Constance in Los Angeles, after she let me think I'd helped her solve the HappyBurger Murder Case, before she invited me to come back to New Orleans with her, we took a trip to Las Vegas.

It was, maybe, the best day of my life. The case was closed and I wasn't sure I'd ever hear from Constance again.

Instead, she asked me to drive her to Las Vegas the next day. I could hardly sleep that night, and we left early the next morning. She directed me to a big, luxurious, ugly estate on the edges of the city. She went inside and came out a few minutes later, not alone. With her were two men. One of them had Constance by the arm. I never knew what their dispute was about. But I could tell it wasn't going anywhere good.

She'd asked me to wait in the car. Instead I pointed a gun at the two men. I already would have died for her. They let her go.

It was only a few minutes later, when I saw her damp face in the cool car, that I realized she'd been scared for her life.

And it was only years later, when I came across his picture in a pile of photos on Constance's desk, that I realized one of the men in the house in Las Vegas had been Jay Gleason.

White man. White-blond hair. Narrow face.

I never knew what they fought about, and I, and everyone else, lost track of Jay after that day. He'd dropped out of sight. There were rumors that he had had to disappear after running a real-estate con on the wrong men. That he'd hooked up with a man selling fake gemstones out of Phoenix, Arizona. That he'd had an affair with a Baptist politician and had blackmailed him for a small fortune. And a long-standing rumor that Jay Gleason ran a scam correspondence school for private investigation out of Las Vegas.

Like the PI school advertised in the Cynthia Silverton comic books.

The ad I'd answered five days before someone tried to kill me.

———

The plan, as I'd told Daisy, was to put her up in one of the low-rent, likely unpleasant, but safe-enough hotels in far west Berkeley, using the ID and credit card I'd stolen. We were on our way there when the radio spoke up. I'd had it on low volume this whole time and it had been steadily letting out a stream of robberies, homicides, static, and other things that weren't about me.

Now it was about me. Someone had spotted the Lincoln. The
cop on the radio was reporting in to his superior that the Lincoln
had been seen near the Ashby BART station. Even better, he had a
Nevada plate number—RBH444.

"Sorry," I said to Daisy. "We're going there now."

She raised an eyebrow at me.

I popped another pill.

"Let me see your phone for a sec?" I said to Daisy.

She gave me her phone.

I threw it out the window.

"Fuck," Daisy said.

I figured we could beat the cops to the Ashby BART station. I was
wrong. We were a half block away on MLK when I saw the flashing
lights. We drove up slowly, as if we were rubberneckers.

I saw a bunch of cops.

I didn't see the Lincoln.

I drove around for a while and looked for the Lincoln. No luck,
if it was ever there at all. I didn't understand all the talk on the radio,
most of it in arcane bureaucratic cop slang, but it sounded like they'd
lost the car. I took Daisy to a hotel on San Pablo. I asked if they took
cash. The man behind the bulletproof glass said no. No one took cash
anymore. Where did people turn tricks? Where did they cheat on their
spouses? Binge on drugs? All the darkest parts of life required cash.
Saving those mysteries for another day, I paid for four days with one
of Letitia Parnell's stolen credit cards and registered in her name. The
man at the counter didn't blink at her ID. Apparently the dark side
was now run on stolen credit and fake IDs.

I walked Daisy to her room and checked it out. No one had followed us here and, without her phone, there was no way on earth
anyone could follow her.

"So what do I do," Daisy said, "just hang out for the rest of my
life?"

"For a few days," I said. "Just hang out for say three days. Four days. And then one way or another, it'll all be done."

"Yeah," she said. "One of us'll be dead."

"Yeah," I said. "Probably. Hopefully not you and not me."

"That'd be a good ending," she said, trying not to sound scared.

I looked at her, looked at her for real, and she looked at me.

"It's not gonna be you," I said. "Let's just make that deal right now."

She shivered, and then nodded.

I gave her a handful of cash for when the stolen card was cancelled and we said goodbye.

I was going back to the car when Claude called. When he first starting working for me I made him buy three disposable phones and keep them charged, on, and ready, just for occasions like this. So far we'd used two of them. Although those other occasions were not all that much like this. One was a time when I wanted to order some painkillers on the internet and was paranoid about being traced. Another was when I wanted to pretend to give my number to a guy I'd spent the night with in Seattle and couldn't think of a fake one fast enough.

"What's going on?" Claude said. "Are you OK?"

"For the moment," I said. I was about to pull out to San Pablo and start toward Nevada when all the exhaustion and blood loss hit me like a drug and my head spun.

"Whoa," I said. "Wow."

The world outside the car tilted one way and then careened the other—

"Claire, what's going on?" asked Claude. "Where are you? I'll come get you."

The last thing I needed or wanted was to get Claude involved. I didn't want to make this more complicated than it was. And I didn't want Claude to get hurt.

For a quick moment a horrible idea passed through my mind—

that I had already ruined Claude's life, which had been safe and steady before I hired him. And maybe now I would get him killed. I pushed it away.

"Listen," I said. "You have to do exactly as I tell you, all right?"

"Yeah, OK," he said. He knew me and knew my voice and knew when I was serious.

"OK. Grab your laptop, leave your phone, and leave your house, right now."

I heard him rustling around for his laptop and snatching it up. Claude lived near College Avenue in Berkeley, near the campus and not far from downtown Berkeley. It was always busy around there, even at night.

"Now walk downtown. Stay on the busy streets. Find something open twenty-four hours—a restaurant or coffee shop or whatever. OK?"

"I'm putting on my shoes," he said. "Laptop, wallet, keys. All right, I'm out the door, locking the door, leaving—"

"Wait," I said. I felt my head spin again and everything started to go black around the edges. I shook myself and spun back around to real life.

"I need you to find out who owns a Nevada Lincoln with the plate number RBH444," I told Claude.

"What's going on?"

It sounded like his words were coming from a million miles away and it seemed like reality was curling up at the edges.

"Just go somewhere safe," I said. "Just promise me you'll be safe."

And then the edges of everything crumbled away, and it all fell down to black.

CHAPTER 6

THE MYSTERY OF THE CBSIS

Los Angeles, 1999

I counted my meeting with Adam Dubinsky as half an hour. Three hundred and ninety-nine and a half hours to go for my fucking license. Three hundred and ninety-nine and a half hours to go before I could legally do the only thing I was good at; the thing I'd been doing all my life.

I was staying in a motel on an unpleasant strip on Hollywood Boulevard. It wasn't so different from my room in San Francisco. Instead of Chinatown, it was in Thai Town. No cat. Spending time around people who didn't share my language was my best bet, apparently. My room was thirty-nine dollars a night in San Francisco and thirty-six in Los Angeles, and the room in Los Angeles tried to be nice in a way that made it even uglier; in addition to the worn bed and the aging armchair and the sad little writing table there were new, unfortunate, striped drapes. A Thai family—parents, grandparents, three kids—ran the desk. None of them had the slightest interest in me or made any pretense of friendliness. Thank God for small favors.

I didn't really know why I never had any money. I would ask for, and get, a lot for a case. I'd been working since I was a kid. No one came to me unless they were desperate and well prepared to pay, whether they could afford it or not. I didn't have an office and I didn't advertise so people generally found me the way people found a drug dealer or a bootleg movie: ask around; look for people who knew; try to read the signs. By the time a client found me they were usually willing to pay and usually I made sure they did. But I only took the cases I wanted to take and I didn't like to think about money before or after I spent it and I never bothered to collect for expenses or keep track of tax deductions or pay taxes or deal with any of it. So maybe I did know why I never had any money. Those were pretty much the reasons. Also I'd do things like give a couple of hundred bucks to a cop I knew in New Orleans who was out of work or give even more to a lady I met in an Ecuadorean restaurant who was trying to get a dog shelter off the ground. I didn't do those things to be nice so much as for the cocaine-like rush of good feelings and self-aggrandizement that they brought. I didn't try to kid myself otherwise. And now, of course, I wasn't getting paid at all.

Back in my room I opened the file Adam Dubinsky had given me. First I skimmed it and then I went back to the beginning and carefully read every page. Four years ago, in 1995, a man named Merritt Underwood died. Maybe he was murdered or maybe he just had bad luck. Or good luck. The case was never solved. Underwood was an artist and made some money but hadn't acquired a lot of wealth: he'd worked and sold less and less over the years, and spent more time drinking and picking fights with people.

On July 8, 1995, his car was found at the bottom of a valley in

Topanga Canyon. He was forty-four when he died. At first it was assumed to be an accident, but his parents, both doctors in Pasadena, both now dead, were never convinced, and suspected murder. I didn't know why they suspected it. They'd paid Adam Dubinsky to try to solve the mystery of who, if anyone, killed Merritt. Adam Dubinsky was still working on it when they died; first the father, from a heart attack, and then eight months later the mother, causes unknown. With no living client, and no one paying him, Adam had put the case aside in favor of mysteries that would affect the living.

The police had turned up nothing. The highlights from their report were in Adam's file. Merritt was a life-long inhabitant of Los Angeles and his whole world was here in the city. Everyone loved Merritt—until he got drunk, did something stupid, and then they didn't love him anymore. Then they put him outside like a dog that chewed up a pair of cheap shoes: annoying, and doubtless a nuisance, but no one seemed to really hate him, and most seemed to find him cute, and they always let him back in the house.

Along with the report was a set of slides of photographs of his paintings. There were also a few photographs of Merritt himself.

He was a man you might call "burly." I couldn't tell how tall he was from the photos but he was tall enough and pleasantly wide. He didn't mind taking up space. He wasn't particularly handsome. There was nothing wrong with his face, all the flesh was assembled well enough, but not especially or particularly well. He was unshaven for a day or two and his hair looked like he'd probably cut it himself.

But there was something about the way he curled his lips. Some kind of light in his eyes. It was like he didn't know how to hide.

The last photo was a candid shot. It was at a party; there was a crowd of unfocused faces behind him. He was looking at the camera and lighting a cigarette.

The look on his face was a cynical kind of almost-smile. It said a few things at once: first, *Stop taking my picture*. The second thing was harder to put into words. I looked and I looked and finally I figured it was something like: *This is all so fucking ridiculous. But at least we know it.*

I wondered who the *we* was—who took the picture.

I put that photo aside and propped it up on the alarm clock next to my bed. I probably would've slept with him in real life if I'd had the chance.

Also in the file was a list of KAs—Known Associates. That would be where I would start.

There was also a note in the file from Adam Dubinsky's first meeting with Merritt Underwood's father.

Hired Richter Agency. No results.

The file also had a few personal items from Merritt. I couldn't make heads or tails of Adam's organizational method. Along with obviously important things, like a timeline of Merritt's death and the list of KAs there were receipts from dry cleaners and a take-out menu from a sushi restaurant on Ventura Boulevard.

In the back of the file there was a big envelope full of other envelopes. A note on the outside of the outer envelope explained: MAIL 7/11/95. It was the mail that had come to Merritt in the days right before and after he died. Most of it was unopened. Water bills. Bank statements. I guessed Merritt wasn't the type to open his mail promptly. Even the mail from before his death was probably never seen. Ads, bills, and a card from a dentist who wanted Merritt to come in and get his teeth scrubbed.

And a letter. Not to Merritt; from him. It was addressed to a man in New York City named Jacob Heartwell and had come back to Merritt, stamped RETURN TO SENDER. NO LONGER AT THIS ADDRESS.

Merritt had decorated the outside of the envelope with sketches of plants and flowers and insects. I opened it carefully, feeling a tiny bit of electricity as I read a letter written for someone who wasn't me. The letter was hand-written on lined paper with holes for a three-ring binder. The letter was three lines.

You are my friend.
I love you.
I miss you.

That night I walked down Sunset Boulevard through Hollywood and West Hollywood to Beverly Hills. I kept walking. The sidewalk ended and soon I was up in the hills, walking down the side of the road, hoping not to get hit by a Porsche. In the hills people started screaming at me from cars. I'd forgotten that walking in Beverly Hills was a sexually deviant action. Maybe it was a fetish. Maybe some rich LA man would offer me money to watch me walk.

Somewhere a few miles west, if I were to keep walking, down at the very end, was Frank Richter, the richest, most successful PI in the world, and his information empire, a veritable high-rise beehive of detectives. Or maybe more like a nest of wasps. They said Richter had files on more people than the FBI. They said he knew when a pin dropped in Juneau or a baby cried in Brooklyn. No one I knew had seen him in years. The rumor was that since his last wife left him—his fifth, and the fifth to leave—Richter hadn't left his house on the edge of a cliff in Malibu. He saw almost no one and left the day-to-day running of his agency, now the biggest in the world, to a team of lackeys, yes-men, and minions. It was easier to get a meeting with certain presidents than Richter.

But he would see me. I was sure of it.

Car after car of men yelled at me, until, long after dark, I turned around and walked back to my room.

The next morning I made an appointment to meet a man named Carl Avery at his house at noon. Carl was the first KA of Merritt Underwood on the list: peer, friend. Carl was handsome with a few days' worth of stubble and big blue eyes and, judging by the size of his house in Venice, a pile of money.

Venice was cool and foggy and smelled like the ocean. Carl was tall and gaunt with a giant, dull aura that made him even bigger. Merritt had been large, too, according to the file: a bit over six feet and close to two hundred pounds. I figured Carl for the same height, thirty pounds fewer. I made a note to research the ratio of human size to artistic accomplishment.

He opened the door wearing blue jeans and a loose button-down shirt, frayed around the edges. He was barefoot. His hair was short and thick and black, with gray around the temples.

"I thought this was all over," Carl said, looking unhappily at me, after a long explanation of my presence at his door. "I thought everyone had given up."

He sounded like he was running low on patience. Weren't we all?

"Well Mr. Dubinsky," I said, "the first detective. I mean the second detective. Mr. Dubinsky wanted me to tie up some loose ends."

We sat in Carl's studio, a large loft-like structure attached to the back of the house and flooded with light. The light in Los Angeles seemed like it was bought and paid for, like it was something the residents were entitled to. On the walls was a series of paintings that I figured were his that made no sense to me. They weren't beautiful. They didn't make me feel anything at all. At least he was trying. Although what he was trying I wasn't entirely sure. Art was a mystery to me, one I wasn't interested enough to solve.

"So how is it that you knew Merritt?" I asked. "Through the art world?"

I didn't know if there was any such thing as an Art World but it felt like a good segue. At twenty-eight I was still working on questioning people, on listening to them tell me the words that could pierce through their armor; on listening to what came out through the holes I'd pierced.

People wanted to tell you the truth. They just didn't want it to be true, and they didn't know they wanted to tell it.

"Yeah," Carl said. "I mean, we were with the same gallery for a while."

"Merritt was a painter?" I asked, even though I knew the answer.

"Yes," Carl said. "Very sculptural. Very three-dimensional. He did these huge canvases. That's—well, that's one reason things got hard for him. No one could deal with these huge creations. These giant, dark canvases . . . They were like a storm. Like a hurricane. Brilliant. But no one wanted to buy them."

"Was Merritt a good painter?" I asked.

"Well, yes," Carl said. He frowned and looked confused. "Very. But does it matter?"

"Everything matters," I said. "Until we know otherwise."

"Hmm," Carl said. He furrowed his brow. His face was long and thin and he had the kind of wrinkles down his cheeks that could easily be knife scars. "He was very good," Carl said. "Probably the best of us all."

"So you said that was 'one reason' things got hard for him," I asked. "The big canvases. What were the others?"

Carl let out a long attenuated sound from his throat. "Merritt was a difficult person," he finally said, with something like admiration. "We were very close at one point. I loved him. I loved him very much. He was like a brother to me. An older brother. But he was hard to love."

"You said you were very close at one point?" I said. I ignored the bit about him being hard to love, which described everyone, ever. *Hard to love* was a pretty good definition of humanity in general. "When was that?"

"When I was younger," Carl said. "Like, ten years ago? He was on a jury—I was in art school, we had a little senior-project show, Merritt was one of the judges. This was when he was at his peak. Fame-wise. The Untitled days."

"Untitled?"

"The Untitled paintings," Carl explained. "Those were Merritt's best work. I'm sure you know them. You just don't know you know them. They're like air. Just part of the cultural landscape. Anyway, I was enormously flattered that he would choose me. For the show. It was a huge deal for me. We became friends."

"Tell me about Merritt," I said.

"He was one of the greatest artists of his time," Carl said, without hesitation. "Maybe my time, too. And I wouldn't be anything without him. Well, I don't know about that. But I don't know who I would be. He gave me my first big break. And a number of breaks after that. Without Merritt I'd probably be selling shit on the boardwalk. And he was smart. He was probably the smartest man I ever met, in some ways."

"What ways?"

Carl frowned. He thought about it. Really thought.

"He saw things," he said. "Things other people didn't see. Connections. Relationships between and among ideas. The themes of things. That was his strength.

"When he was younger, he had these amazing ideas about painting. He was one of those boy wonders, you know. Got out of art school and he was already a star. Already had a gallery lined up, already selling. But, you know. Artists are difficult. It isn't an ordinary life. You have to hold yourself together, and he didn't. I'm barely doing it myself. You want success and then success comes and it isn't what you think it is."

"What did he drop?" I asked.

Carl looked at me.

"You said he didn't hold himself together," I said. "What didn't he hold?"

"Huh," Carl said. "You certainly take things literally. Well, Merritt's work stopped selling, for one. He dropped that—making money. Untitled, you know, those canvases were . . . they were luminous. They were beautiful. Merritt understood color like no one else. But then every year after that—the next show sold less, and the next less, and so on. It wasn't that the work wasn't as good. It was better. Better than anything he'd done before. Maybe better than, you know, anyone has done before. But it was dark. Hard to sell. And Merritt himself—you know, he was not such an easy sell anymore. That was something else that he couldn't hold on to. He became difficult. Everyone wanted him to return to the Untitled days. That's what they always want you to do. Be young again. Be a child again. We have this cultural prejudice about growing up. But Merritt grew up, and he grew into something strange and dark. Something beautiful. He would fight with people over the silliest things. He drank, he did a lot of coke, but the real thing was that he would just lose it. Just self-destruct."

"Self-destruct how?" I prodded.

Carl sighed a few more times. A young woman with very long brown hair came into the room and told Carl, "He's on the phone for you."

Carl sighed again.

"Can it wait?" he asked.

The woman shook her head. Carl went to take his call. I did nothing. When Carl came back he'd had time to come up with an anecdote and he told it to me.

"Here's an example of Merritt in full self-destruction. Just prime death drive. He was on the way out. This was not long before he died. I hadn't spoken to him in a while. I tried, but. So I heard he was broke and I had my dealer, Dennis Schmidt, try to help. So he, Dennis, sets a meeting for Merritt and this rich collector. Hollywood type, and I'm not telling you his name. But a very, very wealthy man. So they meet for a friendly drink at the Chateau Marmont. The point of these meetings—you know, these people spend a lot of money for these paintings. They are not cheap. And one thing they ask for, in return, sometimes, is a little time with the artist. I don't know. It's ridiculous, but I do it. Maybe I shouldn't. But I do.

"So Merritt meets this guy at the Marmont. And apparently Merritt got very drunk. And apparently the guy—I mean, I know this guy, he is not a bad guy—this guy had some ideas about art that Merritt didn't like.

"So Merritt, who is desperately broke and calling in every favor he has for a sale, for a loan, for any money at all, which I did, which I did for him—and was very happy to do—Merritt strips off his clothes, jumps in the pool stark naked, and then shits in the pool. Sorry. Then he gets out, puts his clothes back on, invites the guy to take a swim, and leaves."

Carl let out another long sigh.

It didn't sound so self-destructive to me. I guess it depended on who you thought your self was and what exactly you would be destroying. Was your self the part of you that wanted to make money? Merritt sounded pretty ready to destruct that. But maybe his self was really the other part—the part that wanted to go swimming.

"I mean, if he hadn't had the accident, or whatever it was," Carl went on, "I don't know what would have happened to him. Past a certain point, nothing ever panned out. Past another point—probably the shitting-in-the-pool point—no one even wanted to meet him. He would say something horrible, show up late, drink too much, insult their taste in art. It stopped being fun. It stopped being cool. You would think people would care about the work. You'd think that would be the thing. But you would be wrong. That's, like, half of what they care about."

Carl looked at nothing and sighed.

"Merritt stopped being marketable," Carl said, as if confessing. "I kind of took his place with that. Being marketable. Being the thing of the year. The flavor of the month. Not the career I wanted, but here we are."

"Do you think someone killed him?" I asked.

"God no," Carl said right away. "I think he was wasted and fell off the road."

"Do you think Merritt will be remembered?" I asked.

"God yes," Carl said just as quickly. "Look, I've told you all the reasons he was difficult. I haven't told you—because you didn't ask—why I loved him. Because I did love him, very much. Merritt had, when he was younger, the biggest heart of anyone I ever met. And that came through in his work. And even later, as he got darker, as life turned him darker—somehow that always came through in his work. His heart. It wasn't obvious, it wasn't easy to see at the time, but in retrospect, it was always there. That was always the main thing about Merritt. Everyone thought his late paintings were shit. Well, not shit, just not as good. But they weren't shit. They were better, maybe. Harder. Like I said, they didn't sell. But what sells isn't always good. Those two things don't really have anything to do with each other. Lord knows I know THAT as well as anyone."

I wasn't sure if Carl genuinely loathed himself or was just being politely self-deprecating. I guessed the first.

"So what happened to him?" I asked. "Why did he become so difficult?"

Carl shrugged. "He came from a decent family, you know. Surgeons, I think. Grew up here in LA. I mean, artists; there's always some kind of fuck-up. You don't do this unless you have some kind of chip on your shoulder. You don't do this unless you have something to prove. So what was Merritt's particular, you know, psychoanalytic quirk that made him what he was? I don't really know. I don't think he ever knew, either."

Merritt's father was a psychologist and his mother was a dentist. In my notebook I wrote *upgraded to surgeons*.

I showed Carl the photo of Merritt. The one of him lighting a cigarette.

"Well, that's him all right," Carl said.

"So who do you think took the picture?" I asked.

Carl shrugged.

"I have no idea," he said. "I doubt it matters. It's just a photo. I'm sure it doesn't mean anything at all. Now, I'm sorry, but I really have to go."

We made our pleasant goodbyes and Carl went to the kitchen and I left.

In front of Carl's house I got out my notebook and wrote: *Picture matters. Picture matters very much.*

CHAPTER 7

THE CASE OF THE INFINITE BLACKTOP

Oakland, 2011

I woke up an hour later in the stolen Nissan. I went through the whole mental ritual again: Where was I? What was I doing? Who was I, exactly?

Accident. Car. Lincoln. Claire DeWitt.

I checked my phone. Claude had texted me the registration address for the Lincoln. It was in a shitty part of Las Vegas near the strip. I knew it well from the Case of the Golden Eggshell, a short little case where, in less than two days, I found out who'd stolen the gold and why. It wasn't money. It's never money. It's always one of three things: anger or love or both.

I sent out little tentacles of consciousness through my limbs.

Pain. Exhaustion. Broken things and sickness and more pain.

If you want to live, some voice in the base of my skull said, *you get up. Now.*

I pushed away all my pain and self-pity, all my exhaustion and sorrow. I pushed away everything except my sheer will to live—that will that had left me so many times before. But now it burned bright enough I thought we might burn down the whole fucking world together, my will and I.

I started the car, swallowed two more pills without a drink, and started to pull out just as the radio crackled with news: the cops had found the Lincoln again. A patrol car had spotted it in the northern end of Oakland and they were following it north.

Now I was wide awake and everything was crystal-clear and focused in high-definition.

I swung the car around and headed back toward Berkeley.

I caught up with them where Albany meets El Cerrito. It was barely dawn. I drove along a parallel road for a few blocks hoping I could see the cops or the Lincoln but I didn't see either until I sped up and then ran a red light at Central Avenue.

There was the Lincoln.

I wished I was better at math. I was going about fifty and the Lincoln about sixty. How much faster would I have to go, and exactly where would I turn, and precisely what moment would I need to jump out of the Nissan if I wanted to turn right and stop the Lincoln in its tracks and catch the driver?

I heard a painful crash from what I thought was the next avenue over. I made the next right and turned the corner and saw the source of the sound and braked: the cop car had crashed into the Lincoln, like the Lincoln had done with me. But the unstoppable iron-framed Lincoln pulled away and tried to keep going. It got about fifteen feet before the car died. The driver got out and ran.

He was a full block ahead of me, and he was running and I was driving.

I couldn't get a good look at his face. All I could see was roughly what Daisy Ramirez had told me: white hair, pale skin, narrow face, slim frame, wearing a button-down shirt and jeans, couldn't get a good look at his shoes.

It could have been Jay Gleason.

It could have been a million other men, too.

He ran north. The cop got out of her car to follow him on foot. I hit the gas and sped toward the scene, hoping to catch him—and maybe run him over—in my stolen Nissan.

But another cop was pulling up in a black-and-white and I didn't really want to interact with the cops just now. I kept driving, swung around the block, parked, got out of the car, and tried to run after him. I could see the man with white hair and the cop up a block ahead of me, and then two blocks ahead, and then three.

He was getting away. I couldn't keep up with him and neither could the cop.

My adrenaline and fear and the uppers I'd taken kept me going for about one minute before my body started to scream at me. My lungs felt like someone was tightening a vise around them. I started to stumble and gasp and everything went gray and in a second that seemed like a year I realized I wasn't running at all, I was falling, and it was like that dream where you need to run but you can't because it's like running in quicksand

something was pulling me down, everything was

and then pushed me down, and then just stopped as I fell down, soft black clouds everywhere

and it all went black.

———

"Hey, miss."

I opened my eyes. The sun was East Bay bright and burned on my banged-up corneas. None of your bullshit San Francisco fog to smooth out the rough edges.

I kinda-sorta remembered where I was and I looked around and saw that I was mostly right. The man with black hair, a cop, a car, running—

I looked around a little more.

"Hey Miss."

Before passing out I'd stumbled into the doorway of a falafel restaurant and likely looked more like a homeless man catching a nap than a participant in whatever it was that had happened two blocks back with the cars.

"HEY."

The person saying HEY was a man standing above me. I looked at him. He looked about sixty and almost as wide as he was tall and spoke with an Egyptian accent.

"Hey," I said. "What's up?"

"My doorway," he said.

"Oh," I said. I was blocking him from entering his restaurant.

I tried to stand up and everything seemed effervescent, maybe carbonated, and I sat back down.

"Just one sec," I said. "Don't worry. I really gotta go. I have things to do."

The Egyptian man sighed and kind of nudged me out of his way with his legs and stepped over me and opened his door and lifted his gates and went into his store.

I tried to keep my eyes open. For all I knew the man with white hair was still looking for me here in the neighborhood, although it wasn't likely. The cops had probably scared him off, and I was likely safe for the rest of the day.

But still. Probably a good idea to get going.

I stood up again. White electric snow fell across my eyes and the street turned upside down.

I tried to sit back down but I was already sitting.

The Egyptian man came back out. He had a paper cup in one hand and something wrapped in wax paper in the other.

He held them out to me.

"Eat," he said. "Eat, then go."

I took them. He turned and went back in before I could say thanks.

In the cup was strong sweet mint tea and in the wax paper was a pastry made of cheese wrapped in phyllo dough. I didn't think I was hungry but as soon as I took a bite I realized I was starving. I ate the pastry and drank the tea.

This time when I stood up, I stayed up.

I checked my pockets. Still had the Taser, twenty-two bucks in cash, and the bottle of pep pills.

I figured heading back to the Nissan might not be wise.

All I had to do now was steal another car.

———

I already looked the part, which made it easy. There was a local supermarket across the street but I knew there was a Whole Foods less than a mile away which I figured would have better cars so I walked to Whole Foods.

Whole Foods had a giant parking lot, and two security guards to cover it. Easy peasy to wander around without them noticing. It took about five minutes before the perfect woman pulled up to a corner of the lot in a black, recent Mercedes with dark-tinted windows.

I shuffled over to the Mercedes and timed myself to approach her just as she was getting out of the car. She was blond and wore gym clothes and was about my age, maybe a little older with Botox.

The first thing she did when she saw me, filthy and bloody, was smile.

"Hi," she said. "How's it going? You OK?"

I noticed a bad, old tattoo of a strawberry on her wrist and I knew she hadn't always driven a Mercedes. She reached into her purse. I figured she was gonna give me a five or a ten. A five or a ten before I even asked. Most people would have run but here was this woman, this woman who needed nothing from me, reaching into her purse to give me five or ten bucks.

I stepped closer and she kept smiling. And then I kept walking to her, arranging myself so she couldn't easily step by me, and then I took the Taser out of my pocket and held it to her neck and said, "I want your car and your purse."

She made a wry look and nodded. She handed over her purse.

"Keys are in there," she said. "Can I keep my phone?"

"No," I said.

Then I opened her wallet and looked at her driver's license.

"Here's the thing," I said. "You seem like a really, really nice lady. But if you call the cops, or report your credit cards missing, before, let's say, somewhat arbitrarily, midnight tomorrow? I'm going be heading over to"—I looked at her license—"1120 Rockridge Ave. and beating the shit out of your kids. So don't do that. OK?"

"Yeah," she said. "OK." For the first time she looked scared. I wouldn't hurt her kids, but she didn't know that.

"Look," I said. "I know this is scary. Just do exactly what I say and everything is going to be OK."

I got in the car and started to drive away and saw her crying in the parking lot and I was going to stop and go back and give her her phone but security came running and I drove away, fast, and before they even got the cops on the phone, I was on my way to the highway with a full tank of gas, a credit card, an ID that could be me on a much, much, much better day, and 562 bucks in cash.

I tossed her phone out the window and in the rearview mirror I saw it skid and crumble across the blacktop until it was nothing at all. As we all would be, one day.

But not today.

———

After nine hours on the highway, watching the sun rise over the desert, stopping twice for caffeine, gas, peeing, and snacks, I pulled off the highway at the exit for Crab Orchard Road, checked the odometer, drove exactly thirteen miles, and then looked for the trail on the right, thinly etched into the sand like a Nazca Line, that I usually missed.

I didn't miss it this time. I made a right on the unnamed trail and drove until I saw the first beaten-up beige trailer, then two more in varying desert-burned shades of white, and then, hidden behind more trailers and a pre-fab barn and a storage shed, a house. The house was handmade and a step above a shack, pieced together from scraps of wood and tin. The trailers all had dramatic brand names: Wildcat; Cougar; Mountain Bear.

A man came out of the shack-type house when he heard me drive up. He had angelic yellow hair to his shoulders and a weathered face that had once been beautiful and he held a shotgun in both hands pointed at the Mercedes.

The windows were tinted and he couldn't see me through the glass of the windshield. He came over and tapped the gun on the equally dark driver's-side window.

I rolled down the window.

"Fuck," said the man with yellow hair. His name was Keith. He looked annoyed.

"I want to spend money," I said.

"Well OK, then," he said, looking a hair less annoyed. "Come on in."

He lowered the shotgun. I parked where I was and followed Keith into his little shack-house. The windows were covered with taped-up, yellowed pages of the *Las Vegas Sun* and the *Los Angeles Times*. Half of the shack was Keith's living quarters—a bed with dirty sheets, a TV, a laptop, and a dirty armchair—and half was his lab: cooking tools and chemistry sets and vats of substances I didn't understand.

"You don't look so good," Keith said. "You OK?"

"I will be," I said.

"So what do you need?" Keith asked. He cleared some papers and books off a couple of old, smoke-scented armchairs and we sat in the chairs.

"A gun," I said. "And something to keep me awake."

"Well, I can help you out," Keith said. "Got a couple of firearms I could spare. And uppers, woo boy, yeah. Yes. Absolutely." He had a gleam in his eye and I knew this would be my one piece of good news this week.

Keith showed me a decent gun right away, a nice little Smith & Wesson with no serial number that probably started off life as an LAPD or LVPD weapon in the last year or two. Out behind Keith's shack-house I fired a couple of rounds at a makeshift target he set up of empty oil and kombucha bottles and it did all the things a gun is meant to do. Keith asked for five hundred bucks. I told him I had two hundred for him now and four hundred more in a couple of days or weeks, for the gun and some pills. He agreed. I paid. Back in the shack-house Keith made tacos with *nopalitos* and *refritos* on corn tortillas. We ate three each as he told me about the pills.

"It's not a stimulant," he said. "MK44. It's not, like, a pep pill. It just makes you not sleep anymore. It makes you focused. They developed it for soldiers. Like in the desert or wherever. They never sleep. Whole battalions of them. They're testing it on civilians now."

I'd heard of it. Usually I figured if the government was giving it out, I wasn't interested in taking it. But.

I tossed back one of the pills with a bottle of water and bought fifty more.

"That's good," Keith said. "You gotta drink water with this shit.

It's like X. Easy to get dehydrated. Also you gotta remember to eat. Crazy. Totally kills your appetite and then you wonder why you're seeing bugs everywhere."

"So if I don't sleep," I asked Keith, "what happens to my dreams?"

Keith laughed and shrugged. "I don't know," he said. "Let me know when you find out."

After I paid Keith and drank some more water and made my good-byes I started driving again. Soon I crossed the Nevada border and I saw my first casino. I pulled in. It was a Wild West–themed place with stores next door and an outlet mall across the street. In the vast multi-acre parking lot was an amusement park–type ride, like a roller coaster–type appliance at ground level, that made me wonder if I was dreaming. The ride was broken. The parking lot was less than half full. All around was plain undeveloped desert.

The casino was cool and dark and quiet and continued the Wild West theme. Shabby, aging, plaster-of-paris cowboys lurked in the corners, and a large papier-mâché bull/buffalo/undefined mammal hung out by the ladies' room. There was a $9.97 buffet. I paid $9.97 and ate coffee, fried chicken, and fruit salad. At the little strip mall next door I found a store called 99c + DISCOUNT PLUS SAVE U MONEY. At 99c + DISCOUNT PLUS SAVE U MONEY I bought a pre-paid phone for thirty-five bucks and a white T-shirt and a paring knife. The phone came with sixty minutes free.

In my car I changed into my clean new white T-shirt and called Claude. I told him everything, as briefly as possible. Someone tried to kill me, followed the clues to Las Vegas, was OK for the moment.

It seemed unlikely that whoever had arranged this would have an immediate back-up plan. I'd solved a lot of murder mysteries. Never met a murderer with a solid back-up plan. Not that murderers never tried again, but that it usually took them at least a few days to reorganize everything. More likely a few weeks and most likely never.

I would still be very, very careful.

"So why are you in Las Vegas?" Claude said. "And who's trying to kill you? What's going on?"

"Well, if I told you," I said, "it would ruin my big denouement at the end."

I told Claude I would text him a list of things to do and that he should do them immediately. He agreed and we got off the phone. I figured I'd already pushed my limit with my stolen ID and credit card and I tossed them out in a trash can in the casino parking lot. Back in the casino I bought a large fancy coffee drink with an extra shot of espresso at a Starbucks knock-off and popped another two pills. I also bought a large white tote bag that said VEGAS in pink, a large bottle of water, some peanuts in a cardboard canister, and a pair of cheap aviator sunglasses.

In the hallway of the cool dark casino I texted Claude:

1. call Nick Chang

Nick Chang was my acupuncturist, doctor, and friend. He lived seven blocks away from me in Chinatown. He was also fluent in most Chinese dialects and could stumble his way through all of them.

2. tell Nick to call the guy who lives on first floor of my building named Billy Zheng, and explain to him how to get the emergency kit out of my safe (Nick knows what this means)(so will Billy)(Billy doesn't speak English great so that's why Nick)
3. Tell Nick to tell Billy to deliver the package to Nick at his shop.
4. You go pick it up from Nick and mail it to KITTY McCAIN at NERO'S INFERNO LAS VEGAS.

I'd owned the building I lived in in Chinatown for nine years. The Case of the Knife in the Heart paid for it. When I bought the building, paying actual cash, the first thing I did was find Billy

Zheng. Billy was a professional thief and a minor con man who spoke little English and many kinds of Chinese. We weren't friends but I knew him and trusted him. I'd offered him a deal: I'd give him cheap rent and he would deal with stuff around the building and, more important, we would provide a last-resort line of defense for each other when needed. I'd bailed him out of jail twice and given him cheap rent for nine years. He ought to do what I was asking now quick.

5. When u are done: go to Bix Cohen in Oakland find out whatever you can about the Cynthia Silverton comic books. Try to find who printed. Also you need to scan & send the last issue for me. Bring tools, use if needed.

Bix Cohen was the book dealer who had a complete set of all the Cynthia Silverton comics. Claude was charming and erudite and Bix would like him; if I'd thought about it, I would have introduced them on purpose. I could see them as friends. Claude knew that tools meant a gun; if Bix refused, Claude would force him at gunpoint.

———

I'd figured the Lincoln would be a dead end and it was. But I had to see it for myself. The address was a shitty little fourplex apartment building on a shitty block not far off the strip. I saw a few classic cars, all in bad shape, up and down the block: a 1963 Mustang, a beat-to-hell Jaguar from the eighties, and a couple of Mercedes of various ages and origins.

On one corner was a prostitute, trying to look tough and sexy. But it didn't take more than a second look to see she was as exhausted as me, maybe thirty years old with circles under her eyes and a lifeless face.

She was trying, though. Trying to hold on to what life was left.

I went over to the prostitute. She frowned at me. I asked if she knew who owned the old cars.

"Sure," she said. "That guy in there." She pointed to the address I had for the Lincoln. "I think his name is Romeo? He's got all the cars."

"What's he like?" I asked.

She made a face and I could tell the face meant: *OK, but watch yourself.*

I thanked her and went to knock on Romeo's door. Romeo wasn't in but his wife, Alicia, was, and she let me in. The apartment was neat and clean and much of it was covered in plastic, excluding a large Santa Muerte altar against the far wall.

"You want a car?" Alicia said. "All for sale."

Alicia was a little younger than me, probably from Mexico or Guatemala, and hard as nails.

"Maybe," I said. "You sell a Lincoln Continental lately?"

She shrugged. "You wanna buy a car, I can sell you one."

"Well, I may get a car," I said. "But first, I'd like to know about the Lincoln."

"I think you should leave," she said.

"Well, OK," I said.

I put my hand in my VEGAS bag as if I were looking for my keys. But I wasn't looking for my keys. Instead I pulled out the paring knife I'd bought at the 99-cent store and grabbed Alicia by the hair and held the knife to her cheek.

The Taser might have needed a recharge and I wasn't chancing it.

Up close she was wearing much more makeup than I'd noticed. I pressed the tip of the knife down and pricked her cheek until a tiny drop of blood came up.

"Now look," I said. "I admire you for keeping people's secrets. I really do. But I bet you'd rather keep your life."

Alicia was scared—her face was turning pink and her heart rate was going through the roof—but she didn't show it and kept her expression poised and bitchy.

"Yeah, OK," she said. "Just let me go and—"

"Yeah, no," I said. "No one's letting anyone go until I get what I want."

"OK," she said again. "Some guy with blond hair came and bought the Lincoln two weeks ago. Two weeks today. He said his name was Albert but I didn't believe him. Albert Holiday. He gave me an address, but I don't think it exists. It's in the kitchen there in the drawer. He said he was buying it for parts, but it ran. The Lincoln. Ran just fine."

I eased up on her a little and took the knife off her cheek. She breathed a big sigh of relief and I felt her body relax. But I still kept one hand on her arm and the knife just off her skin.

"Tell me about him," I said. "Whatever you remember."

"He, he scared me a little, you know?" Alicia said. "He didn't have to try. Didn't do anything. Just scared me. And he thought he was smarter than us. With the fake name and all that bullshit. I didn't need to hear his whole bullshit story. We just sell things here—cars, washer/dryers, whatever. Good things. Fixed."

I figured that, despite turning her back on me, Alicia was a good judge of people.

"What was the whole bullshit story you didn't need?" I asked her.

"Just bullshit," she said. "That he collects classic cars and that the Lincoln was SO SPECIAL and we were SO SMART to salvage it. Well, it's not so special, and of course Romeo knew that. Everything and anything about a car, Romeo knows. I knew that too. That's all I remember," she said.

"Do you think he was a local?" I asked.

She thought for a second and said, "Yeah. He seemed like he lived here. Said he was just driving by and found the cars. That part seemed true."

I let her go but kept my knife high and ready and said, "Address, please."

She went to the kitchen to get the paper. I kept a close eye on her. I wasn't sure which of us would win in a knife fight. But she came back with a registration paper with a name and address written on the back.

"Copy it," I said, gesturing with the knife. She copied the name and address onto a piece of paper and handed it to me: 2567 College Drive.

"Word to the wise," I said. "That car was used in vehicular attempted homicide in Oakland yesterday. The cops'll come around soon. So get your shit together."

"Shit," she said.

"Yeah," I said. I liked her. "Sorry about all this."

"Yeah, it's OK," she said, although it wouldn't be wise to say anything else to a crazy woman holding a knife in your house. "No problem."

I left and drove to the address Alicia had given me for "Albert Holiday." Just as Alicia suspected, the address didn't exist. I took College Drive until it ended in the desert. It was part of a subdivision that looked like it had been built of Legos and dropped into the desert, which was maybe not so far from the truth.

The last house on the last strip of College Drive was 1082. There was no 2567 College Drive. I parked and jumped the fence and walked around the house to see what was behind 1082, the last house on the street.

Behind the last house on College Drive was the desert. The vast expanse of underworld in between the meadows and the angels.

Up above, on the edge of the desert and the suburbs, a hawk was flying high in the air. Close on its tail was maybe a crow, maybe a raven. The crow or whatever it was was trying to get the hawk to leave. He kept diving at the hawk and giving her what looked to be a peck or two before the hawk would fly out of the crow's line of attack.

But then the hawk would start to circle again and the crow would attack again and it would start all over again.

The first time, and the second and the third, the hawk did nothing. But after the fourth time the hawk flew up high, higher than the crow could fly, and then with what I figured was just about everything the hawk had she came down plumb-line straight to the crow and hit it with such force it tumbled down out of the sky, bracing itself just before it hit the desert floor.

I don't know if the crow was dead.

But you could be damn fucking sure he wouldn't be bothering the hawk anytime soon.

CHAPTER 8

THE MYSTERY OF THE CBSIS

Los Angeles, 1999

When I left Carl's studio the fog had cleared up and the sun was shining on Venice. I didn't know exactly what Carl and Merritt had been to each other. Or if Carl had been anything at all to Merritt. But I knew that Merritt occupied a lot of mental and emotional and maybe spiritual real estate in Carl.

I left my car in front of Carl's house and walked down to the boardwalk. About half the shops were closed. I called the Richter Agency from a pay phone on the boardwalk. Phone booths were becoming rare, but I didn't trust cell phones and the rates in my room were painfully high. The lowering sun gave the phone booth a warm yellow glow. I put in three quarters to start.

I asked to speak to Frank Richter. No one would say yes and no one would say no. I didn't blame them. It was like calling up Procter & Gamble and asking to speak to Procter. I was persistent and got bumped upstairs a couple of notches. More quarters. More people saying "That won't be possible, but . . ."

Every time, I said the same thing: "Tell him I'm a friend of Constance Darling's." Some people knew who that was and some did not—less at the bottom, more as I inched up toward Richter himself. People like Constance and me existed on a need-to-know basis.

Finally, five dollars and fifty cents in, I got a man on the phone who seemed to be at the top of the mortal heap.

"I can't promise that Mr. Richter will be in touch," he said. "But I will try my best to deliver the message."

He didn't ask for my number. We both knew that if Mr. Richter wanted to talk to me, he would know how to find me.

———

I stopped off at an office supply store and bought an expensive, official-looking notebook with complicated columns to keep track of my hours. Then I went to a pawn shop on Santa Monica Boulevard and bought a slide projector for thirty dollars and a decent-looking hunting knife for ten. After that I got fish cakes and pad thai from a Thai restaurant next to the pawnshop and took it all back to my room.

In my room I ate and recorded my hours thus far in the expensive notebook with descriptions of what I'd done with those hours ("11:50–12:30—buy notebook + pens") and then I set up my slide projector to shine on the door and turned out the lights and looked at slides of Merritt Underwood's paintings. There was a set in Adam's file.

Like Carl's work they were, as far as I could tell, paintings of nothing. Just colors, mounded up on the canvas. But while Carl's paintings seemed quiet and sly, Merritt's howled. I could see why they'd be hard to sell. Piles of red and black paint yelled at you, accused you of a crime you may or may not have committed. Nightmares bloomed. Buried memories were revealed. There was no defense. They weren't things you'd want in your house.

———

That night I woke up at the edge of night and morning for no particular reason. The best hour of the old day and the worst hour of the new one. No reason I could name, at least.

I lay in bed and thought about how much better life was the last time I was in Los Angeles. How, in the days in between meeting Constance and moving to New Orleans with her, I'd been so full of hope I'd trembled with it. So full of hope it felt like I'd swallowed the sun.

Finally I got out of bed, and when I did I saw that something had been slipped under the door to my room: a piece of creamy white, heavy, deeply textured paper, cut with a sharp edge into a five-by-eight note card. Across the top FRANK RICHTER was printed in black ink, all capitals, in a squarish font; underneath was his logo, an all-seeing eye, never closed, never at rest. Underneath was written, by hand, an address in Malibu and a time—4:44 p.m., the day after tomorrow.

There was no RSVP.

If Richter invited you, you went.

———

The next day I had breakfast in a café on Vermont and then looked in a bookstore for a while and bought a paperback true-crime book. I hadn't spoken more than four words to anyone since I'd met with Carl three days ago, and my tongue felt stiff and fat in my mouth. After breakfast I drove up to meet Linda Hill in her white Spanish-type house in the Los Feliz hills near Griffith Park. Her name was in the file as a KA; she'd run an art gallery that had represented Merritt for years.

Linda Hill was about fifty and had long gray and blond hair. San Francisco was famous for its hills. I felt like the fact that Los Angeles was just as hill-blighted was some kind of national secret. Why were the Los Angeles hills so arcane, so occulted to the world outside? People talked about Los Angeles as if it were New York spread out and deformed, melted like hot cookie dough on a pan. I didn't know until I got there that the city was a web of mountains and valleys and canyons, starting out wet and cool and drying itself out into desert as it headed east, unlike anyplace else on earth; a maze of dead-end streets that were never parallel and curved in and across themselves like snakes. There was an energy to Los Angeles that was sharp and would cut you if you didn't recognize it. Every grain of sand in the beaches and desert buried under the city was a little razor, ready and willing to wound.

But if you saw it for what it was, I was learning, you could maneuver in between the knives and glide through the city, like a needle in a record. You just had to keep your eyes open for synchronicity, and never expect kindness. Just shut up and be grateful when it appeared.

———

I sat with Linda Hill on her deck on the hill, surrounded by bougainvillea and jasmine. Hummingbirds buzzed in and out of the flowers. A jade plant bloomed under the bougainvilleas. I'd never seen a jade plant bloom. I didn't know it was possible.

"He said he tried to help Merritt?" Linda Hill said. "Huh. That is not my recollection. Carl helping Merritt? I don't know. Maybe. It could have happened."

"So what is your recollection?" I asked.

"Well," Linda said, "my memory is that Carl was— Do you know artists? Do you know what they're like?"

"I don't know," I said, although I was pretty sure I did, and I was pretty sure they were exactly like everyone else, only more so. "Tell me."

"Well, there's a cycle they go through," Linda said. "They have their heroes, you know. You go to art school or you do your work or whatever and you find inspiration from people—from artists who are already working, who are a few steps ahead of you. But then," she said, one eyebrow raised, "an artist, he—or she—has to grow up. They have to make their own work. When Carl got out of school, Merritt was who he wanted to be. Merritt was who he wanted to attach himself to. And Merritt—he was dumb enough to think that meant Carl wanted to be his friend."

"He was wrong?" I guessed.

Linda let out a long and cynical laugh.

"Carl didn't want to be Merritt's friend, no. He wanted to devour him, and spit out his bones. Merritt's problem was that he wasn't interested in things like that—star-fucking, power plays, psychoanalytical warfare. Merritt, how can I put this—well, I'll use a cliché: Merritt had some *joie de vivre*. He wanted to be this big art star, and for a long time, he was. But he didn't care about other people. Not in the way that people like Carl care. I think Merritt was like you."

"Like me?" I said, confused.

"Like how you obviously don't care what I think about you," Linda said. "And I mean that as a compliment. It's refreshing. That was Merritt. He was not engaged in petty crimes against other artists. That was not his thing. Merritt was in a war with history. And I would argue that in his war with history, Merritt won. He's gone, but his work will stay. I have about two hundred grand of my own money in his art, you know. A good chunk of my retirement fund. Anyway, he didn't get into that scene. Carl may have had it out for Merritt, but Merritt didn't care about Carl. Most artists, they're like crabs in a barrel."

"What?" I said. "What about crabs?"

"It's an expression," Linda said. "Crabs in a barrel. One tries to get out, presumably to some kind of a better life, and the other crabs will pull him back down. They actually do this, you should see it some-time. It's really pretty extraordinary. Although, who knows, maybe the crab majority knows something the escapee doesn't. Anyway, artists can be like that. You stay with your peer group. Life pushes you down into the barrel. Life does not push you toward the original idea, toward the breakthrough. It pushes you to what's marketable. What's mediocre. It pushes you to be Carl. But Merritt wouldn't let that happen. He just didn't have it in him to be mediocre. Everyone else was kind of racing to the bottom, but he just wouldn't go along. And, you know, that makes it better for everyone. It really does."

I verified the basic chronology with Linda: Merritt went to art school in the early seventies, finished in the late seventies, and by 1980 was poised to become the next big star. Then his work took a turn for the dark, his demons got the better of him, and his reputation started to head downhill, along with the price of his work. By the time he died in 1995 he was on the margins of the art world, not entirely out of it, but no longer at the center.

I showed her the photo from Merritt's file. She smiled when she saw it.

"That is Merritt to a T," she said. "That look. I wish I had a copy."

"I'll make you one," I said. "If I can. Who do you think took it?"

Linda turned the photo over, saw nothing, shrugged.

"Probably Ann," she said.

"Ann?" I said.

"Oh," she said. "Carl didn't tell you about Ann? Ann Davidson?"

"No," I said. "Could you tell me about Ann?"

"Yes," she said. "I'll tell you about Ann."

Linda told me about Ann.

"Wow," Linda said. It seemed to make her a little sad. "Well, Ann Davidson was an artist and for a few years there, she was a very big deal. That sounds horrible. I mean, hopefully everyone's a big deal to someone. But Ann was a big deal in the cultural sense."

"She was a painter?" I asked.

"She was an *artist*," Linda said. "She could absolutely paint. She was a wonderful painter. But her heart was not really in painting. She made these sculptures—she made them out of things like oil barrels and suitcases. She called them her hives. Little beehives. I didn't represent her, but I loved her work. And we were friends. Now, Ann, she really hit the sweet spot. Good work that was also commercially viable. And a lovely person, to boot. I mean, look, I'm sure she was crazy on the inside. They all are. That's what makes artists wonderful. But whatever kind of crazy she was, she transformed it all into her work. That's the best kind.

"But back to Merritt—they really fell for each other. They were going out for like two years. Three? Four? I think they really loved each other, honestly. But, then, you know, they were both difficult. They never lived together or anything like that. I don't know if they were exclusive. I mean monogamous. It could have been like an open thing."

"How were they both difficult?" I asked.

"Oh, God," she said. "I don't know what was caused by the alcohol or what was a result. But he almost seemed— I don't know if this was some kind of, you know, psychoanalytic death drive thing or he was just a fuck up. Or maybe he just couldn't handle the attention. I really don't know. But he'd get a good thing going and then he'd screw it up. Do you know about the teaching thing? At USC?"

I did not know; Linda told me.

"So someone gets him a job teaching at USC. When I say 'gets him a job,' I mean—I mean Merritt is a man who didn't file a tax return for ten years. Someone from the IRS came to his studio. They were going to take his paintings. So not the world's most responsible man.

"So he shows up, starts teaching—I came by one day and it was wonderful. Merritt had the biggest heart. He's telling the kids they're wonderful, they're perfect. He's telling them, you know, paint from your eternal soul. Paint from the part of you that never dies. He's bringing in all these guest lecturers—I think he got Schnabel to come in. Ann, of course. I think maybe even Basquiat before he died. Cy Twombly came by one day, spent the whole day with the kids. I think he even did a sketch in class. It was the eighties. But then he never did, you know, the real teacher things. He would die if he heard me say that. Of course he thought what he was doing was teaching. I mean he was *actually* teaching, right? Conveying knowledge to his students. Of course, that isn't what they pay you to do. And he didn't do anything else—didn't do the paperwork, didn't file grades, which he thought was obscene, grading someone on their art. His word—obscene. So of course he was fired. But you know, I heard that a bunch of the kids, after Merritt left, they left school and never went back. He ruined it for them. In a good way. They just left and made art for the rest of their lives. That was what an enormous kind of a person he was. Just huge."

Linda smiled. You could tell she missed Merritt.

"So what happened to Ann?" I asked.

"Well," Linda said. "She became huge herself. Not just art-world huge. She was very pretty, a very attractive woman, and the world wanted her. She did a *Vogue* spread. People wanted to take her picture. People wanted her to model things."

"How was Merritt with Ann's success?" I asked. "Was he jealous?"

"Oh no," Linda said. "He loved it. Loved to see her career take off like that. She was the one who was not always so thrilled with it. I think. I don't know. She'd gone from doing these little shows, where ten or twenty people would show up, to this whole universe of fame, and I'm not sure that really interested her." Linda made a face. "Sorry, I don't mean to be so negative. It was just the last thing we talked about. I shouldn't let one bad day color the whole thing."

"Talked about it when?" I asked, still not entirely sure what it was.

"Well, Ann and I had dinner at Musso & Frank's about a month before she died—twenty-four days, actually—"

"Wait," I interrupted. "She died?"

"Oh God, yes," Linda said. "Sorry. God, I didn't mean to bury the lede there. Yes, Ann died. A car accident."

"Like Merritt?" I asked. I felt like I'd fallen behind.

"Well, they were both car accidents," Linda said. "This is Los Angeles. That's how people die. Did you ever go to an emergency room here? In LA?"

I had, and I knew what she meant. You'd wait eight or ten hours because a new car accident kept taking your place in line. But Linda said they weren't related. Ann died two years before Merritt. She died in a drunk driving accident on Hollywood Boulevard.

"I mean, she was the drunk one," Linda clarified. "Horrible."

"Wow," I said. I let that sink in for a minute and then: "So you were saying. The last conversation you had with her."

"Oh yes, well. She was feeling down. Like I said, I shouldn't let one day ruin all my good memories of her. I just don't want to think she was so unhappy when she died."

"But what was she so unhappy about?" I pressed.

"Well, not SO unhappy," Linda said. "At least, I don't think so. She was just—it was just a moment, and I'm sure it would've passed. But people were jealous. They were mean. She lost a lot of friends."

"Anyone stand out?" I asked.

"No—yes. A few. This stupid cunt named Marcy Evergreen," Linda said. "They used to be close and then when Ann became such a big deal Marcy wasn't nice. You know, people are strange. Or maybe not. But their reactions aren't always what you expect. And then there was the logo."

"Logo?" I asked.

Now Linda sighed. "This company. Something to do with computers. Or advertising. T-shirts. I don't know. But they took one of her hives, one of her drawings, and basically changed it around a little and stole it for their logo. She talked to a bunch of lawyers, and I don't think she got anywhere. But her heart was broken. Her work was very important to her. She did NOT want it used to sell things.

"People work all their life to get recognized," Linda said. "What they don't realize is that once they get recognized, they're not themselves anymore. Not in public. Not to anyone else. They're someone else. And that's what people recognize. That's who everyone falls in love with. That's who they want. People like Ann are constantly changing. But the world wants just that one incarnation of them, over and over again."

We didn't say anything for a moment. Two hummingbirds fought a few feet from us. I thought about how much I wanted to enjoy the sunshine and the hummingbirds and the flowers. Enjoying life as it unfolded was always hard. Since Constance died it seemed physically impossible. It was all just a long, infinite, blacktop of things you'd regret not enjoying later.

CHAPTER 9

THE CASE OF THE INFINITE BLACKTOP

Las Vegas, 2011

Las Vegas was eighty-five degrees and as dry as the desert it was but inside Nero's Inferno the air was cool and dark and almost damp, more like a cave than a royal domain. I didn't know if the rumors about extra oxygen in the air at casinos were true, but I did perk up a bit after waiting on line for the desk clerk for five minutes, and by the time I was at the top of the line, I had energy and vitality to spare—although the planned-to-excite gambling sounds and the bright colors and the uppers and the coffee and the CIA pills I'd bought from Keith were likely also contributing to the busy, busy buzz.

At the desk I told the clerk, a white girl about twenty-something with black hair and a pretty face with pink, rounded lips, that I wanted to see Jonathan Markson in security.

"I'm sorry," the girl said. "This desk is for reservations only. We have an information desk—"

"But you have a phone right there," I said, pointing at her fancy multi-line phone. "So you could call him on that."

She frowned. "We're only supposed to use that phone for checking people in."

"Sometimes life hands us lemons," I said, "and then we make lemonade. And phone calls."

"I don't know what you're talking about," she said.

"That's OK," I said. "Call Jonathan Markson's office, tell him Claire DeWitt is here, and he'll know."

She gritted her teeth and called the central operator who put her through to security who put her through to Markson's office.

"Right," the girl said. "OK. I'll tell her."

She hung up and looked at me.

"Mr. Markson is busy at the moment but asked me to relay that—"

"Right," I said. I wrote my new phone number on a scrap of paper. "You can call him back and tell him I'll see him in about ten minutes. And I'm expecting a package here for Kitty McCain. Please call me right away when it comes."

"Sure," she said, sweetly, as if she was talking to a crazy person. I wanted to say *We'll see who's crazy*, but I wasn't sure that was a bet I would win. Maybe in ten minutes she'd find me out on the floor and say *Well, we've now proven it's you*.

Maybe that would be the story of my life. *Look who was crazy after all.*

I walked through the casino floor and found the roulette tables, and then found the security cameras—one or more over each table. I sat at a roulette table, next to a small gaggle of middle-aged convention men, making sure I was in full view of the camera.

I put ten bucks on zero black. While everyone's eyes were on the wheel I swiped half the chips from the conventioneer next to me off the table and into my hand, where I paused for a second before sticking them in my packet. I lost my bet. I went to another table and repeated the whole thing. Spanish tourists drinking whiskey and cracking jokes about the ass of the young woman at the next table over. I wasn't sure what was so remarkable about her ass but I owed her a cut of the four hundred–odd bucks' worth of chips I pocketed from the men from Spain.

It was at the third table, with the girl with the remarkable ass, that I placed a handful of chips on red to win and a man in a suit came over to me and gently took my arm.

"Mr. Markson says he apologizes for the delay," the man in the suit said, "and will be happy to see you now."

The man led me around a few corners to a service elevator, which we took up to the tenth floor.

Jonathan Markson's office was giant and done up Nero-style with antiques that may or may not have been real and a giant mahogany desk that wanted to pass itself off as something from Versailles. A wide window behind him looked across the city. There was about thirty feet of floor between the window and the door, as a crow might fly. Or a hawk.

Markson stood up from behind his fancy desk, gentleman-like, when the man in the suit brought me in. Markson was also in a suit, and an expensive one, with shoes that probably cost more than cars I'd owned. He held out a big hand for me to shake. It felt like shaking hands with a gorilla. A gorilla who hated me and wished I'd get the fuck out of his city, but was too much of a gentleman to say it. That kind of gorilla.

"Claire DeWitt," he said, with fake enthusiasm. "How wonderful to see you."

I gave the man in the suit the chips I'd earned. Markson thanked the man in the suit and he left.

"Wow," I said when the man was gone. I sat in a fancy gilt chair across from Markson's desk. He looked more smug than angry. I wasn't sure what that meant.

"What a surprise," I went on. "That you're here. In your office. 'Cause I wouldn't have expected that, considering how fucking busy you were like twenty-nine minutes ago when I tried to get you on the phone."

"And I apologize," Markson said, "for the misunderstanding. What can I help you with?"

"A room would be nice," I said. "Under the name Kitty McCain. And I'm expecting an important package later today or tomorrow. Very important. Can you please make sure I get a call as soon as it comes into the mail room?"

"Of course," Markson said with a look on his face like maybe I was joking.

"And I could use some cash," I said. "A loan. Or a gift would work."

Now Markson definitely seemed to think I was joking. He almost smiled, and even looked a little arrogant. I crossed my legs and leaned back in the expensive chair.

"You are in the fucking business of cash," I said. "You are literally sitting on top of the biggest fucking ATM on planet earth. And considering our past—"

What I implied, but did not say, was *considering our past where I helped you break up a gambling ring that had bilked you of close to four million, considering that I of my own free will have kept their means of doing so secret for eleven years—*

"I would think five fucking grand and a room," I went on, now with my own arrogant little look, well fucking earned as far as I was concerned, "would not be a very big deal."

Markson thought for a minute, frowned, realized that I was right and he was wrong, and then opened his desk drawer and took out a stack of hundreds as high as my forearm. He counted out fifty one-hundred-dollar bills and handed them to me.

"A gift," he said, through a tight and unhappy jaw. "And your room will be ready in ten minutes."

I'd never known if I could trust Markson. I didn't know any better now. But it was in his interest to avoid trouble, which, in this case, meant giving me what was needed to mollify me until I left.

Outside his door, a bellhop was waiting to show me to my room. The room was a suite, and the suite was giant and full of ridiculous things—hot tub, whirlpool, chili-lime peanuts, serrano-maple-sugar popcorn, the *LA Times*, the *New York Times*, *USA Today*, ashtrays that could break a skull, oceans of tiny bottles of alcohol, and a coffee maker with infinite combinations of coffee, tea, cocoa, and yerba maté.

I gave the bellhop five bucks and then I went down to the mall in the basement of Nero's and spent some of my five grand on three new pairs of underwear, three new T-shirts, a pair of boots, two pairs of jeans, and a black satin jacket that cost more than the rest of the clothes combined. In a convenience store, still in the mall, I bought antibiotic cream, eye drops, hair product, and a blank notebook. The shops were bright and loud under a fake blue sky painted on the ceiling. I also bought a laptop for three hundred dollars and a few burner phones.

I brought my new clothes and goods up to my room and ordered a French dip sandwich with a salad and fries from room service. I took off the clothes I was wearing, which were filthy and specked with blood, and put them in the garbage can in the bathroom. I swallowed another pill from Keith and took a long shower. When I got out of the shower I put hair product and antibiotic cream on the appropriate zones.

I looked at myself in the full-length mirror in the bathroom. My face was red and angry but luckily red faces weren't rare, and that alone would not make me interesting.

My bigger cuts were healing up rough. Across my ribs and down my left hip and thigh was a great wild mess of blue and black and green and purple.

I looked like shit. But with clothes on, I didn't look like an accident victim, at least. I just looked haggard. That gave me a half step ahead of anyone who was looking for an accident victim.

I got dressed. Room service had come while I was in the shower. I looked in the mini-bar and wanted a real drink but didn't think I could stomach it and settled for a Heineken.

I ate the sandwich and a dozen or so of the french fries and a few bites of the salad. I felt improved afterward. I wasn't actually planning on sleeping but after lunch my eyes started to close and I was finding them near impossible to open, despite my strongest efforts and my multiple pills, until my phone rang. And rang.

I woke up. It was Claude, of course. No one else had this number.

"You found out about the comics?" I asked.

"Yeah," Claude said. He sounded distraught. I woke up the rest of the way and stood up and popped another two pills with the last of the Heineken.

Every bone in my body shrieked. *We are tired*, my bones said. *Why won't you let us rest?*

I bit my lip, hard, to talk back to my bones.

The good news was that Claude had the scans and was on his way home to send them to me now. The bad news was that, otherwise, he hadn't accomplished much.

As Claude talked I saw something tiny dart around the room, near the closet, out of the corner of my eye.

The little darting thing rushed toward me, a tiny white blur.

"Bix is trying but he doesn't, you know . . ."

"Know what he's doing?" I suggested.

"Exactly," Claude said. "I don't think I do, either."

"OK," I said. "We know they were printed in Las Vegas, in 1970-something to 1980-something, by a printer that may or may not still exist, right?"

"I think?" Claude said warily.

"Actually, that is a YES," I said. "So what kind of printing was it? Most likely, full-color offset. How many were printed? Well, given the lack of copies on the internet we can guess not many, so we can look for a short-run press, which is probably all there is in Las Vegas, anyway, printer-wise. The big printers are in cheaper places. So, first, check with the short-run full-color offset printers that exist now that also existed in, let's say, 1979 through 1989. And they will know, and be able to tell you, about the ones that no longer exist."

Claude agreed that this was a good plan and agreed to execute it.

The little darting thing stopped about a foot in front of me.

I bent down to see it.

It was a mouse. A tiny white mouse.

I also told Claude to rent me a new car under a different name from a fancy place that would deliver and would do it now.

"Oh," he said. "And one more thing."

"Yeah, Columbo?" I said.

"The lama wants to talk to you. He texted me twice."

"OK," I said.

Like in the movies, I hung up without saying goodbye.

I was interested in pursuing a conversation with this rodent but instead I called the lama back. I'd been working on a case with the lama when I'd started my day, twenty-four hours ago in Oakland. It seemed like a lifetime ago.

When I first met the lama his name was Chuck. He used to stay up all night to surf the first waves of the morning and sleep during the day. In between he would get high and pick fights and get kicked out of punk shows for being a dick. He was another of Constance's charity cases. He'd thought he was a detective. Constance knew better.

"Hey," the lama said.

"Hey," I said. I was going to ask if he knew this mouse but then I realized probably no.

"So Andray called," the lama said. It was the case we'd been working on; a mutual friend, Andray Fairview, was missing. Apparently he'd been found.

"Yeah?" I said.

"He's in Taos," the lama said. "You missed him."

"OK," I said. "I'm kind of busy with other stuff now, anyway."

I thought about telling him the whole story but the idea of it exhausted me. I looked at the mouse. His face was vague at first. I thought maybe I needed glasses. But the closer I got, the more his face became distinct and clear.

"Hey, I almost forgot," the lama said. "I had a dream about you."

"Yeah?" I said. "What was that?"

"You were in the desert," the lama said. "And you were, like, some kind of goddess of fury out there. Like Medusa, snakes coming out of your head, the whole bit. Total rage."

"Yeah?"

The mouse darted away again. I whipped my head around to look for it.

"Yeah," the lama said. "It was like, a scary thing," he went on. "But not a bad thing. It was something you needed to do. A lot of trapped energy being released."

As the lama talked, the mouse came back. Slowly, with mouse-ish hesitation, it walked toward me and stopped about a foot away from me.

I bent down and then crawled down and then laid down on the floor on my stomach until I was eye to eye with the mouse. I saw that it was holding something in its tiny, uncanny, little mouse hands.

"The whole desert was shaking," the lama said. "It was kind of amazing."

The desert will shake, I thought. But for now the mouse leaned back on its rear paws and held its full little hands out to me.

In its hands was a book.

"Claire?"

"Yeah?"

I recognized the yellow cover, the cranky white man on the cover. It was, of course, a copy of Jacques Silette's *Détection*.

The mouse opened it to page forty-five.

"A mystery is like a termite: even if you don't know it's there, it creates holes in your foundation, leaving you off-kilter and unsupported, never understanding why your house is such a frightening and confusing place to be.

"Sometimes the solution is to rebuild your house. Sometimes, it's to set your house on fire."

Jacques Silette never made it to Las Vegas, but right before he lost his daughter in New York City, he stopped in Atlantic City for the night and loved it. He wrote a long rhapsodic letter about it to his friend back at home, a butcher and amateur vintner named Acel Dumont.

"A monstrous rainbow beauty of electric neon. Dollars and coins fall from the sky in a starlit eternal night. A never-ending meteor shower of hope crushed and reborn, reborn and crushed, inhaled and exhaled. Every supposedly desirable nugget of capitalist material in Europe is here duplicated and made available to anyone with forty-nine cents: a good steak; a cigar; the illusion of a library with wallpapered books; fancy dress and what they call 'fine brandy.'

"But here there is a shimmering illusion of a society that is, in its capacity for hope and optimism, far superior to anything the world has known before. The gambling is nothing. It is a lived metaphor for a real hope: the hope that maybe someday, maybe tomorrow, even *after the dice fall*, *even after our mysteries are solved*, we can be happy. Because now, we can only be happy in that moment when the dice are in the air, when everything is a mystery, when we can continue in petty ignorance."

CHAPTER 10

THE MYSTERY OF THE CBSIS

Los Angeles, 1999

Before I left Linda Hill she gave me a banker's box full of Ann Davidson on loan—slides, auction catalogs, magazine articles, prints, and photographs. Back in my hotel room that night I looked at photos of Ann's work. Her sculptures were odd and busy. Most of them were containers with birds and bees and flowers inside. They started off as little cigar boxes of cardboard and paper and then became trunks and suitcases and finally they changed into big, welded, fantastical sculptures in her last years. Like Linda said, Ann liked beehives; she also liked vines, snakes, nautical ropes and knots, and endless repetitions of shapes in a specific swirling, curling, sinister, vine-like pattern.

She also painted. Her paintings were different from Carl's and

Merritt's—Carl and Merritt painted colors and shapes; Ann painted people and animals and plants and insects and things that were combinations of all of those categories: a woman who was half wolf and part bee; a flower that was equal parts vulture. Like her sculptures, her paintings looked like nature had taken over. But somehow, in Ann's rendering of it, nature was a little smarter and a little wittier and a little more compassionate. It seemed willing to cut you a break, if you were paying attention.

The next day I went to the library. The newspapers from when Ann died were recent enough to be on the internet. I paid a few bucks to use the terminals. I found Ann's obituaries from the *New York Times* and the *Los Angeles Times* and a long profile of her in *ARTnews*. I printed them all out for two cents a page. One hour and two bucks later I had fifty pages to read and an empty stomach. I went to an Armenian falafel place for lunch and read about Ann Davidson's life. And her death.

Armenian falafel is its own strange beast. Ann was born in Mississippi. In one interview she said she'd grown up in Bay St. Louis, a small, unwealthy town on the coast; in another she said she'd come from an estate outside Oxford. I figured neither of those stories were exactly true and the exact truth probably didn't matter much—at least not to me, not right now.

The stories all agreed on the rest of it: Ann got into CalArts on a full scholarship, packed up, moved to Los Angeles, graduated, got in a group show right after graduation, and sold every piece. There was success, defined: selling for double. After that she got a top dealer and, as one newspaper mention put it, with no small disdain, "the stars aligned and the magical alchemy of the art world—turning one's creative vision into cash—was at Ann Davidson's fingertips."

I printed out three photos of Ann, which later that night I would tape up to the wall of my hotel room in chronological order. One was a photo of her from that first group show just out of art school in

1983. Ann looked small and young and glowing; she had short dark hair and wore a short black dress and chunky black shoes. Her arms were bare and white.

The next photo was from a few years later. She was older now, and although she of course wasn't taller, and not much fatter, she somehow looked bigger. Maybe it was her energy that was larger; she seemed to take up more space in the room. Or maybe she'd just learned how to pose for the photos without giving quite so much away. In the first picture she looked a little wide-eyed and maybe too grateful; in this second picture, a professional photo taken in a studio, she kept more to herself. Her outfit was again a black dress, but this one more polished and stranger, her hair was longer and arranged just so. Her arms were bare in this photo, too, and she'd begun her tattoos, images that would become nearly famous in their own right—vines and flowers that curled up her arms, fantastical and organic. The flowers, I would read later, were flowers she'd invented. She'd planned to eventually make a book of them—a field guide to the flora and fauna of her own imaginary landscape. She died before that happened. In the picture she had a kind of half-smile on her face— a kind of knowing look that seemed to see more than it revealed.

The last photo was from a few months before she died. It was from *Vogue*, part of a photo-essay of female artists modeling expensive clothes. Barbara Kruger in an Armani sheath. Kiki Smith in a Dolce & Gabbana corset dress. And Ann Davidson in a Galliano gown. They each had their own double-page photo standing in what was either a very tidy woods in the South of France or a very elaborate set. Around each of the women was a little tribe of taxidermied foxes and squirrels and robins and blue jays and one very large hawk.

I didn't know much about clothes but I didn't think the dress Ann was wearing was something a person was actually supposed to wear anywhere other than a photo shoot: it was black and voluminous, with layers of fabric and lace pushing the outer layer out easily a foot on either side. The dress had no sleeves and you could see her arms were now etched with pale vines and flowers.

In this photo Ann seemed huge, as large as the trees. She looked directly at the camera, and didn't smile. Her eyes were perfect and said nothing except maybe a little tiny *fuck you*.

She looked like a sculpture. But not one Ann would make. A sculpture made by someone else. Someone not as interesting as Ann, and not as good an artist.

By the time I was done reading, it was time for my date.

———

I reached the heavy iron gate that stood between the world and the house in Malibu at 4:28.

Deuteronomy 4:28: "There you will worship man-made gods of wood and stone, which cannot see or hear or eat or smell."

I sat in my car and did nothing until 4:34, when I pushed the button on the intercom just outside my car window. I figured at least ten minutes to drive up the driveway and go through security but the driveway was short, and there was no security, just a housekeeper, and at 4:41 I was sitting in front of a glass wall overlooking the gray and angry Pacific, at the largest wooden table I'd ever seen, made from what seemed to be a single piece of wood. The Pacific made the Atlantic look like mother's milk. The house was large and though I wasn't sure I thought likely concrete. It was cruel and modern, as if beauty had been made illegal. Maybe it was less heartbreaking on a sunny day; the rest of Los Angeles was bright and hot but out here by the ocean it was overcast and chilly.

For three minutes I sat there and watched a seabird dive into the ocean again and again, trying to hook a fish he just couldn't catch. It was like watching a movie. At 4:44 I heard a voice behind me.

"The DeGraw case bought me that view. Back then I wasn't sure if I'd ever make any money again. I put every last cent of it into buying this land. Took five more years before I could afford to build the house."

I turned around.

Frank Richter was older than I'd imagined. He was a tall man with a long face, bones struggling to stand up, gravity pulling his flesh down. The last known photo of him was from the seventies, and somehow I'd expected to see the same open, life-full face, only older. But age isn't just time passing. It's time breaking you—your will, your heart, your beliefs. Richter's breaks were written in the deep wrinkles in his skin, in his tired posture, in his large, sagging hands.

The DeGraw case was famous, and not just for the money at stake. Many saw it as a turning point—the first time Richter worked for the wrong side. The side with money and Washington connections. The case that made Richter realize he could use his skills for something more useful than the truth. Depending on how you defined *useful*.

There was a rumor that Richter had once been a Silettian. I didn't know if I believed it or not.

The seabird kept diving in, trying to grab his fish. Maybe there was no fish.

From a brutally plain sideboard Richter took out a bottle of scotch and poured us each a glass. He sat down next to me. We both watched the ocean and drank. I wondered what he was punishing himself for—living alone, in this brutal house, drinking the ugliest drink in the world. It tasted horrible but it didn't feel half-bad; he poured another for us both and I knew I'd pay for it as I tried to navigate the cliff-side curves back to Hollywood.

"Constance spoke very highly of you," he finally said.

"Thank you," I said. I didn't say she was the only one who ever had.

"So one of my men worked on this case," he said. His lackeys had told him what I wanted. "Tell me about it in a few words."

I thought for a second and then I said: "Someone died."

Richter waited for me to continue and when I didn't he laughed. When he laughed his face lit up and he looked like a different man.

"You think someone killed him," he said.

"Maybe," I said. "I don't know enough to know yet."

"So you think my man was wrong?"

"I don't think anything," I said. "We were hired to look into it. So we're looking into it. If you could ask your guy to talk to me, that would be helpful. That's all I was hoping for."

I said it as if it were not a big deal, but it was one of the biggest deals in the world. The Richter Agency did not cooperate with anyone, ever. Even the CIA had to kiss ass to get anywhere and even that didn't always get them far.

I didn't have much faith in whatever little peon they'd put on the case. I didn't have much faith in any PIs other than myself. What Richter was good at, and what I wanted, was information: police reports, social security numbers, surveillance footage. None of that would solve the case—if it could have, Richter's man would have solved it. But it could save me weeks of excruciating legwork and boredom, and things would be revealed I'd maybe never even think to look for.

He didn't say anything for another long minute. For the first time I noticed that what I thought were natural fluctuations in the wood surface of the table was, in fact, a very faint and fine etching across the whole table: a sundial; an evil eye; writing in Enochian and Hebrew; numbers like 444 and 888 and sigils I didn't understand.

"OK," he finally said. He made a little nod of his head. "Go to the office tomorrow. Not here. The office in Beverly Hills. They'll be expecting you. I'll tell them to give you full access."

I raised an eyebrow. Full access at Richter was unheard of.

I didn't know exactly what had happened between Constance and Richter. I didn't even know how they knew each other, or when they had met.

But once Constance called the agency and got Richter on the phone within four minutes. She asked him questions and he answered. This was regarding the famous Clue of the Golden Butterfly—the clue no one but Constance recognized, the case no one but Constance could crack. And I knew that a set of first-class tickets to and from Los Angeles—tickets she didn't use—showed up on her doorstep a few days later.

Richter's last known public appearance was just about the time of the unused tickets.

Richter poured us each another scotch and we turned around and looked at the gray ocean. I tried to think of something to say, something clever but also deep, something that could maybe pierce his armor, something that could weave a cord between us, no matter how thin.

But I didn't think of the thing to say, the thing that might cure what ailed us, the thing that might bind us together—might bind me to anything—and instead I finished my scotch silently.

When I turned around, Richter was gone, and I was alone.

———

"Meeting Merritt was pretty much the best thing that ever happened to me."

The woman telling me this was Tiffany Stockton, thirtyish. We sat in a sidewalk café on Sunset Boulevard in Silver Lake. Tiffany was one of the art students Merritt had convinced to drop out of school when he taught for one semester at USC.

"There were four of us who dropped out," Tiffany said. "Me, Gail McCort, Alex Rahm, and Clay Jackson. People made it seem like Merritt ruined our lives. That's why he was fired. I mean, one of many reasons why he was fired. But people made it like we were these immature children led astray by this equally immature man. *The Prime of Miss Jean Brodie* or something."

I hadn't read *The Prime of Miss Jean Brodie*, but I got her drift.

"So what was it," I asked, "if it wasn't that?"

Tiffany sighed. She looked like the exact opposite of everything every mother who named her daughter Tiffany hoped for. Tiffany's hair was dyed black and cut into a severe Louise Brooks bob. She wore a black garment that was kind of like a dress but shapeless and wide, and ended at an odd point above her knees. She didn't smile often and everything she said had a kind of seriousness to it that you might have been able to laugh at except most of what she said seemed to be true.

"He talked about . . . about the system of school, about the systems of society and culture, and how art had the opportunity to disrupt those systems. But if you let those systems eat you, you lose that potential. You cannot bite a hand while you are eating out of it. You cannot disrupt a system while you contribute to it. You have to pick one."

"So what was the hand he wanted you to bite?" I asked.

We both sipped hot, fancy, coffee drinks in big white cups. It had been cloudy and cool when we ordered our drinks and then the clouds had spun away and the sun had come out and now we were sitting in the hot sun with hot drinks and too many clothes. Which, in the scheme of things, was not so bad.

I took off my jacket and hung it on the chair behind me. The sun on my arms made me hotter.

"Merritt wanted us to aim higher than creating a valuable commodity," Tiffany said. "Which was pretty much the only art education I'd ever had. I was always very talented. I know you're not supposed to say that out loud, but it's true. It's an ability. Like some people can run or play soccer. I could paint, draw, whatever. And from a very young age, I was basically taught, by well-meaning people, that my worth as a person came from the praise I got for my art. And that, eventually, my art would be worth whatever dollar amount someone wanted to put on it. But, I mean, if you create art, that's a piece of your soul. So to everyone else in my life, everyone before Merritt, the only question was: exactly how much can you sell your soul for?

"So to give you an example of how that worked out for me, my sophomore year, the semester before I met Merritt, I had a real fuck-up in my sculpture class. I overreached on this welding project and I really screwed it up and I actually had to take an incomplete in the class. And the teacher, who was a dick, and I think hated women, was, like, judging me. Like, instead of helping me fulfill my creative vision, he judged me, found me lacking, and refused to help me after that. So at the end of the semester, I was . . .

"Look, all my life I'd been judged by this one thing, right? So when I failed at that one thing, having no idea that that's what real artists do, having no idea that was part of the process, that failing was sometimes necessary, I, well, I hated myself so much that I got so wasted, over the course of three days, that at the end of the three days—well, I OD'd and ended up in a hospital on suicide watch."

She looked down a little. I didn't tell her I'd been there. I didn't tell her I was still there. I didn't tell her: I hate myself that much every day. I didn't tell her: the only thing that saved me is gone and never coming back. I didn't tell her: I will be there again, and I will be there so often I will come to believe it's my natural habitat.

"So how was Merritt different?" I asked.

Tiffany let out a rare smile. "Well. The first thing Merritt said to me—said to me, personally, not the class—"

Tiffany stopped and looked up and I realized she had tears in her eyes. I could tell she didn't want to cry in front of me and it was a minute before she could go on.

"He came over—you all kind of work in a circle in class, it's like the movies—he came over and he said, 'This is really good, and you're obviously very talented. But now, I want you to make the worst painting you can. I want you to just completely fuck this up. Just loosen up your horizons of what you ought to be doing.' And I did—"

Now Tiffany started to cry outright. Her nose turned red and her eyes and forehead scrunched up.

"And that was the hardest thing I'd ever done in my life. I spent all semester on it. Making the worst painting I possibly could. Just totally fucking up everything I'd worked for all my life. Just diving into it. Just really coming to terms with how much I hated myself and my own art. How disgusting I really thought I was."

"So what happened?" I asked. "Was it the best panting you ever made?"

"No," Tiffany said. She finished crying and even smiled a little. "It was horrible! Like seriously the worst of the worst of art school—which is really saying something. But when I was done, I was still me. I was still Tiffany Stockton. After that, I knew I could fail and live. And I knew I could take risks, like I had with the welding, and that sometimes those risks wouldn't work, but I would be a better artist, and a better person, because of it. And the next painting I did after that, that was really good. Like, way better than anything I'd done before. And I knew that who I was was not entirely dependent on my results. I am who I am because of who I am, not because of the commodities I generate or even the, you know, the sacred objects that I generate. I am not my results. I am my process."

I let that sink in for a long minute and realized that I agreed with her.

"You left school after that?" I asked.

"Yeah," Tiffany said. "Between the welding bullshit and Merritt—it all became very clear. Also, I know this won't seem relevant, but bear with me: after I left, I started going to temple. I'm Jewish. And I began to really understand, the way Merritt wanted me to understand, that making art is not like making another commodity. It's not a popularity contest. When you're making art, real art—sorry for being pretentious, I know I keep apologizing, sorry—you are not participating in capitalism. You're participating in mysticism.

"Merritt didn't just tell us to go out and, you know, get high or run away from home or whatever. He told us, this school is teaching you to sell art to upper-class America. I—Merritt—I am here to teach you how to communicate with your soul. He told us that we should hold the highest standard possible for ourselves, no matter what the people around us wanted. That we should be like those hot dog commercials—he loved those commercials! You know. We don't answer to the supermarket. We don't answer to money or grades. We answer to a higher authority."

I asked her how Merritt's advice had worked out since she left school. She said it had worked out pretty well.

"My life isn't perfect," Tiffany said. "It's hard. It's really hard. Especially once you decide not to make money your priority. That does not make it easier." She laughed. "But it's good. And the best way it's good is that my art, the thing I do every day, is not my enemy. It's my best friend."

We were done with the interview and we finished our coffee.

"Hey," she said. "This all reminds me of a joke. A really good joke. What did the guru say to the hot dog vendor?"

"I don't know," I said, and suddenly we were both smiling.

Tiffany started to laugh in the bright hot sun and I did too. Suddenly I saw him in her. Merritt. He had left something of himself, something I'd seen in his art and his pictures and his story, behind in Tiffany, and she loved it and held it close. She'd figured out how to lose him and keep him at the same time.

And Merritt, I saw now, had figured out the ultimate puzzle—how to live forever. How to leave enough of yourself behind, even if it was scattered in little pieces, that your presence on the earth was no longer temporary, but permanent.

"Merritt loved this joke," Tiffany said. "So the guru goes up to the hot dog guy. Hot dog guy says, 'What can I get you?'

"And the guru says, 'Make me one. With everything.'"

———

I woke up the next morning at nine to the hotel phone ringing.

"I'm calling on behalf of Christopher Collins at the Richter Agency. He was wondering if you'd like—"

"To talk to his assistant?" I said. "Not really. Can you put him on the phone."

I heard the woman on the phone grit her teeth, but she said, "Of course," and put me on hold while she found Christopher Collins. He was the Richter PI who actually worked Merritt Underwood's case. As it were. As famous as the Richters were for collecting information and hiring the brightest minds of the Ivy Leagues, snapping up the Skull and Bones men just before IBM and the CIA got to them, I didn't know how much they actually investigated. Never trust a corporation with your life or your case.

While I was on hold I peed and brushed my teeth and put on a pair of pants.

"Claire DeWitt," a man's voice said a minute later, full of fake good cheer and a bad imitation of friendliness. "What an honor."

I knew I had a reputation and I knew he'd heard of it and I knew no one would be particularly fucking honored by meeting up with that reputation in the flesh.

"I bet," I said, not being in the mood right now, and never having been in the mood, for this particular kind of bullshit. "So Mr. Richter said you'd be cooperating with me on this."

I heard him smile a fake and tight smile and say, "I was told that we're giving you full access, which is not common around here. Not common at all. Came right from Mr. Richter. Whom I've never met, by the way. So whatever I can do, just let me know."

"How about I come by and look at the file?" I said.

"OK," he said brightly. "How about, let's see, Friday at—"

"How about now?" I said. "How about right now? Or more like a few hours from now?"

"Of course," Christopher said. "How about twelve thirty? You can come by, get the file, see the place, and then we can have lunch."

"Sure," I said, figuring I would cut out after I got the file. "Sounds great."

We hung up with bright goodbyes, and I got to work.

———

The Richter headquarters were in a big glass tower nestled snugly on the border of Beverly Hills and Century City and whatever came next, within spitting distance of a dozen other big glass towers that radiated black arts and dark power—banks, talent agencies, law firms. No one had picked this location by accident, the meeting point of ley lines that stretched back to China and dragon lines that flowed around from London and Paris.

Christopher's office was on the eleventh floor. He had a long title that I didn't understand, but from the size of his office, I could tell he was on his way up, but not at the top yet. I guessed he was my age, twenty-nine. He was handsome if you like that kind of thing: clean boys, fake boys, boys who kept their hair trimmed and never let their hands get too dirty. I did not.

We went to a conference room that had a bang-up view of the other glass towers, plus a couple of golf courses. We sat at the large conference table. On the table lay a thick manila folder, brimming with well-organized papers. It was the case file.

I reached for it. Christopher pulled it away.

"First," he said, still holding on to his fake smile, "I need you to sign something."

"Sure," I said.

He put a piece of paper with lots of writing in front of me. I signed it at the bottom and slid it back across the table to him and reached for the file.

Christopher looked at my paper, and then snatched the file back.

"I need you to sign YOUR name," he said. "Sorry if I wasn't clear."

"Oh," I said. "My name." I'd signed it Alice I. Wonderland. Usually no one checked. He gave me another piece of paper, identical to the first. I wondered if he always brought a few copies in with him or had anticipated me fucking the first one up. This time I read it. It was a standard nondisclosure form and I signed it with my own legal name.

I slid it back across the table. Christopher looked it over carefully, nodded, and then I took the file. This time he didn't stop me.

"Thank you," I said.

"So," he said. "Wow. Claire DeWitt. So far it's all true."

"I guess," I said.

"Can I ask you something?" he asked.

"OK," I said, since it seemed like it was happening anyway.

I thought he was going to ask me about my tattoos or if I really believed in the crazy book or if I'd really killed two men.

"I was wondering," he said instead, "if you ever came across anything in the antiquities world?"

Of course I knew what he wanted. One of the first things Constance taught me was that as much as people would laugh at us—us Silettians, us misfits, us mad ones—for each of them, a day would always come when they stopped laughing, and asked for favors.

"And the louder they laugh," Constance said, peering at me over the edge of a cup of coffee, chicory steam curling around her face, "the more they'll think you owe them."

We were in the Rue de la Course on Carrollton, waiting for a meeting with a bank manager that would never come. The café smelled like coffee and chicory and chocolate and flowers. Days later would we find out the bank manager had shot himself rather than answer Constance's questions.

"Fortunately, I don't owe anyone anything," I said in the café, trying to sound clever, hoping to sound tough.

Constance raised an eyebrow. "You owe everyone the truth," she corrected me.

Now I sat in a sterile, expensive conference room in Beverly Hills across from a man who I knew had laughed at me before and would likely laugh at me again before the sun had set.

"Gee," I said. "You mean like the Case of the Curse of the White Pearl of the Tomb of—?"

"We always called it the Jackson Affair," Christopher interrupted, with a little smug tinge, as if his name for it had any relevance at all.

"Sure," I said. "But when I *actually worked* the case, with *Constance Darling*—well, Constance and me, we called it the Case of the Curse of the White Pearl of the Tomb of the Lost Golden Lotus. When we actually *solved the case. Together.*"

Christopher took me to lunch at a fancy place in Beverly Hills. I got poached salmon and french fries and he got meat and I told Christopher a little about the market for stolen art and how to find it. He tried to tell me some things but I knew his things—things about bills of sale, about international treaties, about auction-house records.

"You met him?" Christopher said. "Richter?"

I told him yeah I did. Christopher asked what he was like. I was a little drunk and I said he was just like everyone else. Taller, maybe. Christopher asked about his house, Richter's house. I told him it was big and modern and very expensive. I didn't tell him that the man and the house were both so lonely it hurt. I didn't tell him about Richter and Constance, about the things I did know and didn't know. Richter hadn't told me anything especially confidential but his whole existence was, obviously, some kind of a secret, and he'd been kind enough to let me in for twenty-two or so minutes, and that seemed worth respecting, possibly.

After lunch we stayed in the fancy restaurant and drank a bottle of wine and then another. Christopher asked me about Silette. About how I found the book. If it was true that we didn't bother to collect evidence and prints and things like that.

"Well, no," I explained. "We do. We just look at it all differently."

Although by then there wasn't really any *we*. It was me and a few other people around the world, some of whom, like Hans Jacobson, would be there if you needed them, maybe, sometimes. But only if you really, really needed them.

"Then how do you . . . ?" Christopher said. "I mean, at Richter they teach you to, you know, stick with evidence. 'Facts are king' and all that."

Facts are king was Richter's famous motto and lone piece of advice to his operatives.

"Yeah. We don't really see it that way," I said.

Christopher looked confused and so I dragged my chair so we were closer and reached over and put my hand on his chest. Under his clean dress shirt was another clean shirt and under that was his chest, flat and hard, a layer of muscle built up so I could just barely feel his ribs under the flesh. I figured he was going to the gym a couple times a week and maybe a hundred push-ups in the morning before work. Under his young, taut chest I felt his heartbeat, strong and dull and too-steady. Even his own heat was embarrassingly innocent, like a little boy.

"Close your eyes," I said. "Stop thinking."

He closed his eyes. But his eyes moved under the lids and I could tell he was still thinking.

"Stop thinking," I said again. "You were made for better things than thoughts. Feel my hand."

I felt him feel my hand, felt his chest rise to meet the heat from my palm. His breathing and his heart slowed as his thoughts slowed. I tried to help, pushing a little heat into him, pushing a little of my breath into his. Constance knew all the advanced techniques; she had taught the lama and they had both tried to teach me. I'd learned a little and Christopher, with his lack of defenses and deficit of knowledge, was easy.

I leaned closer to Christopher.

"What do you know here?" I whispered into his hot ear. "Feel my hand. Feel your bones. Feel your tendons and your fascia. Something in here knows."

Christopher's breathing slowed. His heart deepened, tripped, dug in with each beat.

I moved my hand down to his belly. Like his chest it was tight. He was holding his flesh in place with his will and control; holding himself up and keeping everything else out.

I leaned in to Christopher and brought my lips to his ear again.

"You know something here," I said. "Where your *nadis* cross at your spine. Where your *kundalini* sleeps. You know something here."

I felt something rise in Christopher, something shudder and come to life, incrementally, with fear and hesitation.

"There is a snake coiled at the base of your spine," I whispered to Christopher, dragging my hand, the warmth I now shared with him, the pieces of him it carried, down to his lower belly. "And there is nothing that snake doesn't know. You just have to let it speak."

Christopher fell into something black and frightening and I kept whispering in his ear.

"There is nothing you have to do," I told him, as Constance had told me. "Nowhere you have to go. All things are known to you and all things are known to all. Knowledge is your birthright. All you have to do is grab it—"

Christopher's eyelids flew open and he looked at me with his eyes open wide and his mouth in an O and all of a sudden it was all back: the restaurant and the noise and the food that had fallen away. Something had scared Christopher, scared him bad, and he shut the door as soon as it opened.

"Wow," he said, trying to shake it off. "Cool."

But he shifted in his seat and I could tell it was the furthest thing in his mind from cool. He'd learned something, and whatever it was he didn't like it.

Psalm 52:3: "You love evil rather than good, and falsehood rather than truth."

After lunch we stood outside the restaurant surrounded by people older than us, people in suits and expensive dresses and shoes that looked like no one had ever worn them before today. A valet was getting Christopher's car. He'd driven us from Richter to the Beverly Hills restaurant. We should have walked. Christopher drove a Saab. I didn't know what to make of that; I didn't know where a Saab fit into the cosmological anthropology of cars in Los Angeles.

Christopher's apartment was clean and dull and looked like an old person lived there. Everything was expensive and perfect. Almost as soon as we got back to his place I knew I'd made a mistake. In the restaurant I thought I'd seen something in Christopher, maybe felt it—something better and darker and richer and more interesting, something worth my time, something worth fucking, something worth sleeping next to, something you could maybe trust a little. Something that could not be faked.

But in his clean apartment as he made us drinks I remembered that everyone had that inside them. It didn't matter what people had inside. It mattered what they decided to share with you. What you could reach in and steal didn't tell you anything at all.

Christopher treated sex like a test of skill; no parties would leave without orgasms and answers; nothing would surprise; the plan would be fulfilled to the letter; no rough edges would irritate.

Afterward, I never wanted to see him again. I pretended to fall asleep until he did, and then I got dressed and looked around the house for stuff to steal. I found nothing worthwhile aside from a few old prescriptions of painkillers and antibiotics, and I left and drove back to my hotel room and took off my clothes and got into bed and pretended to sleep there.

CHAPTER 11

THE CLUE OF THE CHARNEL HOUSE

Brooklyn, 1986

I t was the aftermath of the Case of the Broken Lily. October 1986. We were decompressing in Tracy's father's apartment in the projects. Her father was in a bar somewhere. Her mother had been dead since she was two.

The case ended on a rare hopeful note. Amber Schwartz, fifteen, our client, had won her rightful inheritance from her grandmother because we'd proven that Amber's stepmother had, in fact, altered the terms of a lease from 1969. The inheritance consisted of a dresser full of costume jewelry, two old cats with fleas, and rights to a rent-controlled apartment on Thompson Street. Amber loved the cats and she loved the apartment, the only home she'd ever known. Now she would likely be able to keep it the rest of her life. She paid us with the dresser and the costume jewelry in it. We sold the jewelry for forty bucks and the dresser for two hundred. Everyone was happy.

Except Tracy. She was restless. But her restlessness seemed to have a focus. She'd checked the mailbox on the way up to her apartment. Now, as we sat in her bedroom with cigarettes and whiskey-spiked coffee, she checked the mail again. Kelly was already drunk and seemed not to notice. This time Tracy seemed to hit pay dirt: she came back in the apartment with a thick pile of catalogs, bills, and a letter.

The first strange thing was that she didn't want me to see the letter. Of course, she didn't try to hide it. She was too smart for that. Like the Edgar Allan Poe story, she left it in plain sight; she brought up the mail, tossed it on her bed, and didn't look through it.

No one checks the mailbox and then doesn't look at the results.

It was strange but not that strange. People mailed each other letters then. Some of those letters were private. We had other friends. We had boyfriends. We had cases.

I noted it in my mind, and then I left it alone. Or tried to.

After a few hours we were drunk and tired. Kelly wanted to go to Brooklyn Heights for Chinese food. Tracy said she wanted to stay home and sleep. We hugged and kissed and exchanged I-love-yous and Kelly and I left.

At 9:17 we left her apartment and started down the long hallway toward the stairs. At 9:18, on the third step on the stairs, I stopped.

I couldn't stop thinking about the mail. The mail Tracy had been so eager to check but barely glanced at once she had it.

"My keys," I said. I looked in my pockets.

"What?" said Kelly.

"Shit," I said. "I can't find my keys. I think I left them in her apartment."

Kelly rolled her eyes.

"I'm gonna run back," I said. "Meet you on the street out front."

Kelly rolled her eyes back into their proper place and trotted downstairs.

I turned around and went back to Tracy's apartment.

The door was locked. I knocked.

She answered.

"Hey," I said.

"Hey," she said.

"Keys."

"Come in."

I went inside. Nothing had changed. It had been less than three minutes.

"Can I look in your room?"

"Of course."

She sat on the sofa as if she were watching TV. As if, since the two minutes I'd left, she had been watching TV. But the TV wasn't on.

I went in her room and didn't look for my keys. I looked for the mail. It wasn't on her bed.

I pretended to look for my keys.

"Fuck," I said. "Found them. In my bag. In the pocket. The inside pocket."

"Ha," Tracy said. She was looking at the TV. It was off. Finally she got up and turned it on. *Three's Company* sparked to life.

"Sorry," I said. "I'm going."

I went to the sofa and leaned over and kissed her goodbye. When I did, I saw: on the sofa next to her was the mail. On top of the mail was the letter. She'd started to open it and then put it back down, probably when I knocked.

"See you tomorrow," she said.

"OK."

I left. I never figured out what the letter was, and I'd forgotten about it over the years.

And maybe it was time twisting reality into what I wanted it to be but I was almost sure, now, twenty-five years later, that the return address was a PO box in Las Vegas.

CHAPTER 12

THE CASE OF THE INFINITE BLACKTOP

Las Vegas, 2011

I was on my way out of my hotel room when another bellhop knocked. He had a big padded FedEx envelope for me from Claude. I went back in, made more coffee, and carefully slid the contents out and looked it all over.

Christmas for outlaws: a passport and ATM card and credit card in the name of Kitty McCain, along with a bunch of memorabilia I wouldn't need—photos of Kitty's kids, utility bills, a lease for an apartment that did not exist in Albany, California. Those were for another kind of emergency. And thrifty Kitty had somewhere between five and ten grand in the bank that no one would be tracing, following, or watching.

When I opened my cheap new laptop, I found another gift: Claude had sent the scans of the last *Cynthia Silverton Mystery Digest*.

At the Nero's Business Corner Conveniently Located by the Emperor's Lounge I printed out the scans Claude had sent me. Once printed, it took me a few minutes to find the ad—the one I'd answered a few days before the man in the Lincoln had tried to kill me.

BE A DETECTIVE!

Money! Excitement! Women and men admire detectives. Everyone looks up to someone with knowledge and education. Our home-study course offers the chance to earn your detective's badge from the comfort of your own home.

The address was a PO box about a mile from the strip.

I walked across the street to the Excelsior, walked through the casino and the lobby into the parking lot, stole a Toyota, stopped to buy another burner phone at a convenience store, and got back to work.

The address from the ad in the Cynthia Silverton was a PO box in a strip mall on the corner of a loud, busy six-lane avenue and a short, quiet, forgotten street of one run-down apartment complex, two shabby and possibly-abandoned houses, and four empty lots.

The mall had a bright streetlight and a few permanently closed storefronts and a few that were open in general but closed at the moment. A party supply store. A battery store. A tropical fish store.

And a postal shop. The kind of place with PO boxes. This was where I'd mailed the letter to. The reply address from the BE A DETECTIVE ad.

Why had it ever existed? And why was it still here more than thirty years later?

Let's say it was Jay Gleason's PO box. Let's say he'd tried to kill me yesterday. Let's say he was maybe getting ready for a second attempt now.

Why? What did it all mean?

The parking lot held thirteen spaces. Each was empty. I parked

across three of them and got out of the car and went over and looked
at the PO box place.

Morning had not yet really begun and maybe once the day was
in full swing it would be less ominous, but I doubted it. In any case,
closed strip malls had their own strange aura, radiating failure and
boredom on the surface, promising potential secrets and treasures
underneath. The mailbox place all the more so. It had a plate glass
window with an accordion security gate pulled shut over the glass. I
went over and peered in. Up close it looked exactly like it had from
a distance: like a shabby little mailbox place with mailboxes along the
left wall and shipping supplies on the right.

The lock on the door itself was a cheap little number I could have
opened in a minute or two with a ballpoint pen. The lock on the gate
was different. It was a real lock, an expensive lock. And new.

Behind the locks the shop was closed. Not just for the day. Closed
for a long time. Inside was a row of mailboxes leaning away from the
wall and a dusty sales counter. From the dust around the place I was
guessing it'd been closed to the general public for a few years, at least.

But the floor was different. I couldn't make out distinct footprints,
but the more I looked at the floor, the more I saw that it was less dusty
in the middle, more so around the edges.

I stared at the floor for another minute. I was missing something,
but it was a minute before I knew what.

The mail.

There was a slot in the gate and behind that a slot in the door
for mail. Obviously, a mailbox joint, even a closed one, would get
a lot of mail. Obviously they would also get flyers and circulars and
coupon booklets.

There was nothing under the slot. Just an undefined area of about
a square foot or two. An undefined area with no dust.

Someone was still picking up the mail.

Someone had picked up the letter I'd mailed to this address.

And someone who looked an awful lot like Jay Gleason had tried to kill me after I'd sent that letter.

———

I texted Claude the address and asked him to find out who owned the building and who leased the space. I walked around for a while but didn't see anything else interesting.

In the cool gray morning I went back to the hotel. In the early dawn the strip was empty and peaceful. The sand under the asphalt breathed with relief. At dawn the casino was as quiet as it ever was, just the light murmuring of addicts and the hum and ding of the machines.

I couldn't think and I could hardly see. I went back to my room, drank some water, made myself eat some peanuts, took a few more pills, and checked my email on my phone.

Claude had sent me a very good list of short-run printers that were around when the Cynthia Silverton comics were published and were still around now.

I started again.

———

The first printer was not the place. It was run by a short, cheerful, Orthodox Jewish man named Ray. Ray was kind and invited me into his messy office and insisted that I sit down and talk to him like an actual human being, which was the last thing I felt like at the moment. I knew I should slow down inside, loosen the gears that were wound so tightly inside me. I was rushing through everything, missing the signs. But I couldn't. I was scared.

I showed Ray the scan I'd printed out of the comic book. I liked his office. Stacks of letterhead, business cards, and brochures towered around us. It was like a cocoon of paper, a hedge against the outside world.

"Not us," he said after a few pages. "Very creative work. Very nice. You're sure it was done here in Las Vegas?"

"Well, no," I said. "But I strongly suspect."

He took the papers and looked at them carefully, and then looked again.

"Bound?" he asked.

"Stapled," I said.

"You know the print run?" he asked.

I didn't.

He looked it through a third time, closed his eyes for a moment, and then opened them and said, "Try DeLuxe over in Henderson. Not technically Las Vegas but everyone over there says that's where they are. For the prestige. Everyone wants to say they're in Las Vegas, but no one wants to really be in Las Vegas."

I thought that was a pretty good summary of everything else, too. I thanked him and left.

DeLuxe was also the next stop on Claude's list. The office was actually in the same building as the presses, which, through a few layers of cinder block, produced a pleasant hum/vibration that seemed to slow my gears a little. The office side of the building was spotless and organized, with no towers of ephemera, which made me distrust it immediately.

The manager's name was Rob. He wore a pale blue oxford shirt, undone at the neck, and khaki-type pants and short hair. He reminded me of a man I'd read about in a story once; a man whose hands stay clean no matter what happens to him or what he does. By the end of the story the man kills a woman and rips open her torso and plunges his hands inside to see if they'd come out covered with blood. But as he pulls his hands out from her bloody interior, somehow they come out spotless and pure. But the man is, of course, no longer a man, or at least no longer the kind of man he was a few pages back, and so the whole thing is for naught, as he's now something like a monster. Although one with very clean hands.

I didn't think Rob had plunged his hands into any bloody torsos recently, but I didn't really like him anyway. He had all his information on a computer and in three and a half minutes confirmed that the Cynthia Silverton comics had not, in fact, been printed by DeLuxe.

I stood on one side of a high reception-type desk. Rob stood on the other. I missed Ray and his messy office and yarmulke.

"So I guess that's it," Rob said, trying to smile.

I didn't move. An idea was scratching at the edge of my consciousness, almost ready to hatch.

"If there's nothing else," Rob said.

I still didn't move. The idea scratched a little harder and pushed and—

Rob gave one more good solid try of getting rid of me.

"I guess we're—"

But I interrupted him. "Just one more thing," I said. "And it would be such a huge help."

He gave me his almost-smile again.

"Well the thing is," I said, trying to make up a decent story as I went along, "I'm making a movie. I'm making a movie about those books. And if I could talk to someone who printed them, it would be great to get you guys in the movie. When I come back with the crew. Next month."

"I'm sure," Rob said, "we can find a way to help you out."

I asked Rob if I could speak to the oldest person he had working on the machines. I didn't know the printing lingo but wished that I did. Rob said yes anyway.

He opened a door off the reception area that reminded me of the door in car rental places that separated the garage from the office— like a door to another world, one with more dirt and loud noises and higher ceilings. The next room—the printer's work floor—was far more interesting than the first, filled with giant machines and men and women doing interesting things to and with the machines. I took out my phone and shot a bunch of pictures for the nonexistent movie. I couldn't hear Rob over the sound of the machines but he gestured me toward a little break room toward the back.

I went to the break room. There was a big table, some folding chairs, an electronic time-card register, and a kitchenette. A woman was in there. She was about fifty or sixty and wore a light blue smock, stained with black smudges, over stretch pants and an oversized T-shirt with a drawing of a hummingbird on it. Her hair was curled in a way I hadn't seen in years. The hummingbird's tail had been jazzed up a bit more than nature would have.

The woman sat at the break table eating pasta with tomato sauce out of a plastic container. She had, apparently, been wearing pink lipstick before she started eating, and the base of the tines of her plastic fork was smudged pink.

She smiled at me.

"I like your shirt," I said.

She looked down to remind herself what shirt she was wearing and smiled.

"These guys!" she said. "Can I tell you something?"

"Please do," I said. I sat down at the table, a few chairs down and across from her.

"I started feeding these little guys a few years back," she said. "I live in the Mayfield Parks. I'm sure you don't know it. It's a little mobile home community just eleven miles out of the city limits. My kids say, 'Mom, why don't you just get a real house already? You know we'll help.' I tell them, what do I need all that space for? All the cleaning. I don't want to clean. I'd rather spend my time with these guys. So anyway, out in the desert, people don't understand, that's ground zero for these guys. People think of hummingbirds, you know, in the gardens, in the forests. But boy do we have plenty in the desert. So anyway, a few years back I started putting up some feeders for these guys out in front of my house. Now, the first day, no one came. The second day, one little guy came. The third day, about four little guys came. And then by the fifth day, I had so many they were fighting over the sugar, and I had to put up another feeder.

"And now look."

The woman reached into her pocket and took out a phone and tapped through to something and then handed it to me.

I took her phone. It was warm from her hand. On the phone was a photo of the woman standing in front of a tidy mobile home. She wore loose, cheap, shorts, her hummingbird T-shirt, and dark sunglasses. Her right hand was upturned in front of her, with her palm cupped. In the cup of her palm was a spoonful of sugar water. Perched on either side of her hand was a small green and red hummingbird, iridescent, drinking the sugar water.

"Wow," I said, and meant it. "What do they feel like? Their feet?"

She smiled and made a gesture like a shiver was going up her spine.

"Scratchy!" she said, laughing a little.

I laughed with her. It was the first time I'd laughed since the crash.

"Can I show you something?" I asked.

"Of course," she said. "I would love that. Here I am on my break and it's so nice that you're here."

I showed her the Cynthia Silverton pages.

"I think these were printed in Las Vegas," I said. "In about 1980. Do you have any idea who could have printed them?"

She looked at them very carefully and then looked again.

"Well aren't these something," she said. "I do not know who printed them. It wasn't here. See these gutters?"

She pointed to the inner margins of the pages, where there was a series of small colored circles I hadn't noticed.

"That's the color proofing. We don't do it like that here. Never did. We do it in the bottom margins. But I can tell you who does know."

I looked at her.

"Howie knows," she said. "I'll bet you a silver dollar. Howie knows."

Rob came in the room. Trailing behind him was a fiftyish African American man with a confused look on his face.

Rob said, "Well, this here is—"

"Oh Rob," the hummingbird lady said. "We don't need Peter. Hi, Peter."

"Hey, Mattie," the fiftyish African American man said to the hummingbird lady.

Now Rob looked confused, and a little annoyed. So did Peter.

"Peter's the oldest person here," Rob said. "You asked for the oldest person here."

"I don't understand," Peter said.

"Well, just," Mattie said. She turned to me. "Peter hasn't been with us that long. He was in die cutting up until just four years back. Right, Peter?"

"That is true," Peter said.

"Sorry, Peter," I said.

"Sorry, Peter," Mattie said.

"So how can I meet Howie?" I asked Mattie.

"Well," she said, "if you want to meet Howie, you can come to church this weekend. That's how I know Howie. From church."

It turned out Mattie knew Howie from church, and from nowhere else. She didn't know his last name or where he lived. "We're not that kind of church," she said. "No offense." What she did know was that Howie had worked at different printers for forty years in a dozen different jobs, collected vintage printing equipment, and had self-published a book on the history of printing in Nevada. Mattie knew this because they both went to the potluck after church on Sundays. Somehow they'd gotten to talking, and their mutual interest in printing had come up, and now it was a regular after-church topic.

Nearly every Sunday they spent a few minutes talking about Howie's many projects or the latest industry scuttlebutt.

"And you know," Mattie said, "he's very much the authority on the topic. I'm lucky he's in my church or he probably wouldn't talk to me!"

But she said it with a little chuckle that said *Of course he'd talk to me! He's Howie!*

"So do you think you can film here?" Rob asked.

"Yes," I said. "So I could come on Sunday?" I asked Mattie.

"Of course," she said. "But we have a prayer group tonight. He isn't always there, but we could try."

She got my number and texted me the address. "But don't give him any of that monkey business about a movie." She laughed. "Not in church! You'll burn a hole right in the floor. Maybe we'll all just fall straight down."

Rob looked to the floor, and looked confused. Mattie and Peter laughed, and kept laughing as I left.

CHAPTER 13

THE MYSTERY OF THE CBSIS

Los Angeles, 1999

The Richter file on Merritt's case was a living paradox, full and empty at the same time. Here was Merritt Underwood re-created as a series of numbers—what he paid for his house in Topanga, his bank balances, his test scores from art school, the amount of cholesterol per liter of Merritt's blood. There were about three hundred pages to sift through, many of them redundant and most of them useless.

I looked at his grades from art school. An incomplete for photography. An A on his senior thesis. When Merritt died his blood alcohol level was .5. His iron levels were low. His testosterone was high.

It was 128 pages into the file before I found something interesting—a report from the mechanic who examined the car Merritt was driving when he died. The Richter report on the accident was technical and dull and useless. All I took from it was the name of the mechanic—Marcus Mikkelson—and where to find him.

I tracked Marcus down in his garage in Atwater Village. The Water it was At was the Los Angeles River, a trickle through a paved riverbed across the street from the garage. He was a plump, seemingly happy man about forty with nightmarishly bad teeth who remembered every gear and belt and screw of every car he'd worked on.

"Oh yeah," Marcus said when I asked him about Merritt. "I remember it very well. I don't need to look at the file. Tires were ripped to shreds. Both the right tires. Horrible, just horrible. Guy's driving down the canyon, it's midnight, from what I gather he'd been drinking, shouldn't've been behind the wheel to begin with, and then both right tires go out. Bam. Bang. Heads right off the cliff, down the canyon, crashes at the bottom. Terrible. Just terrible."

"You think someone could have rigged the car?" I asked.

"It's possible," Marcus Mikkelson said. He looked at his hands, which were black with oil and soot. "Cops searched the area, found nothing, no glass, no spike strips, nothing like that—"

I started to interrupt him, but he stopped me.

"But that doesn't mean it isn't possible," he said. "Here's what I think: I think something—coyote, deer, gravity—shook some rocks down from the mountain. Like"—he held up his hand in a circle, to indicate rocks around Ping-Pong ball size—"but not circular. Shale-type rock; I'm no geologist, but you know what I mean: pieces of rock with sharp edges. Little knives. So I think, small rocks on the road, too dark to see them, too drunk to see them, no room to avoid them anyways, drives over them, in course of doing so kicks them back down the mountain, so to speak, blows out his tires, loses control of the car, and bang. Horrible. Terrible. Goodbye."

———

I drove out to the freeway and over to Topanga Canyon, in between the meat of the city and Malibu, to see where Merritt lived. The canyon, which was really the side of a steep, mountainy, hill, at first look seemed like unspoiled wilderness. But everything is spoiled.

After some twists and wrong turns I found the house where Merritt had lived and the road where he had died. The house was gone. There was a construction site where it used to be. Spoiled and spoiled again. Out in front of the site was a two-pronged sign stuck in the dirt for pool designs. Maybe the humans of Los Angeles would miss Merritt, but its real estate developers would not.

Next I found the spot where Merritt had driven—or was pushed or manipulated or otherwise forced—off the road. There was a little pull-over landing about thirty feet away and I pulled over and parked and looked down the curve of the road. Thirty feet away and I could barely see the spot on the edge of the curve. The road hugged the mountain and was just wide enough for two modern cars to pass each other and if one of them was a wide-load truck you'd have a problem. There was no guardrail. On the other side of the road—the side that wasn't a mountain, or as they called it in California, a hill, was a cliff that went right down to the bottom of the canyon, about a forty-foot drop into eucalyptus and sage.

It would be an easy place to fall.

It would also be an easy place to get killed.

———

Ann's old art dealer, Carol Vines, lived in Beverly Hills, retired, rich, and bitter—not bitter from work, but from death.

"Everyone's gone," she said. We sat in her backyard, which seemed to go on for acres. Carol drank gin and chain-smoked. It was 11:00 a.m. I drank iced tea. I would drink in the morning if it made me feel better, but it didn't, just left me confused and angry by the afternoon. "My husband died not long after Ann. In between Ann and Merritt.

They were both close friends. Then my sister that same year—the same year as Merritt. Then—well. That doesn't matter. That's not what you're here for."

"Did you like being an art dealer?" I asked. It didn't have anything to do with the case. I was just curious if life had brought her any joy.

She nodded. "Loved it," she said, and I was reassured. "I just couldn't do it anymore after everyone died. I'd rather drink. Anyway. Ann. You asked if she had friends. Well, she knew a lot of people. I don't know if any of them really knew her. I don't know if they were friends. She was odd. That's the thing about creative people, why I loved working with them—all crazy, but each crazy in a different way."

"How was Ann crazy?" I asked.

Carol thought for a long time before she answered.

"Ann kept her crazy to herself," she finally said. "The best kind. She kept it all inside and let it build up and build up until it all came out in her work. And sometimes, you know, in her life." Carol smiled a little. "She wasn't one of those people who loved drama or seemed especially emotional. But somehow there was always activity round her." Carol made a little marionette motion with her hands. "Like a beehive. Well, Ann and her bee thing, you know. Always some kind of situation. Other women did not like her. Well, I did. But she was distant to women. She wanted to be left alone and make art. She went to parties, she wasn't a recluse. But she didn't like to do press, even when she did do it, didn't . . . how can I put it? She didn't want to be caught. Didn't want anyone to pin her down and really take a look at her. And once you reach a certain level of, maybe not fame, let's say renown, you're going to get attention, and you're going to get a lot of it.

"Now men, men never really see women at all. The more famous you are, the less they see you. That's one thing I know. You can spend a lifetime around men without them ever really seeing you."

Carol was starting to get drunk, which was not a bad thing for an investigation or, I figured, her day.

"What do they see?" I asked.

"They see one of two things," Carol said, with no malice. "They see someone who can solve all their problems—someone who can make their dick hard, make them rich, make them grow their hair back. Or they see the mean old lady standing in between them and all of that. The witch. That's me. You don't believe me now, but wait until you're my age. You will. You'll see how fast you change from one to the other. And Ann, Ann didn't fit into either category, and that made people uncomfortable. And it made her very uncomfortable, too, I think—always being looked at, never being seen."

"What about Merritt?" I asked. "What did he see?"

Carol thought for a minute. "Merritt was different. Well, like I said, they're all different. But Merritt didn't mind Ann's success at all. He saw her. Really saw her. Everyone wants to know why the men do so well in this business and the women have such a hard time. Well, it's the wives. Men have them. Women don't. They make it all work. Now Merritt, he was no wife. But he had some security about him. Some confidence. He didn't mind if she got more successful than him. He didn't mind driving her to an opening or doing some laundry or whatever. I mean, I don't know who did the laundry. I don't think he was ready to be Mr. Mom. I just mean that he knew who he was. He didn't have anything to prove.

"That being said, their relationship was rocky. Very much in love, but rocky. Never monogamous. Neither of them was ready to settle down, and if you're not ready by thirty or forty or whatever they were, I don't know when you will be."

"What about Ann's death?" I asked. "Do you think she was drunk?"

Carol shrugged again, this one more of a life-is-complicated shrug.

"Well, they say she was. She was drinking more, that was for sure. I don't think Merritt was a good influence on her in that regard."

I asked about Carl Avery.

"Carl and Merritt were close," Carol said.

"What about Ann?" I asked. "Were they close?"

"Oh, that," Carol said. "They worked it out."

"Merritt and Ann?" I asked. "How did they work it out?"

"Merritt and Ann and Carl," she said.

I stopped.

"What?" I said. "Sorry, I mean—Merritt and Ann and Carl?"

"Well Carl," she said. "That guy—that's exactly what Ann wanted to avoid. Exactly what she didn't want. Carl Avery is bloodless. Talented, but bloodless. Everything about him—now *him*, he wanted a wife. What I just said? About how men see women? Him. That's him. Carl needs a woman to complete him. He needs a woman to be his blood. To bring him to life. But Merritt, Merritt had everything he needed. He *loved* Ann. He didn't need anything from Ann. Good artists—the best artists—are wild animals. They're not ordinary people. Carl didn't have a wild bone in his body."

"Wait," I said. "So what went on between Carl and Ann?"

"Nothing went on," Carol said. "Carl was in love with Ann."

"Carl was in love with Ann?"

"*Love*," Carol said, with a third shrug. "I mean, call it what you want. But he wanted her, wanted to be with her."

"Carl and Ann?"

"Oh yeah," Carol said. "I thought you were a detective. Yeah. Carl and Ann."

———

I called Linda Hill, Merritt's art dealer, one more time.

"I was wondering about Carl and Ann," I said. "About that thing they had."

"Oh my God," she said. "I forgot all about that.

"It wasn't really a thing," she went on. "Well, Carl wanted it to be a thing. He had feelings for Ann. God, I can't believe I forgot all about this. Well, I guess I can believe it, because it seemed like a big deal at the time, but it all came to nothing. You know, Ann and Merritt were not a traditional couple, because he was so nuts, and maybe she was, too. And neither of them was interested in, you know, family-type stuff. But they were very much together. And Carl, he thought—well, who knows what he thought? But he had designs on Ann. And after she died, he blamed Merritt."

"Blamed Merritt how?" I asked.

"Oh, not that Merritt had killed her or anything like that. But that Merritt was a bad influence on her. And I think, if I remember right— Oh, I don't know what happened. They had some kind of a fight. Carl and Merritt. Some kind of a big blowout, I think, over it. But they fought all the time. I can't remember it all. Merritt and Ann are gone. There's no reason to carry this stuff around in my head anymore. It's over. Let someone else keep them alive."

For now, that someone else was me.

———

For no reason I drove down to the end of Santa Monica Boulevard and found myself at the bright and shimmering Pacific. In Santa Monica I ate a sandwich at a vegan café and looked through the Richter file again. There was a timeline: as far as Christopher had been able to put together, Merritt had last used his car the night before the accident, coming back from a party in the Hollywood Hills. The address of the party was typed neatly under the item. Mulholland Drive.

I drove across town to Adam Dubinsky's office, where I exchanged a few uncomfortable formalities with Adam and used his reverse directory. While I used it Adam spoke on the phone to someone in what I thought was Ukrainian but I wasn't sure. Adam sounded frustrated and defensive. Maybe that was just his accent. Maybe that was just what Ukrainian sounded like. Before I left I remembered to ask Adam if he knew anything about some of the odd things in the file—especially the letter. The letter that had been returned to Merritt.

> *You are my friend.*
> *I love you.*
> *I miss you.*

"I really don't remember," Adam said. "That's kind of your job now."

Adam gave me one of his non-smiles and did something with his forehead to indicate that I was annoying him.

"Cool," I said. "Right. Thanks. Very cool."

The house on Mulholland Drive wasn't in the reverse directory, so I'd gotten my daily dose of *fuck you* for nothing. I left Adam's office and drove up to the house. According to my map, it was fourteen miles away. The map did not show, unless you knew what you were looking for, that those fourteen miles were mostly uphill about forty-five degrees. I didn't know Los Angeles well enough to know, until I got there, that this was moneyed territory; I was just beginning to understand that while other cities organized themselves on the horizontal plane, Los Angeles neighborhoods went up when they went up and down when they went down.

And the farther up you went, the tighter the security. I found the address. There was a bald man in a black suit standing guard at the start of the long, uphill, drive. At the end of the long drive was a pair of large, strong, iron gates. They were not decorative.

I stopped by the bald man and rolled down my window. He approached.

"Help you?" he said.

"Who lives here?" I asked.

"That's personal information," he said, which was stating the obvious, but there was nothing to be gained from judging his capacity for subtlety. Everyone's got a job.

"Well, here's the thing," I said, and then I told him the thing— that I was working for Adam Dubinsky, that I was on the Merritt Underwood murder case, that there was a party in this house a few days before Merritt died.

He asked if I had a card.

I pretended to look in my wallet. "Shit," I said. "I ran out."

I'd never had a card. I wrote my name and the hotel phone number on the back of one of Adam's cards and handed it to the bald man.

"Maybe someone on your team could check me out," I said. "Give me a call."

"Maybe," he said. "We'll see."

———

It was a few days later that I got the call. James Voorstein. A security guy. I knew who he was. He protected politicians and celebrities and other people who could afford him.

"I know Adam well," he said on the phone, making it clear that Adam's good name was the only reason I was getting a call. "What's the story?"

I told him the story. He listened carefully and asked perceptive and particular questions, some of which I answered and some of which I couldn't.

"OK," he said at the end. "I'll talk to the homeowner. If he agrees, I'll set up a meeting. If not, there's nothing I can do for you."

He called again the next day: the homeowner agreed. He would see me. Time and place to be determined.

"It's Anderson Schmidt," Voorstein said, and let that sink in.

"Wow," I said. "OK. Thank you."

When we got off the phone I went downstairs and drove to the library downtown. I asked a librarian in the art department if she knew who Anderson Schmidt was. The librarian was in her thirties and wore cat-eye glasses and Dr. Martens boots. She seemed to be a specialist.

"You mean the artist?" she said.

"Yes?" I said, realizing I probably did.

She made a face of something like bliss.

"Do you want to see the books?"

I did want to see the books. She came out from around the counter and walked me toward the shelves.

"You like him?" I said as we walked.

"He's my favorite," she said. "Everything he does is so playful. So tangible. But also beautiful. It's like he's spiritual and childlike at the same time. I mean—I'm sure he would say child*ish*, not child*like*. I have no idea what he would say. But yes. My favorite living painter."

I didn't really understand any of that. I asked her something else.

"If you could meet him," I said, "and ask him one question, what would that question be?"

She thought and thought until we reached his section. I wondered what it would be like to have your own section in the library.

The librarian pulled out a pile of books for me, big heavy books with glossy color pages. I asked her to show me her favorite paintings of his and she did. They looked like cartoons. Like cartoons made by someone who wrote graffiti. I saw what she meant about them being childish, in a good way.

"I would ask him," the librarian finally said, "if he would sleep with me."

———

Two days later Anderson Schmidt met me at Chez Jay in Santa Monica. Everyone at Chez Jay seemed to know him and seemed to be happy to see him. Anderson had messy hair and giant hands. His clothes were expensive and didn't fit him right and his nose was sunburned. He was one of the most successful artists of his generation, and by far the richest in Los Angeles.

"Boy," Anderson said, after ordering a corned beef sandwich with extra pickles on the side and a beer, which I immediately imitated, sensing genius at work. "Merritt Underwood. I haven't heard that name in years. What a guy. Such a character. Such a gifted SOB."

"So you liked him?" I asked. Our glasses of beer came and they were cold and perfect. I knew I'd been right to copy Anderson's order.

"Oh, I loved Merritt," Anderson said. "What an SOB. He was nuts. NUTS. Total alcoholic. Total crazy man. But he would give you the shirt off his back. Boy, did we fight. Cats and dogs."

"What'd you fight about?" I asked.

"Everything," Anderson said, smiling. He seemed to really relish the memory. "But mostly art. I met Merritt when he was young, but I always felt like he was my equal. Intellectually, I mean. If I thought anyone else was my equal artistically, I'd have to kill them."

"Really?" I said.

"Yes," Anderson said without hesitating. "But Merritt wasn't, so you can cross me off your list of suspects. Very talented, but he was Merritt and I'm me. And I'm better. Usually."

"Who should be ON my list of suspects?" I asked.

Anderson shrugged. "Everyone else? Life is mysterious. I'm sure I don't have to tell you that."

He did not.

"So there was a party," I said. "A couple of days before Merritt died?"

Anderson nodded. "Back then we had parties every week. Almost every night. Before we got old." But you could tell from the way he said it that he didn't really think he was old. "Had I known . . ."

Of course there was no way to finish that sentence—had he known Merritt was going to die just two days later, there was likely much he would have done differently.

Everyone dies. And everyone is always surprised when it happens. I couldn't understand it. It isn't a secret. It's not like no one ever told them.

Then again, when Mick, Constance's other assistant, told me Constance was dead, I didn't believe him. I didn't believe him the second time. The third time, I smacked him across the face, as hard as I could, and my fingernail cut his cheek and left a scar.

"So the party," I began again. "What was that like? You had parties like that before?"

"All the time," Anderson said. "Merritt had his place in Topanga; Paul January had a big warehouse in Santa Monica; Carl Avery was in Venice. We'd paint all day—well, all afternoon—then one or the other of us would head over to the other's studio around eight or nine and start drinking. If we hadn't started already. I was married to my first wife. Trina. She was insane. Obviously. Only an insane woman would marry me. My current wife is almost as crazy, but she likes to stay home. We stay out of trouble. Most of the time. Anyway. We had parties often. The other painters would come, women"—I noticed that for Anderson, these were two separate categories—"and students, whoever was around. We had a blast. Usually ended with a fight, but that's what men do."

I got the impression Anderson liked arguing with people. I guessed he would refer to it as "locking horns" or "going mano a mano" or "duking it out."

"What do men do?" I asked, although I was pretty sure I knew. They did what women did, but worse, and thought murder was a good way to solve problems.

"Good question," Anderson said. "You have to realize, I'm speaking strictly in the mythopoetic realm here. In real life, men and women aren't that different anymore. But in our fantasies, you know, we're MEN." Anderson made a weight lifting–type gesture and laughed. "And as men, we have this burden, you know, of trying to separate right from wrong. When to use force and when to seduce. Well, I don't know why I'm trying to make it a male thing. I guess that's just how we all thought of it. I'm sure my wife wouldn't agree with that. Anyway—"

Anderson made a gesture for more beer and someone brought us more beer, like magic.

"—Merritt wanted to make something meaningful and so did I, and so we fought, because we thought that was what men did. We didn't know how else to show that we loved each other. Now I know better. Now I tell the people I love that I love them. I tell the people I hate that I hate them. Life is much better this way. Easy to do when you have a million bucks in the bank. Not so easy to do without it."

I was getting a little drunk from the beer and I thought Anderson was probably right. I'd done well with telling the people I hated all the ways in which I hated them, even with nothing in the bank. Not so great with telling anyone I loved them. I'd said it a few times and it had never ended well.

I'd never said it to Constance. She knew anyway. I knew she did.

"So who else was at that party?" I asked. "Anyone in particular fight with anyone else?"

"Honestly, it was not an exciting night." Anderson sighed, wrinkled his brow. Something a little bit broken showed on his face and I could tell he'd gone over that night, his last night with Merritt, a million times. "My wife at the time, Trina, she was there. Merritt. Paul, of course. Jenny O'Donnell, she was always around back then. A bunch of kids from my studio. These two girls Paul picked up in Hollywood, they were from Argentina. The stained-glass guy, what's-his-name. A couple of other people, but we hardly knew them. No one important. Not unimportant existentially. Unimportant to our little scene."

"So there were no fights?" I asked again.

Anderson frowned. "Not that I remember. Listen, I was drunk. I mean I GOT drunk. There's a lot I could have missed. Merritt changed after Ann died. He was quieter. But quieter for Merritt—I mean, he started off LOUD. Quieter, smaller Merritt was still very, very big. Still caused all kinds of trouble."

"Can you kind of track the night?" I asked. "Can you tell me what you remember?"

"Sure," Anderson said. "Merritt showed up around nine. Maybe ten. I don't remember what—I mean if we had plans or if he called first or just showed up. Like I said, we did this almost every night. Joan Shapiro—I think she was still there from the previous night. My wife did not like that. Trina. Mike Kelly came around. Ray. Merritt came around a little later."

"Did he come alone?" I asked.

"No," Anderson said. "Not alone. With some girl. Some actress. Rebecca something. They seemed to be having fun. Nothing serious. I don't think Merritt was serious about anything after Ann."

"Did you know Ann?" I asked.

"Know her?" Anderson said. "I introduced them! Ann and Merritt. I gave Ann her first show. Little group show I put together in Venice. She was a genius, and I'm very proud to say that I was, as far as I know, the first person to say that out loud. She was from this little town in Mississippi. Missouri? Still in art school. We showed her first Beehive piece. That was what she called them—*Beehive #1*, *Beehive #2*, and so on. This one had actual bees in it—somehow she, I don't know. Preserved bees. Formaldehyde or something. Smart as a whip. Enormous talent. And boy, did she have opinions. Didn't care about, you know, the art world or the oil crises. But get her started on bats or Freud or the history of the flower business. STRONG opinions. She was probably the most curious person I ever met."

"So why did you and Merritt fight?" I asked. I'd finished my lunch and felt pleasantly high from the meat and the fat and the beer. It was the most relaxed I'd been since I'd come to Los Angeles.

"Because, as talented as that SOB was—and boy, was he ever talented—he didn't want to play the game. He didn't want to duke it out. He didn't want to fight for his place in the world. He thought it was beneath him to worry about whether his work sold, if it got reviewed. And you know, it probably was. But that's what the world needs."

"People who stand by their art?"

"Oh, no," Anderson said quickly. "We've got enough of those. People who want to keep everything pure and contained and then no one ever sees it. No no no. We need people who'll do what's beneath them in order to do what needs to be done. People who have vision and are unwilling to let the mediocre steal that vision. People willing to get down in the mud and fight. Because, you know, the bad guys are winning." I thought we were both a little drunk now, because I was starting to agree with him. "They're winning every fight, all the time. We, people like you and me, we've totally conceded the lower three chakras. The whole bottom triangle. You and me and Merritt and Ann—the good guys—we gave up too easy, moved on to the higher chakras. We gave up the war. The good guys, we don't need to elevate. There's enough of us up there. We need to crawl down in the mud, and plant some lotus seeds."

"So that's what you fought about that night?" I asked. "Lotus seeds?"

"No," Anderson said. "Actually, I don't think we did fight that night. Not that I remember. We did have a heated discussion about politics. Merritt didn't care about politics. I think that's disgraceful. I think it's your civic obligation to be utterly fucking furious about politics. Anyway, we did talk, but no big fights. In fact, I don't remember any big fights that night. Not even with Carl. Maybe a little fight."

Something pierced through my haze of beer and meat—at first I thought maybe it was a ray of sunlight from outside the restaurant, or a blast of cold air from the vent.

But then the feeling, which at first I thought was just a little shiver, didn't stop.

Instead it grew.

And it grew.

"Carl and Merritt fought a lot?" I asked.

"All the time," Anderson said.

"About lotus seeds?" I asked.

"Fuck no," Anderson said. "About art."

"And?" I said. There's always an *and*.

"And I don't know what else," Anderson said. "There is no *and*. I don't know what happens when other people are alone."

I thought that was a pretty profound statement, but I put it aside and asked a dumb question.

"So what did they fight about that night?" I asked. Because now I was sure—they fought that night.

"According to Carl," Anderson said, "they fought about politics."

"Politics?" I repeated. It was another dumb question. I was getting good at them. He'd just said Merritt didn't care about politics.

"That's what Carl said. But look, when artists fight, it doesn't matter what they're fighting about," he explained. "Paint. Women. Politics. They're really only fighting about one thing. The same thing. The only thing men ever fight about. Women, too, probably."

"So what are they really fighting about?"

"What we're fighting about," Anderson said, "is who's better. That's all that matters to artists. We pretend to be decent people, or at least interesting people, but we're not. All we care about is one thing: being the best. All the crazy stuff—the drinking, the sleeping around, and the going after money, being little bankers—that's what they are now, little bankers, little painting hedge fund managers—all of it is just so we can keep working. Eating, breathing—all so we can keep working. So we can be better. So we can be the best. And luckily," he said, a giant grin spreading across his giant face, "*I am*."

———

That night I dreamed about Ann. I imagined her standing far in the distance on a kind of dream highway. The road was perfectly straight and long, with no cars. Ann stood at the horizon, in a sharp and shiny black suit from a film noir, one arm bent, one finger curled to invite someone forward. She smiled a smart, crooked smile.

I woke up at 4:44 in the morning with a dark, wet feeling. I lay in bed and I couldn't sleep.

Usually solving a mystery brought on a nearly-giddy feeling, a feeling of rightness and satisfaction, almost like happiness. A sense that the world was right on its axis. But now I just felt dark and sad.

I lay in bed until I was sure of what I wanted to do. I thought of Ann and Merritt and soon my face was hot with tears. I thought of what was lost without them. I thought of the holes in the world that they could have, should have, filled. The seeds they planted and those they would have planted, had they lived.

Finally I was sure. I stopped crying, got up, made some coffee in the little hotel coffee maker, got dressed, left my hotel, got in my car, and drove to Carl Avery's house in Venice.

Carl wasn't home. The lights were out and there was no car in the driveway. I sat on a broken chair on his porch with my .45 and waited.

It was a cool night but not cold. Los Angeles was darker at night than any big American city I'd ever been to. After an hour a raccoon ambled its way across the yard, stopping to dig for a root or a mushroom only to leave off in the middle and waddle its fat little ass as far away as it could get when a car approached.

The car was Carl's. He parked the car, got out, and clumsily made his way to the door. Good. He was a little drunk. That should help. He stumbled up to the porch.

"Hello Carl," I said.

He gasped and dropped his keys. "Whoa," he said. "Wait. Are you that detective girl?"

"Yeah," I said. "I am."

He looked at me as if he didn't know why I was there.

"What are you doing there?" he said. "I mean here."

"I'm here," I said, "to talk about the night you killed Merritt."

Carl froze in place, and sobered up fast. His face went through at least three quick permutations: shock, fear, shame.

I probably didn't need to, but I pulled out the .45 and pointed it at him.

Carl sighed and shook his head and looked utterly disgusted. I wasn't sure who he was so disgusted with—me or himself or the world as a whole.

"OK," he said, drunk again. "You might as well come in. But put that thing away."

"OK," I said.

I went in.

I did not put that thing away.

———

Inside we sat where we'd sat last time. Carl stared at all his half-done paintings. I couldn't quite read his face at first. I'd had many denouements in my life but I wasn't sure I'd ever seen a murderer like Carl. Usually they denied it or started justifying it or cried. Carl was quiet and still.

Carl looked at his paintings. I looked at Carl. I'd had weeks with the case and an hour with the raccoon to think about my angle and it was time to try it out.

"Merritt ruined Ann's life," I said. I didn't believe it. But I was pretty sure Carl did. "He might not have exactly murdered her, but—"

"Oh, right, sure. He killed her," Carl said, looking at his paintings. But he said it with a strange little snort, a kind of horrific mirror image of a laugh. "He ate away at her. She gave him chance after chance and every time, he broke her heart. Every year she became a little less. He chipped away at her until there was nothing left."

"That's where people like us come in," I said—us gentle men and women, us defenders of honor, us cops who chase down pirates. "People like Ann need to be protected."

"No," Carl said. "You mean monsters. Horrific, unforgivable monsters."

He kept looking at his paintings. I looked along with him, trying to see what he saw. All I saw was paint.

"That's what I told myself," Carl said. "To cover up my jealousy. My loneliness. I wanted what Merritt had. I wanted to BE Merritt. So I made him into this shitty person. I mean, he was a fuck-up. I didn't make that up. He was a disaster. Jesus. That was because he was an artist. All artists are fucking disasters."

He made a gesture with his hands. It indicated something like *look around, this room, this house.* I wasn't sure what I was supposed to see. But what I did see was an orderly studio and an orderly house and paintings stacked neatly against the wall. There were no disasters. No messes. Maybe Carl meant that he was never really an artist. Or maybe he thought this *was* a disaster.

I'd planned to draw a confession out of Carl by pretending I agreed with him. Pretending I saw things how he saw them.

But Carl didn't need me to do any of that. His confession had been waiting.

All I had to do was let him let it out, not stop him.

"Yeah," Carl said bitterly. "That's what I told myself. If I didn't save Ann, no one would. Merritt used her. He emptied her out like . . . like an ATM. He just took. Took and took and took. Merritt ruined her. Ruined her life. She was dead less than ten years after meeting him. That's what I told myself. That getting rid of him was this noble fucking deed."

Carl made another ugly sound.

"I just wanted him dead," Carl said. His face was sad and haunted in the dark and hard to look at. Hard to see. "He was better and he was always going to be better. I did love Ann. I did have feelings for Ann. Some kind of feelings that were, if I am to be believed about anything, ever, real. They seemed real to me. When I saw her with Merritt—it was like proof. The ultimate proof."

"That he was a better person?" I guessed.

Carl looked at me like I understood nothing.

"That he was a better painter," Carl said. "Everything about her was . . . Ann was perfect. She was like the ultimate fucking prize."

I'd never met Ann, of course, but I knew that wasn't true. None of us were perfect. No one was complete. People weren't designed to be pure; everyone needed parts of everyone else: money, time, sex, labor, tears, attention. We were all filthy; all contaminated by each other. Ann had needed all of those things. That was what ruined her. That was what ruined all of us. There is no escape from the pain of other people. They would ruin you and you would ruin them.

Not that it mattered now.

"I was an idiot," Carl said. "After the party at Anderson's, I knew he wouldn't go out the next day. Merritt. He'd be sleeping, or too hungover to drive. And I knew that to get over it, he'd have another drink—you know, hair of the dog. And of course, one drink would be four, and then five.

"It was all on impulse," Carl said, seemingly in shock at his own ability to murder. "I planned it all in about three minutes, and then went through with it before I could stop myself. We'd gotten in that fight, the night before. I told him, straight up, 'You killed Ann.' And he said, I remember exactly, 'You have no idea what you're talking about.'" Carl made an indignant little sound in his throat. "No idea?! I knew Ann first. No, not really. But I knew her work first. I knew her work before we even met."

It was too late to explain to Carl that it wasn't a numbers game. That it wasn't a game at all, at least not the kind with points and a score. But I said nothing and let him fill the silence.

"I couldn't stop thinking about it," he said. He quoted Merritt again: "I had no idea what I was talking about?! Like I'd never even known her? I just couldn't—it was just the last straw. Merritt always thought he was so much better than me. So much better than everyone. And he was. As an artist. But as a person? Fuck him. Just fuck him and fuck that. I couldn't be a better painter, but I could be a better person. Or so I deluded myself. Deluded myself to justify the wound to my ego. He'd ruined her life. Who knew who else's? Who would be next? He wouldn't stop. He'd just suck the life out of some other girl. So I just . . . decided. I don't know. I didn't even decide. I just did it."

Carl looked at me and as he told me his horrible story I could feel and see something draining out of him as he admitted the enormous awfulness of what he'd done. When I'd caught him at the door he'd looked kind of like a man; now he was looking more and more like a corpse; like an animated, moving corpse, come to visit from the land of the dead.

"Of course I see now," Carl went on, "that it was all just horseshit. Just horseshit and jealousy. But at the time. At the time I worked myself into this . . . moral indignation. I just felt in some inarticulate way that it was the only thing to do. That I'd be doing the world a favor by getting rid of him. That's what I was building toward, all those years. Only one of us could live. So I planned it all out just like that. I knew he'd sleep late, so I called him late, about four—late enough for him to be up and have a few more drinks. I said some stuff, stuff about Ann. About his career. Then I gave him time to drink. Time to get dumb. I called back at six. That time I really just let him have it. We got into all of it—Ann, fame, money, everything. I goaded him into it—he said he would meet me down in Venice at eight that night. I knew he'd just stay home and drink until then. So I went up to his house, went up the driveway, and cut away at his tires. I had this little knife with me, a kind of bowie knife, and I just cut, cut, cut. Never all the way through. There's a whole system. I found it in a book. A detective novel. I was so angry I barely remember doing any of it. I mean, I did do it, I know that. But I was in such a rage—it was like I was someone else."

"Who were you?" I asked, out of curiosity.

Carl crunched up his face when he thought about it. "Someone who didn't . . . Someone who DID things. Someone like the people in detective novels. Men who do things without obsessing, without fussing over every little detail. Without second-guessing myself all the time." He thought for another long moment. "All my life it seemed like, like I was trying. Like I was working. Like life was my job, and I was failing at it. But that day, with Merritt—it seemed so real. More real than anything else ever had. Like I was really alive. The way other people were.

"But afterward—I could remember that it felt good, but I couldn't feel it again. Like pain. Once, I broke my arm. It was so stupid, I don't even want to tell you how. But then later, after it hurt—I mean, after it healed—it was like I was aware of the fact that it had been incredibly painful, but I couldn't really ever feel it again. It was like that.

"Anyway. I cut his tires and"—Carl made an ugly, dead, smile and tossed his hands in the air—"it all worked out perfectly. Merritt got in the car, he was drunk, blew out his tires in the canyon . . ."

The odds of his shitty little plan working were about a million to one. You can spend a lifetime studying fate and change and trying to figure them out. And then someone like Carl goes and has the luckiest day in three thousand years.

Or the unluckiest.

"As soon as I heard he was dead," Carl said, "I knew I'd made a . . . Jesus. *Mistake* isn't the word. It was unforgivable. Unconscionable.

"I won," Carl said. "I won. And I lost the best friend I ever had. And I—a man who has devoted his life to art, to this only thing, to this—I killed the best artist I ever knew. Over something . . . something I'd made up. A fucking lie I'd invented to justify myself. To justify my jealousy. Ann? I hardly even knew Ann. She wasn't even real."

But she was real. Maybe she was never really real to Carl, or even Merritt. But she was real.

Neither of us said anything for a while. Carl started to cry. I sat next to him and held his crying, shaking hand as I called the police, and as we waited for the police to come Carl put his head in my lap and sobbed and I stroked his hair. When the police came he went without arguing.

In that room with him, the solution rolling out before my eyes, for a short moment I'd felt the way he'd described—alive. Like I wasn't rehearsing, like this was actual, real life, and my place in it was inevitable and secure. Like I belonged here as much as anyone else.

And I knew that, also like Carl, with his broken arm, I wouldn't be able to hold on to it after it was gone.

In my mind's eye the rest of my life poured out ahead of me: black tar on an endless road, dark and alone. It would be a long series of empty moments that took me down an infinite highway to nowhere in particular. Happiness would always be around the next corner—but never here, never now, never on this road.

———

In the days after I busted Carl I didn't feel much of anything in particular. It wasn't an interesting case and he wasn't a particularly noteworthy adversary.

There's the mystery and then there's the case, Silette wrote. This was no mystery. This was a case, and a dull one.

And now it was closed. I had my four hundred hours. Or so I thought. I typed up all my time sheets and brought them to Adam. He was sitting at his desk, as usual, smoking cigarettes and shuffling papers around. I don't remember ever seeing him do anything else.

I sat in front of him and gave him my ledger. Adam smoked and looked at the pages. He wrinkled his brow a little and tapped out some addition and subtraction on his fingers as he looked the ledger over.

"You're short," he said.

For a quick moment I thought he meant my height. Then I realized he meant my hours.

"I don't think so," I said. "I was very careful. I bought a calculator."

"I see that," he said. "But you're one hundred and eight minutes short."

He handed the papers back to me.

"The case isn't done," he said. "You have one hundred and eight more minutes to go."

There was no arguing. Unless I wanted to argue with him for one hundred and eight minutes and make up the time that way.

"OK," I said. "But I think this case is done. Is there something else I can do for you? I don't mind going over in hours. I can do a few days' work on another case if you have anything. I don't mind at all."

"I don't think so," Adam said. "This is the case. And you have nearly two hours left to go. So why don't you go and do that, and then when you're done, come back, and I'll sign your paperwork."

"OK," I said. "I'll do that. Thank you, Adam."

He made his tight little non-smile and said nothing and I left.

———

So I had an hour and forty-eight minutes left. I didn't know what to do for an hour and forty-eight minutes.

Carl confessed to everything all over again pretty quick once the cops and the lawyers started in on him. He wasn't a tough guy. Just a frightened and jealous man who'd made some terrible mistakes. I didn't really care if he went to jail. I didn't think he was gonna turn around and kill someone else all over again. But maybe he was better off now. Nothing to hide, no secrets. We should all be so lucky. Although being out of prison was pretty nice, too. Either way, I'd solved the case. Not my problem.

A few days after he confessed, later in the day after Adam told me I was short, Carl was on the cover of the *Los Angeles Times*. For reasons that were opaque to me, he was being walked into the police station by Christopher Collins. Christopher Collins from the Richter Agency. Who hadn't fucking solved the case then and hadn't fucking solved the case now.

I skimmed the copy—murder, confession, blah blah—until I got to the last paragraph.

"The case was solved by an agent of the Richter Agency, Christopher Collins, who specializes in cold cases. 'I was hired for this case over eight years ago,' Collins said, 'but the case isn't solved until it's solved.

" 'Richter never rests.' "

CHAPTER 14

THE CLUE OF THE CHARNEL HOUSE

Brooklyn, 1985

Tracy had been quiet all day. It was the aftermath of the Case of the Gilded China, and I could tell the case had hit her hard. Late that night, when the air was cold and calm under its own silence, we sat on the steps of a row house across from the projects where she lived. Our breath was cold in the night air, white against the black sky.

"So yesterday," Tracy said. "I mean last night. At the hospital. I was talking to the man—the witness."

Tracy paused and didn't say anything.

"What'd he say?" I asked.

"Well, that once—before all this happened—he was at the end of his rope. That's how he put it. Like there was an actual rope, and there he was, at the end. Under that rope—you know, it was just nothingness, I guess. Just blackness. Anyway, he had a rope, and he was at the end of it. And he didn't know what to do anymore. He said he couldn't keep living and he couldn't die. He was frozen. So he went and he lived in, like, in some rooming-house-type place. He had a room in this place and for a year, he didn't leave his room. Every night he would stand at the window and try to will himself to jump, and every night he couldn't do it. Every night, he didn't have the courage to jump.

"And then, one night when he was looking down, doing his usual thing, his little chat with death—that was what he called it, his nightly little chat with death—he said he realized something. He realized that you can try as hard as you want to escape who you are, but eventually, you realize there is no escape. There's nowhere to run, and nothing to run to. Nothing ever really changes. The state of life on earth is exactly what it is, and the only chance of a happy life is accepting that. Accepting life as it is. And knowing that there is no escape. And that's the only freedom he's ever been able to find."

I didn't know what to say. I put my arms around her and told her I loved her and told her we'd feel better tomorrow. We never felt better tomorrow. But I said it because I didn't know what else to say. Accepting life as it was, without rage, seemed maybe possible for some enlightened other people, in another place, with a better reality. Not for me. Not for us.

Less than a year later, Tracy would disappear, taking with her all of our best tomorrows.

A year and a half later, Kelly and I analyzed every memory, dissected every clue she had left behind. I reminded Kelly about the man in the rooming house.

We were in Kelly's apartment, sitting on her bedroom floor. Kelly frowned. She didn't say anything for a while—she was already starting to speak less, frown more. She went digging in her boxes of papers,

clues, and notes; she dug until she found what she was looking for—
a scrawled hieroglyphic note on the back of a paper menu from the
Kiev Diner: *Open all Nite. We Serve Pierogi.*

"No, no, no," Kelly said. "She told me a completely different story.
A completely different version. It was a woman, not a man. And she
didn't live in some kind of halfway house—"

"Rooming house—"

"She lived in the Plaza Hotel. Like in the book. She said—"

Kelly read the woman's words off the back of the menu, where
Kelly had written them eighteen months before:

" 'After the fire, I was staying in the Plaza, across from the park. At
first I pretended I was looking for a real place. A place to live. Then
I stopped pretending I wanted to live. I couldn't pretend anymore,
and I just stayed there. I had a suite. I wanted to die, but I couldn't
bring myself to do it.

" 'I spent a lot of time looking out the window. I tried to miss life.
I wanted to want to live. Or to have the courage to die already. But I
just couldn't do either. I didn't want to live and I didn't want to die.

" 'I told myself I was hibernating. Healing. But winter passed, and
then the spring, and then, soon enough, it was winter again, and I
was still in the Plaza. I still didn't want to leave. When I felt restless
I would get dressed and roam around the halls, take the elevators up
and down. Sometimes I'd go to other floors and walk around there.
Mostly it was the same, but some floors were different.

" 'Then one night I was sitting by the window—I had a kind of
window seat I would sit in—I was sitting in my seat and the moon
rose up, there was a big white moon and I realized: history isn't real.
It isn't real. Maybe it happened once, but it wasn't happening now.
That who I was yesterday was not at all important to who I could be
today. That every day the world was born again. I could walk out of
that hotel and change my name, change everything about myself, and
never look back unless the mood struck me to do so.

" 'Escape is possible.

" 'So I escaped. And that's the only freedom I've ever been able to find. To give up the past, and create a new life. To start again.' "

I looked at Kelly. She didn't look at me.

"But they're complete opposites," I said. "They can't both be true."

Kelly turned and looked out the window, thinking.

I didn't know what to say, and we never talked about it again.

CHAPTER 15

THE MYSTERY OF THE CBSIS

Los Angeles, 1999

I wasn't above lying to Adam, but it wasn't worth the risk. Back in my hotel room I looked for something to do for 108 minutes. I flipped through the paperwork again. Looked at a catalog of Carl's paintings. Put a bunch of slides back in my slide projector and looked at them. Somehow I ended up looking at Merritt's last paintings, the ones that everyone thought ruined his career, the paintings that were too big and made you too uncomfortable.

I set the slide projector on automatic and in its dim light I looked through Merritt's file again. His paintings had grown on me since I started the case. I would have liked to have one of them, if I had money or a house to put it in. I put aside a slide of my favorite of Merritt's paintings. It was called *Pacific Ocean #12*. It was dark and frightening and there was something in it that I knew but couldn't put into words, and had never known I knew before. I figured I'd take it to a photo lab and get a print made for myself before I returned it to Adam.

Merritt himself had grown on me, too. I was a little in love with him. I put all the papers back in Adam's thin file. I wondered where the file would go when I was done with it. I took out the letter from Merritt—the sweet, drawn-on, three-line note Merritt had sent to a friend in New York and that was returned as undeliverable.

I opened the letter and read it again:

You are my friend.
I love you.
I miss you.

I'd asked Adam about the letter. As far as he knew it had been in Merritt's last mail delivery. Merritt likely didn't see it before he died. No one knew who Jacob Heartwell was. He wasn't in any of the files, at least. It had been on my list of potentially interesting avenues of investigation, but Carl had confessed before I'd gotten around to doing any real investigation.

Who was Jacob Heartwell? If Merritt loved him so much, why didn't he know where he lived? What did love mean to Merritt? To anyone?

Merritt had drawn all over the outside of the envelope. I put it aside. I would ask Adam if I could get it back to the friend Merritt had sent it to, if I could find him. Jacob Heartwell.

I put the letter back in the envelope and put it on the top of the file and there it was, on the back of the envelope. Under and above and mixed in with shapes and curves and lines Merritt had sketched.

A bee. A honeybee drawn with black ink. Its wings were spread wide, as if in flight or about to take off.

My hands shook as I picked up the envelope and looked at the bee. I turned off the slide projector and turned on the lights and looked at the bee again. I went into the bathroom, where the light was brighter, and looked at the bee again. It was finely drawn and from a different pen than the rest of the drawings on the envelope.

The clock ticked. A hundred and eight minutes had passed.

I didn't care.

I'd spent weeks now with Merritt and Ann's work.

Merritt hadn't drawn that bee. Ann had.

And according to the postmark on the envelope, which was from 1994, she'd done it the year after she died in 1993.

Or, I realized, as I rewrote history in my head, the year everyone thought she had died.

———

At first I thought there was no way to date the envelope. There weren't any radical innovations in postal technology in the two years between Ann's death and Merritt's. No fundamental changes to the nature of the envelope.

I looked at the envelope and looked at it and looked at it some more. It was a security envelope, business size and business type, no maker's mark anywhere.

But security envelope meant a pattern and patterns could be traced. I picked it up, carefully, and looked at the pattern inside. A web of green wavy lines in a repeating pattern of about a half a square inch, set against itself at conflicting angles.

———

"I don't understand," the man on the other end of the phone said. "We're not an archiving company. We're a paper company. We make paper."

"I understand that," I said. I was sitting up in bed in my hotel room. I'd gotten up at eight, had two big Thai coffees and a churro for breakfast, and gone to the Hollywood library. Merritt's envelope had been plain, with no plastic window. Fortunately, paper manufacturers didn't come and go frequently. It was a good solid business where the main players mostly stood still for fifty or more years at a time. From the phone books in the library, I made a list of envelope manufacturers in the American Southwest. Of course the envelopes could have been sent from anywhere, but everyone likes to save on shipping costs and you had to start somewhere. I got my list together and then I went back to my hotel room and started making calls.

Now it was 2:00 p.m. My hands were shaking and my temples were throbbing. I'd planned to keep going until I had an answer, but now I realized that wasn't going to work. After this call I would break for lunch. The idea of another Thai lunch alone was not appealing, which was another reason I hadn't stopped.

"I completely understand what you do," I said. "I am actually a detective. A private eye. And I am on a very important case concerning a murder that happened in 1995."

"Huh," the man said. The last person had hung up on me. The one before him had called me crazy, and then hung up on me. This one sounded just interested enough to keep listening. "A detective?"

"Yes," I said. "I'm trying to solve a very important mystery, and I think you could help."

The man took a deep breath in and out.

"Is this one of those TV shows?" he said. "Where they're gonna come out with cameras and start laughing at me?"

"No sir," I said. The man was in Bakersfield, which was a few hours away driving and a few galaxies away in every other way.

Another deep breath in and out.

"So what was the question?" he said.

I explained again what I needed: if he might have sold this envelope and if so, when—the only defining characteristic distinguishing it from other envelopes being the security pattern on the inside. A crosshatched repeating pattern of green wavy lines.

The man didn't say anything for a minute.

"Are you there?" I said.

"I am," the man said. "I just. I mean."

"I know," I said, gritting my teeth against the reality of the fifty more phone calls I would need to make that day. "It's an unusual request, and—"

"No," the man said. "No, that's not it at all. I just can't believe you're asking about that envelope. Green ink? Little wavy lines in a repeat about half an inch wide?"

I looked at the envelope.

"Yes," I said. I felt my heart start to beat a little harder and I wasn't as hungry or tired anymore.

"Well I'll be damned," he said. "That is us. And I can tell you exactly when that came into production, because it was the first thing I did when I got hired here. See, when I came on here—I'm a manager, I been in paper all my life but before *that*, I was in drafting—well, I'll get to that—see, OK, let me start again."

"Sure," I said. Suddenly this envelope man was the most enthralling man in the world. I grabbed a pen and my notebook to take notes.

"When I started here," the man said, "we were buying our security paper from, well, I probably shouldn't say who, but I will tell you they were overcharging us. So I go to the president's office, third week on the job—I am sweating bullets, let me tell you—and I hand him a piece of paper. Now, this was the old president. The father. Tough man. I hand him a piece of paper that I stayed up all night working on. He looks right at me and says, 'Son, what the heck is this?' and I say, 'Sir, that's our new security paper. Because I cannot in good conscience allow you to continue buying from' —well, if you know paper, you can guess from who. Then I showed him my spreadsheets. I'd crunched all the numbers, done all the comparisons. Stayed up two nights in a row doing the math. That was one of the longest moments of my life right then, waiting for an answer.

"Well, long story short, we went into production on my paper the very next week. And we told you-know-who to go to hell. And to date, I've saved this company over 164,000 dollars since then by making our security papers in-house."

"Wow," I said.

"I know," he said. "I still can't quite figure out where I got the balls to do it. Pardon my language."

"Pardoned," I said. "So what year was that? When you started making the new paper?"

"The year I started here," he said again. "1994."

"You're sure?" I said. "You're absolutely sure? That paper went into production in 1994?"

"Absolutely," he said. "October ninety-four. Do you want to know what it's called? The paper?"

"Yes," I said. "Very much."

"*Green Waves on a Day of Dark Fog*," he said. "That's what I called it."

"Wow," I said. "That's very poetic."

"Thank you," the man said, sounding very sincere. "I really do appreciate that. I've never seen the ocean, but I always imagined it looks like that."

"It does," I lied to him. "Just like that."

I thanked him a few more times and we got off the phone.

————

I didn't know what I'd found, or how to make sense of it, or what it had to do with Merritt. But Ann was still alive in 1994.

Here's what I figured: Merritt was writing a letter to his friend Jacob Heartwell. As he often did, as many artists did, as many humans did, he drew on the back of the envelope before he sent it. But when Merritt was writing this letter, he was with Ann, who was supposed to be dead. Not only was she not dead, but she added a bee to the drawing. Was she trying to send a message to Jacob, whoever he was, to let him know she was alive? Or was she just idly sketching? I didn't know the answers. I also didn't know why Ann would have pretended to be dead if she wasn't.

But the envelope was from 1994. She was supposed to be dead in 1993. She'd drawn that bee.

When Adam had handed me the Merritt Underwood file it felt like a cord of dead wood I was going to have to drag around with me until I got my license.

Now it seemed like a jewel box of treasure that all the forces of earth couldn't keep me away from if they tried. Now it seemed like an oyster, with my pearl somewhere in there, waiting for me to discover it.

Now it wasn't just a crime. It was a mystery. *My* mystery.

I started again.

The letter was addressed to a man named Jacob Heartwell. On Melrose I found an internet café and booked an hour of time and searched for Jacob Heartwell. He was a painter who taught at an art school in San Francisco. He'd taught at Parsons in New York for a few years, which was where Merritt had tried, and failed, to get a letter to him. Heartwell didn't look oversized and sex-powered like the male artists I'd met in Los Angeles. He was thin and had a long face and looked sad.

It took nine phone calls over eleven days before Jacob Heartwell would talk to me. Including three times that he hung up on me. Finally on the fourth try I got him to stay on the line long enough to explain that I was a private investigator and I was investigating Merritt's death.

"Oh," Jacob Heartwell said, not seeming to be particularly moved by this. "I thought you were a collection agency."

I thought he was probably right and I was—PIs were the collection agencies of information, tracking down unpaid knowledge debts and bail jumpers from facts. But that was all somewhat more poetic than was called for by the situation at hand so I just said, "No, not at all. Sorry about that. I'm working for—well, we were hired by Merritt's parents, before they passed away. Anyway. Yes. Not a bill collector. Can I ask a few questions about Merritt?"

"Oh," he said hesitatingly. "OK. That's somewhat painful."

"Were you friends?" I asked.

"Yes," he said after a long moment. "But we hadn't spoken in, well, almost two years. When he died."

"That sounds like a story," I said.

"Well," Jacob Heartwell said, "anything is a story if you tell it right. But this one, yes, I think you're right. I think it's a story. Now, the problem with stories is always where to begin," he said.

"At the beginning?" I suggested.

Heartwell laughed. "Fair enough. Merritt and I went to school together. High school. Pasadena. We were both artists. We were both, you know, fascinated with the world. Full of—well, it seemed like rage at the time. Now I think it was just a kind of love. We were in love with the world, and we wanted the world to love us back. Anyway, we were very close. Best friends. Merritt was the first person to know I was gay. And he took me to a gay bar in Hollywood. Hand to God. This straight boy from Pasadena.

"After high school, we drifted in and out of each other's lives, but we were always close. You know what men are like. We don't need to talk every day for our relationships to be real. Most of the time, we don't even need to talk at all.

"And then, he met Ann."

Jacob Heartwell paused.

"You didn't like Ann?" I asked.

"No," he said, and I realized he was trying not to cry. "I loved Ann. And I loved Merritt, with her. Ann and I became very close.

Immediate friends. We went to plays together. Bad plays, usually. She was so well-read. She read like a gay man—Virginia Woolf, Truman Capote, Joan Didion. And when she died, I just could not handle it.

"And I could not handle Merritt. I didn't mean not to speak to him for so long. It had nothing to do with Merritt. I wasn't mad at him. After the funeral I just—I don't know. I needed a new start. I've lost so, so many people. Ann was the last one I could take.

"I couldn't keep going after that. It was end my life or start over. I'd done my part, lest you think I just ran away. I nursed many, many men out of this life. Cleaning, medications, the IVs. I told eleven mothers that their sons had gone. No fathers. Not one father wanted to hear it. My life in Los Angeles had become a funeral.

"So I left Los Angeles, came up here, and started a new life. I've . . ."

He inhaled deeply and sighed.

"I've made the best of it," he finished. "And then Merritt died, and I realized I'd made a terrible, terrible mistake going so long without speaking with him. I was trying to be someone new," he said. "And in the process of doing so, I let go of the best part of myself. I'd lost touch with my family, with—well, Merritt WAS family."

"So," I began, struggling to say something I didn't have words for. "Did you. I mean. After that."

Somehow he answered the question I didn't know how to ask.

"There is no map," he said. "I miss Merritt every day, but as for what I did wrong—starting again is uncharted territory. Everyone has to feel their own way through. But now, every day, I wake up, and I call my sister. And then I call my mother. And then, because I can't call him, I light a candle for Merritt."

That night I tried lighting a candle for Constance. I bought the candle in a drugstore—it was the big kind in a glass jar—and back in my room I thought about Constance and I lit it and nothing happened.

———

I drove over to Adam's office to talk to him about it. I sat across from him at his wide messy desk and spelled it all out for him.

"I don't know what you want," Adam said when I was done.

I didn't know what to say. I didn't know what I wanted either. I wanted to solve the mystery of the bee. I wanted Adam to like me. I wanted Adam to be Constance. I wanted to be happy, or at least to envision what happiness might look like. I wanted to be the best detective in the world. I wanted to take every ounce of pain I had ever felt and condense it and transform it into something terrible and beautiful and throw it back to the world and say *Now do you see how wrong you were? Don't you fucking see it?*

"So should I keep going?" I finally asked.

"I'm not your boss," Adam said.

"Well, it's your case," I said.

"My case is closed," Adam said. He said it as if he were talking to a child. As if I needed things explained to me. Which apparently I did. Adam went on, "Whatever you do next is up to you."

I sat there for another minute and neither of us said anything until finally I said, "Well, OK. Thanks," and Adam gave me one of his little non-smiles and I walked out. Out on Sunset the sun was coming down like an atomic bomb and I realized I'd forgotten to bring in my papers for Adam to sign. My hours. I'd left the papers in my hotel room.

A woman came up to me. She was about fifty, maybe, and wore an old pair of sweatpants and a halter top and plastic flip-flops. She was sunburned and dirty and was maybe homeless or sick or maybe just drunk or very poor. The lines between categories of undesirability were easily blurred, as I knew all too well. Start off as just poor and it was pretty easy to get to homeless and addicted. Start off addicted and it was a short walk to poor.

"You got a quarter?" she asked. I didn't but I had a dollar and so I gave her that instead.

"You're a good girl," the woman said. "You're a nice kid."

They were the kindest words anyone had spoken to me all week. Likely all year. Possibly ever.

I could have gone back to San Francisco. Gotten my hours signed somehow, gotten my fucking little card. I could have given up on California and gone back to New York or Dallas or Portland and worked some cases and made some money. I could have gone to work for Richter.

But I didn't even think about any of those things. They walked into my mind as half-formed and probably wise ideas and then walked right back out.

Instead my mind stayed with Ann. My mind stayed with the bee.

I booked my hotel for another week, and starting looking for Hernandezes.

———

On page 109 of the Richter file was the police officer who'd dealt with Ann's accident. His name was then Officer, now Detective Hernandez.

"I don't think it was me," he said at first. I'd gotten him on the phone by leaving a bunch of lies on his voice mail. Urgent, murder, et cetera. "There's a lot of Hernandezes on the force. And I thought you had information regarding an ongoing investigation."

"Forty-nine Hernandezes," I said, "and I do."

I reminded him again about Ann's case and quickly, before he could hang up on me, reminded him that less than two years later, her boyfriend died in a similar accident in Topanga Canyon.

"That's not really what we call evidence," Detective Hernandez said. "This is Los Angeles. You ever been to an emergency room in Los Angeles?"

"Not today," I said.

"You're waiting nine, ten hours," Detective Hernandez went on. "You know why? Because every time you're up, there's another car crash."

"OK," I said. "It isn't impossible. But you know," I said, "it's a pretty big fucking coincidence."

I heard a big sigh from the other end of the phone.

"Yeah, OK," he said, still half in his sigh. The universal words admitting life was more complicated than anyone wanted it to be. *Yeah. OK.* "I'll see what I can remember and I'll call you back."

"Can we meet in person?" I asked, and added fast: "I'll take you to lunch. My treat. Anywhere you want."

A homicide detective's day is ten or twelve hours of misery. They aren't investigating people who were nice to each other. A decent lunch wasn't the worst offer I could make.

"OK," he said. "Tomorrow if I can, the next day if I can't."

It was four days before he had time for me. Or, maybe, before he had a day dark enough to gamble that anything, even a PI, would be better.

"I'm in Beverly Hills," he said on the phone. It was close to eight o'clock. He sounded lost, like he didn't know where Beverly Hills was. "It's too late for lunch. But if you want to talk anyway. I found my old files. I found them for you."

He said it like it was his last lifeline. I grabbed it.

I met Detective Hernandez at Nate 'n Al's on Beverly at eight forty-five. He was forty-something, worn-out and heartbroken, serving penance for who knew what sins.

"It was a strange one," he said about Ann's case. "Right by the Magic Castle, off of Hollywood."

"Not on Hollywood?" I asked.

"No," he said. "On Franklin. Just by the Magic Castle. I brought you this—"

From a briefcase he pulled out a file folder—the file on Ann's car crash. I felt a rush of endorphins at the sight of it. Before you really saw something, I realized, was the best moment you would have it. Before it could let you down, when the dice were still in the air. For now, the file could be full of mysteries, secrets, solutions, puzzles, everything good.

From the folder he took a printed, generic street map, some kind of cop-form crime-scene-tool, over which he'd roughly sketched the accident. A car smashed into another car, the second one leaving the curved driveway from the Magic Castle.

"Franklin Avenue," he said again. "See this here?" He pointed at the intersection of the two cars. "This always hit me as strange. It was almost as if she was aiming to hit this car. See the angle?"

I did. He meant that Ann, driving down Franklin in the first car, had meant to hit the person coming out of the Magic Castle.

"How fast was she going?" I asked.

"Fast," Detective Hernandez said. "That's another strange thing. Had to've been doing sixty, at least, for this kind of damage."

He showed me pictures of Ann's car, what was left of it. It was sickening to imagine someone had been in there, every piece of its front half broken and twisted and shattered.

"How was the other car?" I asked. "I mean, the person in it?"

"Fine," the detective said. "Which is odd. Look—"

He pointed at the drawing again. Ann's car had hit the other car, a Honda, just at the side of the front end, he explained. The Honda was stopped, waiting for a chance to exit the Magic Castle driveway. The Honda was badly damaged. The driver was fine.

"Who was the driver?" I asked.

"Good question," he said, and rummaged through his papers. He found a name and address, which, against all law and procedure, he wrote down for me.

"So did you ever find out what happened?" I asked.

He knew what I meant: why this happened; what happened before it.

"Not exactly," he said. "She was drunk, driving too fast, hit the car at, like I said, sixty or seventy, head-on. Head hit the windshield, and . . ."

And she died. "From what I heard about her," I said. "This doesn't sound like something she would do."

"I know," Detective Hernandez said. "That's why it's stuck with me all these years. Everyone said they just couldn't imagine her doing something like this. But she did. One mistake, one stupid night, and that was it."

He said the words as if they'd stolen something from him, stolen something he'd believed, maybe the last thing—maybe some belief that there was any order at all.

"What if she didn't?" I said.

He made a face. "I know. I know. But it was all there. Everything fit."

I asked how he ID'd the body.

"Her purse was right there. Husband ID'd her. I mean, by height, weight, hair. Her face was . . . gone."

"Husband?" I asked.

Detective Hernandez frowned and looked at his papers again. "Boyfriend. Merritt Underwood. He ID'd the body."

That was all he knew. He admitted it didn't all seem to fit together as well as he'd first thought but, as I well knew, the truth was not always pleasurable or symmetrical. Life was not algebra.

After we finished eating, I ordered us both mint tea and asked about what had happened in Beverly Hills that day.

"You don't want to know," he said. But I could tell he wanted to talk about it.

"Sure I do," I said.

He looked at his tea. He was aging before my eyes, *ojas* and *prana* leaking out as I watched, chakras winding down to stillness.

"I've worked a lot of murder cases," I said, which was almost true. "I can take it."

We stayed for another hour or two and he told me about what happened in Beverly Hills.

He was right. I didn't want to know.

Driving back to Hollywood from Beverly Hills, late that night, everything seemed seedy and ugly, even the sticky palm trees and the gaudy roses and lurid hibiscus.

I'd kind of wanted to sleep with Detective Hernandez. It seemed like a possible opportunity for something, although I didn't know what that opportunity was. It was what someone would do in a detective novel. But after he told me about what happened in Beverly Hills that day anything like that seemed out of the question, and sex seemed like cotton candy—something for kids having fun when they don't know any better, not something for adults to seriously consider.

———

I went back to all the slides and photographs and catalogs I had of Ann's work. Her work changed over the years. People don't stay the same. They might grow or they might shrink, but all things changed.

I looked at Ann's early work. Probably not the first art she'd made but the first anyone thought was good enough to make a fuss over. The sculptures and paintings she made were fascinating and intricate but the overall impression was muddy, confusing. As she went on, everything got bigger, stranger, more precise.

I looked at the last piece. Linda Hill had said she wasn't making as much art, or at least not showing it as much, in the months before she died. The last big-deal piece she'd done had been sold at a charity auction 252 days before she died.

It was nothing like anything she'd ever done before. It was a piece of rough silver metal, raw and scratched, with graffiti written all over it. The graffiti was in English letters but didn't seem to be any words that I knew. Maybe it was a piece of a car left over from an accident. Maybe a third or a quarter of a bumper.

The graffiti didn't make sense to me and I took the letters and wrote them out and rearranged them and put in breaks between words in different places, until finally it fell into place before my eyes, opening like a flower—

Fuck

Off.

I looked at the catalog where I'd found the piece.

It had sold at auction for $350,000.

She'd never shown a piece in public again.

———

I looked for what wasn't there.

I tried to track down Ann's car but it was a dead end. As far as Detective Hernandez knew it was destroyed after the accident.

I went back to Marcus Mikkelson, the mechanic who'd looked at Merritt's car. I went over the whole scenario with him. The scenario of Ann. She'd been driving at night on Franklin Avenue and hit another car. There were more details in the police report, which I showed Marcus.

There's a certain feeling you get as a detective when you know you've found your person—your paper guy, your footprint lady, your cat fancier. I knew with Marcus I'd found my car-accident guy.

But ironically, just six months later, Marcus died in a car accident himself. He had a heart attack on the 210 heading out to Pasadena. He steered into the guardrail just in time to avoid killing anyone other than himself, and left no mysteries behind.

As I told him about Ann, Marcus listened carefully and asked thoughtful questions, most of which I couldn't answer.

"Is it possible?" he said when I was done. "Yes, it's possible. One thing you learn in this business pretty fast is that anything's possible. But look at it like this: this is a one-in-maybe-five-million shot." He meant Ann's car hitting the other car at that exact angle, killing Ann but hurting no one else. "Now, have five million things happened, making it possible that this is one of them? Are there five million things? Of course. There's far more than five million things out there. Would I keep digging? Absolutely."

I thanked him, and kept digging.

———

The person driving the other car in Ann's accident had been an actress named Barbara Resin. Barbara's address was not far from my hotel, which I figured told you everything you needed to know about where her acting career and her life had gone since the accident.

Except I was entirely wrong. The building wasn't far from my hotel, but the neighborhood was entirely different; Larchmont was like the nice parts of New York City, bustling with well-off people and well-off babies and their equally well-off dogs. Barbara lived in a small, pleasant little Tudor off Larchmont Avenue, with a lawn out front and a couple of rose bushes around the house and two good cars in the driveway.

She did not invite me inside.

"I don't understand who you are," she said after I ran down my shtick—detective, settling the issue for the family, just following up on some formalities to eliminate any misconceptions. Barbara was blond and attractive and looked much younger than her fortyish years—not the way people look after surgery but the way people look when they're happy and well-rested and have some money.

I started again. "I'm a private detective—"

"No, I HEARD you," she said. "But you didn't tell me what you actually wanted."

She was also not dumb.

"Did you know Ann?" I asked.

"Of course not," she said. "It was a completely random accident."

"But I know that it wasn't," I said. "And I know that for years now, you've been carrying this with you. And I know that every day, you say to yourself, *Don't think about it. Forget about it.* But you can't. And it comes to you at the strangest times. When the kids are playing. When you're making love with your husband. You made a huge mistake," I said. "And now is your chance to set it straight."

"Get the fuck off my property," she said.

She shut the door.

———

Ann had no children, no siblings, and no living parents when she died. Her estate went to a cousin who lived in Ventura. I called the cousin. I asked if I could exhume Ann's grave.

"Why?" she asked. "Why would anyone want to do that?"

Something made me bite my tongue. I made up a lie about a suspect, blood alcohol levels, accident patterns. It took a long five minutes of lying, but finally she agreed. She didn't really care. She barely knew her cousin, and her material remains were not all that interesting to her. Then the coroner had to sign off. I begged and pleaded with Hernandez to ask the coroner and finally he did and the coroner said yes. I knew he'd say yes to a cop and no to a PI. I probably would too.

Then it took an undertaker and funeral director and five grand. I didn't have five grand. I found out that people bill you for this kind of thing. They billed me.

Three weeks later the body was exhumed, taken to a medical examiner, and inspected.

The body in Ann's casket wasn't Ann. It was Kate Duvall, a woman with fifteen prior arrests for solicitation and DUI and public intoxication. Her teeth, uniquely flawless, gave her away.

Probably alcohol poisoning, the examiner said. It was hard to tell this long after death, but that was what it looked like and it sounded good to me.

I laid everything out for Detective Hernandez. Ann hadn't been killed that night, and someone else had been buried in her grave. Carl had murdered Merritt over nothing.

We met in Nate 'n Al's again. This time he admitted I had a case. Ann was possibly still alive.

"Nice job, DeWitt," he said, with grudging grudgingness.

"And?" I said.

He shrugged.

"What do you want me to do?" he said. "Track her down? You really think she killed that girl?"

"No," I said. "But she faked her own death."

"That's not really a crime," Hernandez said. "I mean, fraud. But." Which I knew. But still.

"Isn't there something you can do?" I asked.

"Sure," Hernandez said, "There's a lot I could do. But would any of it be, you know, a good use of taxpayers' time and money? No. It's a mystery how the woman, Kate, got in the coffin. Probably found her somewhere, or bought her from a hospital. People do all kinds of fucked-up shit. There's lots of ways to get bodies. You wouldn't believe it. Experiments, black magic, switcheroos like this. It's a whole black market. Anyway. I got eleven murder books on my desk. Fresh. This isn't a priority. It isn't my job to hunt down every little aspect of the truth," Hernandez said. "Maybe that's your job. I don't know. I just try to solve murders. Looks like she wanted to disappear," Hernandez said. "Maybe she had a good reason. Why not let her?"

———

I didn't know if she had a good reason, or what a good reason would be. It seemed like if she was in trouble, she had resources for help.

Carl hadn't seemed like a threat. If women disappeared over men like Carl there would be none of us left. And I was sure Merritt must have been in on it—I figured she was escaping with his help, not from him.

So why would a successful and rich and beautiful woman want to abandon her life? A woman who was marketable, profitable, and attractive to just about everyone she met? A woman with the eyes of Los Angeles and New York on her back? A woman men wanted to sleep with, men wanted to marry, a woman men wanted to solve and to fix? A woman other women envied, and wanted to be, and would imitate, and followed?

The more I thought about it, the more I came up with a better question.

Why wouldn't she?

———

Kate, the woman in Ann's coffin, had a daughter who lived in Venice. We walked down the boardwalk together and I told her about her mother. The daughter's name was Leanne. She was a bartender at a bar on the boardwalk. She fed a bunch of stray cats who lived behind the bar. She was thirty-seven and sun-wrinkled.

"Believe it or not," she said, "I really loved my mother."

"I believe it," I said.

"You know," she said, "this guy I study with. He says at any given moment we're all just doing the best we can. I don't know if that's true about everyone, but it's true about my mother. She did the best she could. She was an alcoholic and a prostitute. That was the best she could do. She worked very, very hard to be where she was. She could have been a lot worse."

I asked her to tell me something wonderful about her mother.

"My mother loved to dance," she said. "When she was younger, and she had boyfriends, she would make them take her out. When she was older, and no one wanted to be around her, she would put on her records—she lived in this little room down on Sixth Street—and dance around by herself, until they would bang on the door and make her turn the music off. Now I do that. I put music on and dance alone in my room. It's . . . joyous. As long as you can move, it's a joy no one can take away from you."

We sat on a bench on the boardwalk and Leanne cried harder and longer than I'd ever heard anyone cry in my life.

———

I went through the files again—mine, Adam's, Richter's. I stayed in my hotel for two days. I ate nuts and yogurt and beef jerky from the gas station on the corner. I read through every interview, all my notes, everything I'd seen or thought or heard.

I found nothing.

At the end of the second day I got dressed, got in my car, and drove around. I drove up Hollywood Boulevard and down to Santa Monica Boulevard. No one had a sign up: *Drugs here. Good facsimile of companionship.*

But you know. You can tell.

I parked on a side street and went into a bar off Hollywood Boulevard where a lot of people my age looked to be coming and going. Inside it wasn't hard to find a hook-up. The bartender sold me a bottle of beer and then pointed toward a girl in the back by the jukebox. I took my beer and went over and put a few songs on the jukebox. The girl was with a boy and two other girls. I caught her eye.

"Hey," I said. "The bartender sent me over?"

She nodded toward the bathroom. I nodded and went in the bathroom and waited for her. She came in in a minute. She had bleached-white hair and wore a short black dress with a white collar and thick black thigh-high stockings and a ring of black makeup around her eyes.

"What'd you want?" she said suspiciously.

"Coke?" I said.

She nodded and introduced me to a guy at the bar who took me into a back room in the bar and sold me an eight ball. In the back room the guy cracked open a bottle of whiskey and we shared it. He tried to kiss me. He did not succeed. His eyes were bright and a little frightening. After the transaction the girl went back to her friends and she asked if I wanted to sit with them and I said OK. We introduced ourselves. I instantly forgot their names.

They asked what I was doing and I said visiting LA. I said I was looking for a friend. Finally I got the white-haired girl's name. It was Danny. "I'm so glad you're here," she kept saying. Later I found out she thought everyone hated her. She was in love with one of the boys and he didn't seem to realize it. Later, as life wore on, I would realize that most people think everyone hates them. The truth is worse; for most people, no one is thinking of them at all.

After that we went to another bar and then back to an apartment in Venice. I didn't know whose apartment it was; there was a hole in one wall and you could see the veins of the building through the hole. Maybe it was a squat; it was dirty and smelled like stale drugs and ashtrays and everything in it was someone else's garbage.

At the apartment were about a dozen people. A bunch of them were in a hardcore band together. They'd played earlier that night in Long Beach and now they were excited and manic and high.

Fuck mysteries. Fuck clues and suspects and victims. Fuck being the best detective in the world. I was done with hope and done with goals and aims and doing and becoming. I was done with it all. Let someone else solve the mysteries. Let someone else pick up the pieces. Let someone else try to make it all fit together.

Maybe I would just do drugs full-time now. Maybe I would marry some man, or be someone's girlfriend. Maybe I would get some kind of a real job or maybe I would give up on jobs and just be a poor person.

But fuck this life. This life was nothing but pain and useless pain at that. Joy might be useless but at least it was joy. Supposedly. So I'd heard.

One of the boys from the band was the kind of boy who never sits entirely still. The kind who's always doing something with his hands and always knocking things over. He offered me speed and I accepted. We talked for a while about his band and a few hours later we were in the back seat of his Ford by the beach doing something that was supposed to be impactful, I guessed, but was exactly like everything else.

I thought about the last time I was in Los Angeles. It was when I met Constance for the first time. It was as if a character from a movie had stepped off the screen and into my life, like a dream suddenly made real.

It seemed like my life could start. It seemed like everything before had all just been the price I would pay for this.

In the back seat of the Ford I thought I would like to find that hopeful girl from six years ago. I would like to take her, and hold her hopeful little face in my hands, and I would like to break that face until I felt her bones snap in my hands. Until I opened her veins and made her bleed, and she knew enough to never smile again. I would go back to that hopeful girl and beat sense and logic and pain into her until she understood, finally understood, that hope was a scorpion, and that if you poked at it, you would be stung.

When we were done we went back to the apartment in Venice. The best drugs were gone and the party was fading. Suddenly exhausted, I curled up on a dirty, damp sofa and started to fall asleep.

I was in New Orleans, back in Constance's house, like I had been a thousand times. Like I'd been every day for a number of days. Stacks of books on every surface and dust on the plaster trim.

But it wasn't like those other days. Nothing looked out of place but something felt horrible and wrong. It was dead silent and the air was tense, like a murder about to happen. I smelled something foul and organic and I looked around and thick filthy black mud was seeping in through the floor, through Constance's good cypress floor, the last real cypress on the block . . .

And then just as I was falling off the high cliff of life into the low and sticky tar of sleep I jerked myself awake with a recoil. I shook off the dream about cypress floors and I thought about honey.

Honey and bees. Bees and beehives.

People change, but they only change so much. Especially when they changed intentionally and willfully and with a reason; you'd think they would understand that in order to change a thing you have to see the thing you were changing—in this case, themselves. You had to at least try. But they never did. People, in my experience, never really saw themselves at all—at best they saw a distorted, reversed, mirror image. And, if nothing else, the messy and fucked-up little pieces that you didn't even know you had would give you away in the end.

I sat up, shook myself the rest of the way awake, and started looking for my stuff. Everyone else was sleeping. I found my things, used the bathroom, and left. Outside the sun seared my eyes and I blinked and squinted. I'd left my car back in Hollywood somewhere. I went through my pockets and found $19.45.

I started walking and soon there was the boardwalk and there was the ocean. I spent four dollars on a pair of sunglasses and two dollars on two cups of coffee, which I drank as quickly as I could, and then got another. I found a bus that took me as far as La Cienega and Sunset. I got off there and got more coffee and walked the five miles back to my hotel.

Back in my room I took off my clothes and took a long shower. Then I dried off, got dressed again, and went back to my files.

I started again.

I looked at Ann's Beehives, projected through the dark against the white door to my bathroom. Some of them looked like real beehives and some, obviously, were some kind of metaphor.

I went back to all of her catalogs. In the last one she had a long artist's statement about the work. I didn't understand all of it. I wasn't sure I really understood any of it. It was a full page of fine-type text. Some of it was about paint and pigments that came from flowers and insects. A lot of it was about bees and matriarchy and the history of beekeeping. There was a long list of citations at the end.

After that I found my car. It hadn't been towed but there were a handful of tickets on the windshield. I threw them out and drove to Chinatown, where I had tea and steamed ginger fish for lunch, and then I went to the library and spent the rest of the day and the next day and the next day reading about bees.

There was no such magazine as *Beekeeper's Quarterly*, as I'd hoped. But there was *Beekeeping Times*. The library had three years' worth of back issues. I read them all. On the third day at 11:11 on the forty-fourth page of the thirteenth issue of the ninety-ninth volume of *Beekeeping Times*, I found a letter to the editor:

To the Editors:

Please note that, contrary to what Mr. Addelson states in his September 15 article "Nothing New Under the Sun: Ancient Trends in Beekeeping," most ancient images of, and references to, beekeepers were not "high-status men" but women. Archeological and scholarly research, combined with ethnographical analysis of beekeeping cultures around the world, confirms that women were always at least as prominent as beekeepers as males. Perhaps, in some spheres, more so. The author may want to examine Emilia Gustav's survey Blood & Wax: A History of Women & Bees.

Sincerely,

KA

Fayetteville, AR

I went back to the artist's statement I'd read by Ann. I checked the citations at the end. There it was in her bibliography, third after R. J. Revice's *Natural Pigments* and Eleanor Vraylon's *The Equine in Art*. Emilia Gustav's *Blood & Wax: A History of Women & Bees*. I was already in the library, so it took just a few minutes to find out that *Blood & Wax: A History of Women & Bees* was not in this library, or any other in Los Angeles. It was not a common book.

Of course, I couldn't prove Ann had written the letter. And I didn't know if anything in the letter—the stuff about bees—was true. Or what kind of person would think it was true.

But I felt I could say for sure that it could have been her. And that if Ann was alive, she would not be in Fayetteville, AR, and would not be using the initials KA.

———

The beekeepers didn't cave as easily as I'd hoped. They were a pretty antiauthoritarian bunch, which I hadn't expected. Only one of the people on the *Beekeeping Times* masthead lived nearby, in Ventura, a little town northwest of Los Angeles.

I drove up there and figured I'd charm whatever I needed out of her with my slick urban wiles.

"If you don't have a warrant," Maggie Simowitz said, standing six feet tall in her white beekeeping gear, "you can fuck yourself, and get off of my property."

"I'm not a cop," I said. "I'm actually—"

"Get off my property," she said. "Before I let my fucking bees out."

I got off her property. I reserved my hotel room in Hollywood for another week. I couldn't get anyone at *Beekeeping News* or any other beekeeping concern to talk to me. I guessed they figured they could live off honey and propolis and fuck the rest of the world. They had bees and honey; we had bad ideas and guns.

Finally, after ten days, I figured out how to get their subscriber

list. I bought it. It took another thirty-five hundred bucks that I didn't
have, and I had to fabricate an elaborate scheme about working for
an upscale marketing agency, involving stolen letterhead and a PO
box that cost me eighty dollars more, but it worked. Eight days later
I got the list in the mail. The marketing company I'd bought it from
would bill me.

It was nine hundred names long.

I assumed if Ann had a new identity she would be smart enough
to stick to it consistently. So I didn't worry about her using a man's
name or having layers of false identity laid into her magazine
subscriptions.

I figured she'd started again.

———

Tyler wasn't his real name. It was good enough for me. I'd met him a
few years back on the Case of the Silent Owl. I hadn't quite believed
him when he told me computers could talk to each other, but now
it seemed to be an established fact. They had talked and were talking
and no doubt were having conversations all on their own, without
any input from dull mortals and their flesh.

Tyler lived in a loft by Skid Row with high ceilings and dirty
windows patched with plywood and wires everywhere: computers,
keyboards, guitars, boxes with dials and buttons and switches, some
of which were musical instruments and some of which were computer things. He was about my age and blond and would have been
attractive if he did things like wash his hair or change his clothes or
cover up the bad math tattoos on his arms.

I went to him with the list of five hundred women.

"So what'd you want to know about them?" Tyler asked.

"Anything?" I asked. "Everything?"

I sat on a dirty sofa near the main computer area in one corner. A
guy slept on another dirty sofa across the room. As Tyler and I spoke

the other guy woke up, scratched himself, noticed me, said nothing, and began brewing a pot of what I guessed was coffee on a hot plate.

"Can I have some?" I called out. "If it's coffee?"

"Yeah OK," the guy said.

"Well, sure," Tyler said, referring to my earlier question and not the coffee. Or maybe also the coffee. "If you have infinite money and unlimited time, that sounds good. Otherwise maybe let's have a plan."

The guy brought me coffee in a chipped white mug with red hearts on it and Tyler and I came up with a plan. Tyler would train his electronics to sift through the women by age and reality—the degree to which he could, with the internet's web spinning into newspapers, county databases, and hospital records, verify any of these women existed. I would pay him five hundred dollars, which I would pay him in the near future. If he told anyone, or I didn't pay him, we were fairly likely to kill or at least wound each other. We'd both figured that out fast enough on the Case of the Silent Owl. So no worries there.

Three days later he came back to me with a list of nine women who could be Ann. I'd spent those three days reading more about bees and reading more about art and generally making a pain out of myself in the library.

This time in the big loft near Skid Row the guy who made coffee was gone but there were two girls on the dirty sofa, not sleeping, sitting up and smoking and talking about other girls they knew. The girls both had black hair shaved around the nape of the neck and tattoos on their shoulder and minimal clothes. They looked about twenty.

"Hey," I said to them.

"Hey," one of the girls said back. "I like your hair."

I thanked her and said I liked her tattoos. I asked if she was going to make coffee and she said no but the other girl said she could and she wouldn't mind some and so she did. I found Tyler in his computer corner.

"Hey," I said.

"Lady," he said. "Girl."

"*Claire's* good," I said. "*Claire* is cool."

"OK, CLAIRE," he said, and he told me about the nine women who could be Ann.

Three of the women I dismissed out of hand. One lived in the dull suburbs of Atlanta, one in the cold suburbs outside of Cleveland, one in a housing project in Chicago. I didn't figure any of them for Ann.

That left six.

While I was there I asked him to poke around and see what was out there about Ann and he did.

"You know about the lawsuit?" Tyler said.

I did know about the lawsuit, but I'd forgotten. An old newspaper article from 1992 glowed on the page: "Artist Sues Technology Firm."

"Well," Tyler said. "Let's look at the lawsuit."

Ann had sued a technology company that did something with computers for using one of her images as their logo. They'd put it on T-shirts. The lawyer asked Ann what the harm was. Even if the designer had drawn some inspiration from her work, so what? Who did it hurt?

(*silence*)

(*silence*)

Q: Would you like to—

A: No, I heard the question, I just—I mean. Do you know what you're asking me here?

(*silence*)

A: Imagine taking a knife. Imagine taking a nice big kitchen knife and putting it right here—(*indicates central torso*). Can you imagine that? Are you all with me? Now imagine taking that razor and you cut. You cut and you cut and you cut—and it hurts like hell, it hurts just like you think it does—and you bleed until you find something inside you—until you find something good enough and pure enough and broken enough that you—that this is the very best part of you, this is the essence of you, this is all of your pain and all of your joy compressed into this little, this bloody little thing, like an organ, like a material manifestation of your soul—you cut and you cut until you find this secret thing, this nameless thing, and at great, you know, great personal fucking expense you cut some more and you tear this fucking thing out of yourself, and you leave yourself bloody and raw, and hopefully everyone else in the room too, hopefully you are all in this together, all of you, you know, traumatized or enlightened or whatever by this.

And that thing we find, that thing we find when we cut, is the best thing we have. It's all we leave behind when we're gone. And your client wants to use it to do the single most boring, useless thing on earth: make money.

(*silence*)

———

I felt there were three things in the world: there was me and there was Ann and there was the mystery between us. And for no reason that made any sense and for no reason I could put into words; even though it was now technically illegal—me not having my license and no longer being under Adam's supervision—; even though it was putting me even further in the money-hole I'd dug for myself, my debt to Tyler growing by the moment, hotel bills piling up and no paying jobs in sight; even though no one had hired me, even though no one cared; even though everyone missed Ann and no one would miss me; even though Ann was loved and I was (at best) hated; even though Ann wanted to be lost and I was praying every day to be found—for no reason at all the only thing that mattered, the only thing that was real, was solving that mystery and if I got hurt or if I got lost or if I died—no matter what came in my way and no matter who came in my way I was going to solve it. I was going to solve it and there was nothing else except solving it, and everything that before the case that had seemed like real life was now just an undifferentiated mass of gray because I had this.

I had a case. I had a mystery.

———

The first woman who wasn't Ann was dead and had last been seen in Maryland. The second had lived in Pensacola, Florida. She had moved and I never found her but I could tell by the sad and wrong color of periwinkle blue she'd painted her house it wasn't Ann. The third woman was a married Korean American woman with four children in Oregon.

The fourth was Ann. I guessed she wouldn't live too far from the sea and I was right. I promised her I would never reveal the place. I haven't and I won't.

Ann's house was about eighty years old. It was a small, plain, gray house a few blocks from the ocean and a few blocks another way from the island's small downtown. Out front was a garden of what I thought were wildflowers and a few fruit trees. It was a lazy place full of nothing. The island was not a resort. People rode bikes or drove small cars or, if they needed them, pickup trucks.

Two chickens roamed around, one red and one black.

I didn't know what to do. A few monarch butterflies poked around at the wildflowers.

There was a fence around the property. I walked down the length of it. At the end was a driveway-type space along the side of the house.

I looked down the driveway-type space between the houses.

The first thing I saw were sparks. There was a gap between the edge of the fence and the start of the neighbor's fence, and I slipped through it and walked toward the sparks.

As I got closer I saw the sparks were coming from a welding set-up. She was joining together parts of steel that looked like some kind of car she was turning into a snake. The thing was about ten feet long and somehow at the same time seemed both like a pile of rusty garbage and like a living, vibrant, snake that might lift its head up any second.

She was older now, with gray curls mixed in with her black hair. When she took off her safety glasses I saw she had lines around her eyes.

When she saw me she knew. I don't know how she knew—no one had ever pegged me for security before—but she did.

"So I guess you came to charge me with something or other?" she called out across the yard. She looked different but in her face I saw some of the hardness from her *Vogue* photo. I wouldn't want to fight her. I would win, of course, but it would be a long and ugly fight before that happened.

Not that I wanted a fight.

"No," I said, frowning. "I just came—"

She looked at me.

"I came," I began again. "I. I came because."

I started to cry.

"Come in," she said.

———

In her house she asked me not to tell anyone what she said or what we spoke about. She said a mystery was not a bad piece of art for her to leave behind. She said after she died she wanted it all to come out piece by piece, like a giant puzzle.

"I want it to have meaning," she said. "And I want it to be delightful."

I ran my theory of the case by her and I had it pretty much right. She wouldn't tell me what I didn't know—where she got the body, how she and Merritt kept in touch, what happened to all her money, when she drew the bee—but she did confirm what I already suspected.

"People kept my secrets," she said. "I owe it to them to keep theirs."

She wasn't surprised about Carl. She'd seen it in the papers, and she'd always suspected him, anyway. I told her the details and she was interested and sad. She cried a little when she talked about Merritt. She told me about opening the paper one day and seeing his death there on the front page, under the fold, like a bad joke. She said she actually looked around the room, thinking for a moment that maybe Merritt was there, playing a trick on her.

Finally she asked the obvious question: "Why are you here?"

I told her the story about the four hundred hours. About how I needed to close the case. I told her about meeting Constance and about losing Constance. About the years spent driving around the country alone, about nights in motel rooms where no one would find me if I died. About knowing no one would miss me when I left the earth. About how wrong I was to think life would ever be different than this. About how I wished to fucking God I'd never met Constance, if it was going to end like this.

"How did you do it?" I asked Ann, finally asking the question I'd come there to ask.

"Do what?" Ann asked.

"Live without Merritt," I said. "I can't keep doing this." I started to cry again. "I can't live without anyone. Just no one. I can't do it."

Ann looked at me.

"Of course you can," Ann said. "Look, you *are*. You're doing it."

"I'm not," I said. "I'm fucking up everything. Everything I've done has been a mistake."

"Yes," Ann said. "Probably. That's what it means to be a person. It means you make horrible decisions, and you fuck everything up. It means you love people, and they leave. It means sometimes no one loves you at all. That's the state of like 90 percent of humanity at any given moment. You don't need to make a religion out of it. You don't need to memorialize everything that hurts. Everything changes, and half of finding peace in life is to stop resisting it. Someone who loved you yesterday doesn't love you today. Someone you loved is gone now."

"I can't," I said. "I can't go through this again."

"You can," Ann said. "You can and you will. You're tough. It's not like you're going to curl up and fade away. You're going to be here either way. But you have to decide to try. To try just a little. To be a little open to something good again."

She could tell by my face I was not encouraged. Maybe she could also tell that I didn't do well with subtleties. She tried again: "When your heart is broken," she said, "you can cling to your old, ugly, broken heart, and let it make you ugly. Or you can let that broken heart fall away and die, and let something new and beautiful be born. Your heart will break again, and nothing will change that. The only variable is if you're going to enjoy life, at least a little, between the broken hearts."

She put one hand on my face. Her hands were dry and calloused and strong. Touching another human being immediately made me feel like I was fucking something up. If I and another person were getting close, it was a sure bet that even as it was happening, I was ruining it.

"Let this make you beautiful," Ann said. "Just a little bit. Just one little inch of you. The rest of you can stay ugly and mean and bitter. Someone loved you. She was your friend. You miss her. Let her make one little piece of your heart beautiful."

I told her I didn't think I could do that. She said she thought I could, and I would. I promised to keep her secrets. She believed me.

I left, and began the five-day drive back to Los Angeles.

In Nashville I stopped at a tattoo studio I knew from the Case of the Haunted Horse Barn. I told Natalie, the tattooist, to make one small piece of my heart beautiful. First she made a box, one square inch, just where my left breast met my sternum. In the box she poked a yellow sun coming up in a pink-and-blue dawn. It was nothing like the rest of my tattoos, which were dark and not pretty: quotes from *Détection*; a fingerprint; a magnifying glass.

That night, in my hotel room, we took a bath together, Natalie making sure my one beautiful inch didn't get too wet, or get hit too hard over the course of the night. I didn't sleep, and when dawn came I got up and looked out the window and watched the sun rise over Nashville and I thought, *Well, maybe I could. Maybe I can.*

Maybe.

———

When I got back to Los Angeles, twenty days after I'd left, I went right to Adam's office to wrap up my paperwork. To get my hours, get my license, and go home.

Adam was gone.

The entire office was cleared out. It was like he had never been there at all. Not even an ashtray was left.

I went back out to the hall and looked on the door again. There was an eviction notice from the sheriff taped to the door.

I went and knocked on the closest door. Allied Natural Products. A woman's voice called for me to come in. I did. It was a big messy office with stacks of boxes everywhere. Most of the boxes were labeled DESSICATED ALOE VERA JUICE DO NOT FREEZE. At a large messy steel desk was a small woman maybe fifty or sixty. A pair of chrome arm/leg braces were leaning against the wall next to her. She smiled at me.

"What do you need?" she said. "You here to see Nate?"

"No," I said. "I'm here to see Adam. Next door. You know what happened to him?"

She made a sad face. "Adam!" she said. "They kicked him out. Guess he hadn't paid the rent in I don't know how long. I mean, he could have fought it. Instead he says, 'You know what, Marie?' That's me—Marie. He says: 'I'm going home.' I booked him a flight—I used to be a travel agent, that's my thing, I just help out here when they need me—anyway, I booked him a flight, he took off last week, says he has no idea if he's coming back."

"Home?" I said. "Where's home?"

"Slovakia," Marie said. "You didn't know? I bet you thought: Lithuanian. That's me. People always get us confused."

I thanked Marie and asked if Adam had left an address. He had. She copied out a long, complicated Slovakian address on a scrap of paper for me and I thanked her again and left.

Out on the street the sun was like a hammer and I sat in my car and turned up the air-conditioning and tried not to break anything, because I would regret it later. I loved my car.

I needed to get my hours approved by Adam, and notarized, to even apply for a license from the CBSIS. To even begin the process.

At least I didn't give up, I told myself, thinking of reasons why I might have believed Adam liked me. Why I was maybe not technically insane for thinking someone could have liked me.

At least I didn't give up.

In my head I tried to compose the letter I would write to Adam when I got back to my typewriter at home.

Dear Mr. Dubinsky,

Hope you are enjoying Slovakia and your family is well. I have completed the additional hours you requested from me, which as you know must be both <u>*approved by you*</u> *and* <u>*notarized by a notary*</u>*. Do you think you may return to the States anytime soon? Would it be more convenient if I came to Slovakia? Do they have notaries there?*

Thank you for the opportunity to work on the Merritt Underwood Case—

I realized I hadn't named the case. I had probably never gotten so far into a case before without naming it. Nothing brilliant sprung to mind.

———

The case was closed—or so it seemed—and there was nothing to do but tie up my loose ends and go home. Or go find a new home, since I wouldn't be working in California anymore. Adam Dubinsky was my last chance at getting my license. But I didn't have anyone else calling up and begging me to relocate to a new state and I'd left a few things back in San Francisco, so I figured I'd head back for a few weeks and think about what to do next. The thought of moving again made something that felt like a lump of coal form in my lower belly.

But here in Los Angeles there was one loose end in particular to be tied up first. And tight.

Back in the Richter building on Wilshire I checked with the receptionist and waited forty minutes before Christopher Collins's assistant came out to smile and apologize and show me in to Christopher's office. She left and closed the door behind her. Christopher was at his desk.

He smiled and stood up and said, "Claire, I—" and I took out my .45 and Christopher got a look on his face like I'd just called him ugly and I hit him with the .45 across the face, where his temple and his high, defined cheekbone met. He whimpered and stumbled down and I punched him across the other cheek, hard, with my fist.

Now he fell down. I remembered what he'd looked like naked: pale and thin, physically strong but spiritually weak.

How he'd been hungry. How I'd let him see me.

Christopher reached for his desk—I figured there was some kind of panic button there—and I kicked him away and then crouched down and brought my face close to his.

"Don't even fucking think about it," I said.

His face crumpled and tears came to his eyes and he gave up. I kicked him again. The red in front of my eyes turned to black and by the time I could see again he was unconscious and bloody. I checked his pulse. He was alive. His face wouldn't be so pretty anymore, but he'd live.

For better or worse.

"Next time," I whispered in Christopher's ear, in case he could hear me, "I'll kill you."

I realized that I was panting and shaking. I sat down on the floor with my knees up and caught my breath. After a minute or two I was still shaking but I could breathe almost normally and see almost clearly.

On Christopher's desk was a red marker. I took all the diplomas and certificates off his wall and broke them over the coffee table. Then I picked up the marker.

On the now-empty wall I took the marker and wrote CLAIRE DeWITT ALWAYS WINS.

Then I left.

CHAPTER 16

THE CASE OF THE INFINITE BLACKTOP

Las Vegas, 2011

Outside the printer's, the sun was beating down on the Nevada desert. The fresh-ish air perked me up enough to realize how close to going down I was. I drove in the general direction of Mattie's church. I knew I shouldn't be driving; the edges of my vision were going glittery and black, and my eyelids were pressing down. The shimmering heat on the road seemed to make my eyes heavier. After a few minutes or lifetimes of semi-developed desert punctuated by liquor stores and closed grocery stores I came across a restaurant that looked like it used to be an International House of Pancakes and was now locally owned and called Holiday Pancake House. I parked in the lot, got out of my car, and my knees buckled. I steadied myself and made inside the cool dark pancake house, where a few scattered lonely men sat alone. None of them ate pancakes. All of them ate small steaks or eggs. I got both, a coffee, and a water, and as the words came out of my mouth I realized, as if on cue, how much was lacking in those things: my stomach growled and my mouth felt parched. I ate and drank and took two more of Keith's pills and had another cup of coffee and felt like maybe, maybe, I could still win.

I paid, left, and got back in my car. I drove around the edge of the desert and the city, in and out of different subdivisions and service roads, about one streetlamp every half mile, looking for Mattie's church. Finally I realized that the church was somehow part of the small, shabby housing complex I'd driven by eight times. I turned up the desert-sand driveway to a courtyard lit by a few spotlights. On either side was a small apartment building, probably six apartments each, low and painted beige-pink. At the end of the courtyard was a smaller building with two or four apartments. I parked my car and walked behind the small building at the end of the courtyard. The desert air was still hot and it was nearly black.

Behind the smaller building was a tiny trailer-type building with dark fake-wood paneling that made me guess the trailer was about thirty years old. Maybe seven hundred square feet. A floodlight above the front door lit up the fifty square feet in front of it. That was the church.

Inside eight people sat in a circle in mismatched folding chairs. Other than that the trailer was bare. In the eight there was Mattie, in the same outfit from work; four other women; two other men; and Howie. I couldn't say exactly why I knew it was Howie, but I did.

I guessed Howie was in his late sixties, white, with a beard and combed-back hair. He wore boot-cut jeans, boots, and a trim T-shirt. He was the kind of man who shrunk as he aged, compacting into a wiry little cricket.

Everyone turned to look at me when I opened the door. As I stood on the threshold of the trailer, the gears spinning inside me slowed down enough for me to realize where I was and what I was doing.

Maybe I was solving my mystery.

Maybe I was solving everything.

"Well there she is," said Mattie. I apologized for walking in late. She told me not to worry about it and to grab a seat. I sat between two of the women, both of whom smiled at me as I sat down.

"Now," Mattie said, "we were just talking about how complicated life can be. We all say we want to be good. I mean, most of us do. You hardly ever meet anyone who says they want to be a bad person.

"But wanting to be good isn't being good. And being good isn't always so easy. Even knowing what good is isn't always so easy. Sometimes what people need isn't really so nice. I mean, you see a little baby crawling into traffic, you don't say well now can you please not. You see a man trying to kill another man, you can't just tell him he ought to be better. He knows that already. I mean, earlier in the process, maybe just being nice is enough. I can think of days where one kind word saved my life. But there's other times when it's just too late for that. We have to make hard decisions. Sometimes the kind thing is the cruel thing. And sometimes we're just looking for an excuse to be cruel."

I don't think I'm going to make it, I said to the mouse. But the mouse was nowhere around.

I was alone.

It was black-dark out through the windows of the trailer. You could feel the heat come up from the desert sand, feel the sunlight trapped there, fermenting into something stagnant and strange.

Mattie went on—

"The older I get, the less I understand. I don't know what it would mean to be really good. I think sometimes we get caught up in trying to tell the world something about ourselves. Maybe even trying to tell ourselves about ourselves, you know, trying to keep up an idea of ourselves we can live with. But I think sometimes we need to stop worrying about all that and just do something. Just look for ways to help and then just try to help. Water a plant. Feed an animal. Help the people you see every day. We don't have to make some big controversy over it, or get wrapped up in some drama. We make things so complicated. All we have to do is just be a little bit better than we are, and keep heading that way. It doesn't have to feel good. You don't have to like it. And you can have your doubts about it, too. You just have to do it.

"God tells us so little, and asks so much. There's this lady in my building. She's got two little kids, one's a baby, actually, and her man left and she's scared. She's really scared about what's going to happen next. So am I. I'm scared for her. There's not a lot of help out there for people like her. So there's a little bowl over there and if you can put something in there for her, please do that. Also, if anyone has a Costco membership, we all know what diapers and wipes and all that cost. I'm sure getting a week or two's worth of diapers would mean just about everything to her right now. I think that could really just change everything for her. I would really, really like for her to believe the world is on her side right about now. Maybe we can make that happen for her. I hope so.

"Well, I guess that's it for tonight. Hope everyone has a good night and see y'all on Sunday."

Everyone stood up except me and Mattie and Howie. The six others chatted about traffic and the weather on their way out.

I was no longer at all sure that this was real and that I wasn't dreaming. Supposedly you couldn't see time in a dream. I looked at my phone. The time was blurry but then I rubbed my eyes and it was less so.

I popped another pill and washed it down with bad church coffee. But I knew that each pill would have diminishing effects. I was likely as wired as I was getting. From now on, if I kept myself standing, it would be pure will.

Mattie said, "Howie, I think you can help this lady with something."

"I'll try," he said.

I noticed that none of them had asked me my name, or anything about me. I showed Howie the Cynthia Silverton pages. He took them and turned the pages carefully, looking over each one.

"Look at the gutters," Mattie said. "Look at the colors. I don't know who could've done it."

Howie looked the pages over for another long minute and then he looked up with a wide bright-eyed smile and said, "Look at this. This right here is something very special, young lady."

None of us were young but we all knew he meant me. Mattie and I looked at him. Mattie's eyes were wide and joyful.

"This little book," he said, "was printed by Songbird Press."

"Well my word," said Mattie. She looked delighted. "Well, just. I mean. Who would've."

They both looked at me, smiling like cats with mouths full of feathers.

"I bet you'd like to know what we're talking about," Mattie said.

"I would," I said. "I really, really would."

"All right," Howie said. "I'm going to tell you about Songbird Press. And I think we might just about blow each other's minds."

Out behind the church a few picnic tables were set up under more spotlights on a patch of gravel. We sat at one of them and Howie told me about Songbird Press. It looked like things were moving around us in the dark desert as my chemical cocktail brought the shadows to life: coyotes; wolves; men; a sea of Rorschach ink.

"Look at this—"

Howie pointed to the same circular marks in the gutters—the inner margins of the pages—that Mattie had pointed at earlier. On another page was a different set of marks in the gutter—a series of small bars in different shades of black and gray.

"You see that?" he said. "Now this right here, this is not a perfect reproduction, because one of many things Songbird is famous for is the colors. Darn near perfect colors. Perfect blacks. This isn't so perfect. But this here, that's their test patterns. No one does it quite like that. God—I mean, gosh darn. Sorry Mattie. OK. So about 1976, there was a man named Pakshee. He's long gone now. Anyway, he was working over at EZ—EZ press over in Henderson—"

Mattie made a little snort-laugh sound.

"They're not the best," Mattie said by explanation.

"It is not a high-quality shop," Howie said diplomatically. "You know what they say: a job can be good, fast, or cheap—you can pick two. Well, with them maybe you'd be lucky to hit one. But to be honest, plenty of other shops in town are nearly as bad. So, this is back in, maybe, 1976? So anyway, Nick Pakshee, he was running the floor there—well, the story is that one day he saw a cocktail menu come off the presses so out of register, with such muddy colors, such ridiculous type—just so shabby, just so bad, just so *shameful*—that he walked off in disgust. He was just ashamed to have anything to do with it. Just sick about the whole thing.

"Pakshee disappeared for about a year after that. I mean, *disappear* is a big word. The authorities weren't involved or anything. Let me put it like this: I sure as—uh, something, don't know where he was for that year. And I don't know where he got the backing. But just about a year later, he had his own shop up and running. It was like something magic, the way it rose up out of the desert. Seemed like it went up overnight. And then all the machinery—every day there was something new. Offset and also letterpress and a little stamping and die cutting and, if I remember right, even some hand binding. I'm not sure if I am remembering it right.

"Now, this was a full-service shop of the kind that just doesn't exist anymore. Your workman pamphlets and menus and all that, but he could also do some very fine printing. Hand-set type. Foils. He had some very fancy people take notice, I tell you. Quality people."

I asked Howie if he knew any way I could find out who had had the comic book printed.

He thought for a long moment and then said, "No. I don't see how you could. Everything burned. I can't imagine anyone had copies of any—"

But for the first time since the Lincoln hit me I felt some kind of certainty in my heart. I knew that he knew more. Life was often cruel and usually unfair and often pretty fucking unbearable.

But now, with my lack of sleep and blood loss and trauma imposing on me what I was pretty sure they meant when they said a natural high—on top of all the drugs and their gift of unnatural highs—now it seemed obvious that as vicious as life could and would be, there was a logic to it. It wasn't a logic a human could understand, but it was there nonetheless, and sometimes, if you let nature and pills open enough doors, you could just barely see the edges of it, see the shadow of the patterns, even if your eyes weren't wide enough to see the patterns themselves.

Howie stopped talking for a minute and looked out at the black desert and then said, "Well, maybe," and I felt my heart skip a beat.

Everything was real and everything was true.

Everything mattered.

I popped two more pills in my mouth and swallowed them with a bottle of water I didn't remember acquiring but was in my hand nonetheless.

The desert sparkled and roared.

I took a third pill to celebrate.

I was solving a mystery.

CHAPTER 17

THE CLUE OF THE CHARNEL HOUSE

New York City, 1985

I t was the Case of the Stolen Seashell. You don't know what little things can mean to a person—a seashell, a paperback book, a piece of plastic jewelry—not unless you're a detective. Then you see. All the big things in life, the enormous transitions in and out of existence, in and out of partnership, motions through and across space—if you trace them back to their origins, all of them start with something small. A look that came out wrong. A misplaced word. One single egg and one lonely, lustful interloper.

The Case of the Stolen Seashell had started off as That Case Where That Lady Stole Her Sister's House. It wasn't until months of work that Kelly and Tracy and I found out its true name and the true origins.

"All I wanted," the lady said, "was to make her see how she had hurt me."

Later, I would learn that was all most people wanted: to make everyone see how they'd been hurt. Eventually I would see that I was one of those people—that huge swaths of my life had been a message with no receiver, a dramatic story in a language no one spoke but me. We were screaming. No one was listening.

We were in a coffee shop in Washington Heights. The three of us and the lady. Tracy leaned across the table toward her.

"She sees that now," Tracy said. Tracy took the woman's hand. "She gets that. Everyone knows that you were hurt. Everyone knows that you were angry. So now you need to give her back her home, and do something else."

The woman nodded and signed the papers and started to cry.

After she signed the house back over to her sister she said, "What do I do now? What do I do now that it's all over? Am I supposed to start life all over again?"

At the time I thought I was young and foolish for not knowing how to answer her question. We were fifteen years old. We didn't know what you do once you've proven your point in life. As teenagers we were holding out hope that adults had this shit figured out; that there was more to humanity than proving a point and baring your wounds and leaving a trail of blood and bone and knocked-out teeth and broken hearts behind you.

"Yes," Tracy said to the woman in the coffee shop with a strange, strong, confidence. "You're supposed to start life all over again."

CHAPTER 18

THE CASE OF THE INFINITE BLACKTOP

Las Vegas, 2011

Howie drove.

I sat in the back like a child as Howie and Mattie sat up front and talked as we drove through the black Nevada night in Howie's 2005 Ford. A few minutes ago we'd turned off the highway and onto a long well-paved pitch-black local road. We were going to see a man named Worth. Worthington Able, known in the trade as "Worth," was a retired print-shop employee widely admired for his skill, knowledge, and love of the black arts. He started his career, Howie explained, in the famous, long-gone, Printer's House out on Sahara Avenue.

"Printer's House did all the top-tier casinos," Howie explained. "Did the keno slips for nearly everyone, menus, everything for the Sands—"

"Back when it was really the Sands," Mattie said, an inside Vegas joke that she and Howie both chuckled at.

"When they closed, Worth went to work for QuikShop—they were a more basic kind of a place. More, you know, like the name would indicate. Then when Pakshee started up his shop, Worth was one of his first hires. Worth worked at that shop from the day it opened to the day it closed."

We were long past the eastern city limits and now we turned off the freeway onto a smaller road that seemed to cut straight into the desert. Howie's headlights sliced white through the black air, skittering across the road like a snake. In a few minutes we turned off that road to an even smaller one and then pulled up near a small house on a compound-type property, not that different from Keith's, where I'd bought my pills and my gun: a few busted trailers; three or more broken cars; a couple of sheds; raised garden beds; date and orange trees out back.

Apparently Howie knew Worth well enough to know that Worth wouldn't be asleep and wouldn't mind us dropping by to say hello at ten o'clock on a weekday evening. And Howie was right. Worth was an African American man close to seventy, wearing blue jeans and a faded button-down shirt and puffy black shoes for old men that made his feet look like big dark marshmallows.

Worth seemed unsurprised to see us and let us in to the main house, which was a double-wide mobile home made immobile and set on a foundation. Inside, the house was neat and plain, and we all sat in the living room area on old, clean sofas and chairs. Introductions were made all around; excitement hung in the air; apple juice was served on a tray; Mattie introduced me and explained what I was looking for; and then Worth began with a proud smile.

"I did indeed have the pleasure of working for Songbird Press," Worth said. "I'm very proud of that. Pakshee and I got along very well.

He was a very eccentric man. Liked to come in at all hours. Liked to set type himself. Have YOU ever set type, young lady?"

"I have not," I said.

"It's very challenging work," Worth said. He talked to me like an affectionate, indulgent, zoo tour guide. "Very precise. Very detail oriented. Not many people enjoy it. Pakshee, he sure did. Loved it. Had a whole collection—a flatbed Vandercrook, a Holt & Brewer platen, a Galloway binding press. Only the best. I think you would say it was his passion. Maintained them all himself. You know, usually in these places—well, they call printing the black arts for a reason. Messy work. Dirty work. But Pakshee kept his machines clean enough to eat off.

"Like I said, we got along very well, me and Pakshee. Same interests. This was not long after my first wife died. I was not eager to go home at night. We'd stay up and talk printing or clean up or tinker with the machines or whatnot. He always had some special thing—some new ink or new type he wanted to try.

"Now, very quickly, Pakshee was doing all the best jobs. He did the menus for all the best restaurants. Business cards for everybody in town. Just the best. Boy, did we have a waiting list. It became like how they say a status symbol. You get your shoes from Gucci or whatever, you get your suits from Italy, and you get your papers all made by Pakshee.

"And then it all just . . ." Worth made a little spinning gesture with his right hand. "Went up in smoke.

"The first fire was November 19, 1986. Could not figure out how it started. The insurance was horrible. Just horrible. Didn't want to pay a bit. But somehow we got it up and running again and then, March 1987, there was another fire. Same scenario. Middle of the night, no one could find the cause. And now the insurance was really horrible. They thought Pakshee was pulling one over on them. Nothing could've been further from the truth.

"February fourteenth was the last fire. 1988. And that time Pakshee said no, we're not calling the fire department again. He gave up. He called me, I came over, and we parked across the street and watched it burn. At the end of the night he turned to me, shook my hand, and left. After that night I never saw Pakshee again, and as far as I know, no one else did, either."

I showed him the Cynthia Silverton comic. Worth took the pages out of my hand and looked at them carefully. Something shifted on his face as he looked at the pages. He looked intent and focused and twenty years younger. For a brief moment I wondered if white moths had gathered around his face and I started to say something and then I realized it was my eyes playing tricks on me. Probably. Maybe it was the moths being tricky. I was trying to parse it all out when—

"Of course I remember this," Worth said, looking up with a wide smile. "I printed it myself."

I looked at him. I realized my mouth was open. I shut it before a moth could fly in.

"Oh yes," he said. "I remember this very well. Best colors we ever did. Just now when I was saying about how Pakshee and I would come in at night and tinker around? Well, more than one night, this was what we were tinkering with. Cynthia Silverton, teen detective. Tiny print run. Yes ma'am, we did every issue," he said. "Even the lost one."

The white moths gathered around his face, kaleidoscoped around the room, nestled in the corners—

"The lost one?" I said. "The lost one? Did you say the last one? The LAST one or—"

"The LOST one," Worth said. "The one that never got sent out. The lost issue of the *Cynthia Silverton Mystery Digest*. Number 201. In fact, if you don't mind digging a little, I can show it to you."

The moths cried and I felt my eyes start to roll back but I shook myself back awake. I felt a shiver as somewhere in my body a deal was struck and my heart and mind and lungs agreed to keep going a little while longer.

We're almost there, I told my organs, as if I were talking to a child. We're almost done.

The moths spun into a kaleidoscope Busby Berkeley fireworks dance to celebrate.

Worth did show me. With bright flashlights, the four of us walked out to one of the trailers behind the house. After some futzing with the lock Worth opened it and shone his flashlight inside. It was filled with what I guessed was printing machinery and cardboard boxes full of paper. Worth stepped into the trailer with a big sigh. It was small, not the kind of trailer people would voluntarily live in. More the type you would haul things in. The boxes were half-full and mismatched and messy but standing up OK.

"Now, these here," Worth said, looking at one pile of boxes, "I got all kinds of good stuff here. Howie, Mattie, sometime we'll go through it all together. That'll be a fun time. But for now I think this young lady would like to see the one thing."

Worth didn't object when I offered to shuffle the boxes around and poke inside as he stage-directed me. As I searched he told me about the lost Cynthia Silverton digest.

"There's five of them," he said. "I'm going to give you one, because I can tell it's important to you, and in thirty years, no one else has come to look for it."

It didn't look so from the outside, but the boxes were well organized inside: finely printed restaurant menus from 1985 to 1990, proclaiming chops and aspics and other things people didn't eat anymore; business cards; invitations to Jerry Jablowski's retirement party and Annie and Richard's wedding; brochures for the Crystal Palace Spa and the Aladdin's new keno; heavy-bond stationery for casino executives and many, many casino lawyers—all of which I would have loved to read and sort through and study if I wasn't scared of being murdered.

As I looked, Worth explained about the lost issue.

"I told you there were five copies of the lost issue. But that isn't entirely accurate. There were no copies of the lost issue, because Pakshee's whole operation burned down before we ever got to print it. That was the last fire. But we'd printed up the proofs, and that's what I have here. The proofs."

As I moved the boxes I felt the life drain out of me from exhaustion and knew I was very close to being done—with the night, with the mystery, with life. But at the same time I felt something reaching up to me from the boxes, some dark and bright force pulling me close, something that was feeding me and keeping me alive.

That thing was the truth.

I'd been moving boxes around for about an hour. I didn't know what I was doing anymore or why I was doing it. I was starting to see things again, this time tiny white frogs jumping around in the dark boxes, multiplying by the moment. I knew they were too ludicrous to be real and I also knew from the shivering around the edges of my vision that more were coming, and soon—

Then I felt it. I knew as soon as my fingertips tapped against the box. The colors and light that were keeping me alive were coming from this box; in this box were all the secrets I was supposed to know and did not, all the words wise people knew and I'd forgotten.

I opened the box and there it was: *Cynthia Silverton Mystery Digest* number 201.

On the cover was the familiar image of blond Cynthia. She stood on Mount Happy, just outside of town, and looked down on the peaceful facade of Rapid Falls. A tear came from one eye. At the bottom of the hill, on the way up, was her nemesis, Hal Overton.

A sound came from my mouth that was something like a gasp.

"The Final Showdown!" the headline exclaimed.

I made another strange sound and the moths came back and they teamed up with the frogs and everything was white—

"Hey little lady—"

And Worth caught me from behind as I started to fall and gently sat me on the floor. Mattie and Worth and Howie made concerned sounds.

Mattie went to get me a glass of apple juice and Worth and Howie held my hands, like good mothers, until I was back in the right time and place.

"It's just a lot," I said, and everyone nodded in agreement.

"I know how you feel," Worth said. "Sometimes the past comes up on us like a ghost. Sometimes life is like a haunted house. But there's no way to leave. You just have to make your peace with the ghosts."

Howie and Worth put together a big shopping bag for me with a complete set of the comics—it turned out Worth had them all, not just the lost issue. Howie drove me back to Nero's. I dozed on the way there, adrenaline kicking in with white-hot panic every time I came close to actual sleep. At Nero's Inferno Howie pulled up the big circular drive and stopped behind a line of cabs twenty or thirty feet from the front door. I thanked him profusely and offered him gas money, which he refused. I asked if I could make a donation to the church and he said yes, but that it wasn't necessary. I gave him two hundred dollars and he seemed shocked, in a good way. I got out of the car and Howie drove off.

I thought about what Mattie had said. How good it felt to think of myself as kind, and how self-serving it was. Maybe it didn't matter, as long as everyone had their Pampers. Or maybe, until we learned to do things for reasons other than imposing our own fucking pain on the world, there would never be enough diapers to go around.

A show had just ended and a crowd was coming out of Nero's. Instead of fighting my way through them I stood and waited for them to clear.

I didn't know what to do next other than read the Cynthia Silverton digests I had in a large, wrinkled Tropicana plastic shopping bag in my hands. I knew I couldn't stay awake much longer. I'd gotten no shortage of leads or clues or ideas since I'd been hit by the Lincoln, but I'd barely begun to put them together.

What I did not have was the person who was trying to kill me, dead beneath my feet. That was when I would sleep again.

Or maybe I would go to my room, sleep for just an hour, and then get up and start again. Just two hours.

I leaned against the wall outside the casino and felt moths flutter around me. The wall was plaster and felt like cool water against my cheek. I looked down and saw white frogs jumping on the diamond-flaked ground, popping like touch-me-nots in spring, but not just all white now; the colors I'd felt before, in the trailer, now infused the little amphibians with light. They swam in the cool lake of the black earth, zipping through the black muddy water in bright skins, slicing through the cold—

And then with a sickening shiver in a deeply rooted piece of myself I had never known existed before I shook myself awake and my own voice whispered something without words into my inner ear.

The translation was: *You are going to die.*

I shuddered awake and looked around. The crowd had thinned slightly, but not by much. I'd dozed for less than a minute.

I didn't see him. But I heard him in my same inner ear, heard him singing for me, calling out for my arteries, my liver. I heard him coming in on the breeze like a whistle or a hum.

There were people all around me. A million targets between his heart and mine.

No more Technicolor kaleidoscope variations and no more white moths; now everything around me was stop-motion slow and crystal clear. The air was dry and the wind was hot and thick and every wave of it brought more of him. Him, he, him—I couldn't see him but I could feel him and he was close.

Jay Gleason. He was coming back to kill me.

I grabbed the .45 from my waistband and turned around. I didn't know where to point it.

I heard people scream.

Two security men came running toward me, one from inside the casino, one from the parking lot.

Then I saw him.

It was a bullshit car. He'd ditched the Prius. Now he drove a blue Toyota from 2001.

Jay Gleason. He was coming to kill me.

He came around the endlessly long cul-de-sac of Nero's Inferno from the same direction Howie had just left, and as he pulled up toward me, the driver's-side window rolled down—

—and out curled a long white arm holding a simple black gun—

—and I aimed and I fired and then he did—

—and I heard a *BANG* and the air around me rushed violently and I felt a horrible ripping across the top of my right shoulder that made me drop my gun just as I felt the kickback from my own shot recoil up my arm and the two met at my shoulder, white-hot.

Blood poured down my shirt and my right arm was limp. I felt pain in the abstract way you feel it when protected by shock. I spotted my gun a few feet away and crawled-ran over and grabbed it with my left hand. I pointed it at the Toyota and shot again, and then again and again. I hit the car every time but I didn't know whether I'd hit the person inside until the Toyota lurched forward and hit one of the columns under Nero's overhang, cracking the plaster column in two. The door opened and a man stumbled out. He was holding on to his gun, but barely. I'd hit him. More than once.

It was Jay Gleason.

I ran toward him in a crooked curve, making a semicircle across the twenty feet between us, hopefully making myself a harder target. But he could barely hold his gun, and he tried to lift it up and point it at me but didn't have the strength. By the time I reached him, the front of his black shirt was soaked with blood.

I stepped closer and grabbed his useless gun out of his hands and smacked him across the face with it. He fell down to his knees.

Around us people screamed and cried.

I pushed my gun against his neck.

"Why?" I said.

He didn't answer.

I wanted to shoot him. I knew what I should do was try to keep him alive, to seduce information out of him.

Instead I lifted up my gun and hit him in the face with it, hard. Blood came out of his nose and mouth and his eyes shut.

I bent down and whispered in his ear—

"Claire DeWitt always wins."

He didn't answer. I thought he was dead but no such luck. The security guards came and broke it all up just in time. For him.

Security guards surrounded us and it was a slice of a moment before six police cars came pouring into the cul-de-sac, officers racing out, guns drawn, ready for action.

But it was over. An ambulance came racing up, sirens blazing.

All the exhaustion of the last few days came crashing down on me like a rough wave, knocking me out so deep I choked for air. I felt myself crumple down to the ground.

"She's—"

"Blood pressure—"

But after that wave came and went and washed me clean there was more exhaustion underneath. The exhaustion of all the mysteries and all the crimes. A lifetime of running and fighting. I was tired down into what was left of my living and beating heart. My liver was depleted and spent; my kidneys could not try anymore. Always trying and always failing. Scrambling for what? For what purpose, exactly? The grief and wear and weariness peeled away only to reveal new etheric and physical levels of fucked-up and worn-out.

"She's coming back—"

"Stable—"

Forty years in the desert. Forty years of clawing my way out of danger just to throw myself back into more. And for what purpose, exactly? I was tired. So tired I thought I could float away and sleep forever. And for what purpose, exactly, had I done all this? All this drama and worry and fuss. Like a cat jumping in the air over its own shadow. Look at the cat! Just look at how clever and foolish! Forty years of being that cat and why?

So tired I couldn't even think about standing. So tired one breath was a full day's job.

Who are you if you're not that cat, fighting with your own shadow?

Who are you if you start again?

———

My eyes popped open. Or tried to. My eyelids dragged across the eyeballs like wood, leaving splinters behind. I saw a small glow of light and then black again.

———

Remember, remember.

———

"I think I was shot," I said to someone in the car.

Laughter. I couldn't see anything. I was shivering.

"I think so too," a woman's voice said. "Don't worry. We're taking you to the hospital."

"I'm tired," I said. "Really really tired."

"I know," someone said. "But it's not over yet, Claire DeWitt."

CYNTHIA SILVERTON &
THE CHARNEL HOUSE GROUNDS

"And so," said Cynthia Silverton, world's greatest teen detective, to the assembled crowd of police, shoppers, and crime victims in the PriceSlasher parking lot, "I think we can all see now that the real villain in this case is our beloved grocer Tommy Madison. But what you probably didn't know is that Tommy Madison . . ."

The svelte teen detective walked over to the balding, portly Tommy Madison and, in one swift gesture, ripped off his face.

The crowd gasped with fear as they saw Cynthia attack, and then gasped again as they saw who was underneath Tommy Madison's life-like mask: criminal mastermind Hal Overton!!

"Sheriff Brown," Cynthia said, with perhaps a hint of smugness, "I think this one's ready for another arrest!"

But Sheriff Brown, along with everyone else, was running for cover. Hal Overton had suddenly manifested, in a cloud of white and strange-smelling smoke . . . a giant white Himalayan tiger!

But the chic and friendly criminology student only laughed.

"I suppose you'd like me to believe that white tiger is real," Cynthia said to her adversary. "But I'm betting it's a tulpa you created with the help of your old friend the Tea-Leaf Reader."

"Don't bet on it," Hal Overton said. "And even if he is a tulpa, don't forget, his teeth can still bite if the flesh is impure."

"We'll see about that!" the fashionably-dressed detective said. "Here, kitty!"

To the surprise of Hal Overton—and dozens of mystified spectators—the white tiger trotted toward Cynthia Silverton and sat down at her feet. Cynthia reached down and tickled the formerly vicious beast under his chin. The big cat lay down and purred. Cynthia knelt down to pet it as it curled over onto its back, exposing its wide white belly for the private detective—and lonely orphan—to stroke.

"We'll see who's so smart next time!" Overton exclaimed.

"We sure will," Cynthia said. "After I perform a banishing ritual on this fella, and send him back to the etheric realms!"

———

And so that was the Case of the Tiger and the Tulpa. After a few days of rest, Cynthia went back to junior college, and got back to work. But Cynthia was barely prepared for the biggest case of her life—the very last case of them all!

It started on her very first day back at school.

Professor Gold pressed down on the remote control in his hand. The familiar *click-whirl-click* of the slide projector filled the dark lecture hall. On the wall appeared an image of a crime scene in a neat, modern, stylishly furnished home. On the plushly carpeted floor were the remains of a family of three—mother, father, and toddler son. Blood soaked the rose-beige deep-plush carpet. DIE PIGS was written on the wall in dried, brown blood.

"Now," Professor Gold queried, "who can spot the clue in this picture?"

"Why, I know," Hank Greene blurted out. "It's the writing on the wall—that's the clue!"

Professor Gold nodded evenly. "That's true, Hank," he said. "That writing is a clue—and for the police, it's a pretty good one. But that's not the kind of clue I'm talking about. Does anyone see another clue in this picture—one that's a little more meaningful to them?"

The students shuffled their pens and papers, unsure of how to answer. Even Cynthia was stumped by this one. For once she hoped the professor wouldn't call on her!

"Cynthia," Professor Gold called out. "Why don't you give it a try?"

Inwardly Cynthia groaned. Gee, would she look like a fool. But if there was one thing Professor Gold had taught her, it was that looking foolish wasn't after all a very important thing in life. Not compared to finding the truth!

"I-I'm sorry," Cynthia stammered. "I don't know where to begin!"

"That's OK," the professor said with a smile. "How about this: look at the picture, and begin with anything that says something to you—anything at all. It doesn't have to mean anything to anyone else but you."

Cynthia squinted and stared at the picture.

"Don't strain," the professor said. "Relax. Let it come to you."

Cynthia was embarrassed at her faux pas—the professor had gone over recognizing clues with her a thousand times—but she quickly recovered. She let her eyes and face relax, just as the professor had taught her. She didn't so much look at the picture as sit with the picture, and let it tell her its secrets.

After a few minutes Cynthia stood up and walked up to the wall, becoming a part of the picture itself as the light shone bits of blood and bone on her neat yellow casual dress.

"This painting," she said, tapping on a simple painting of sunflowers on the wall of the lovely, if gore-ridden, home. "I know I've seen it before."

"Go on," Professor Gold said, encouraging his favorite student.

"It was at the City Museum. I went there when I was a girl. Mrs. McShane took me there when I was sad. That picture—well, it cheered me up a little. I even bought a little postcard of it to take home, so I could look at it again."

"Keep going," Professor Gold said.

"Why it's so cheerful it's almost as if—well, you would think someone in the family wasn't very happy, to need such cheering. And look at this," Cynthia said, moving toward the bookshelf projected on the wall. "Look at these books here—*Curing Melancholia* and *Be Happy*. Someone in this family was depressed!"

Professor Gold smiled, but Cynthia needed no more encouragement. She was on a roll!

"And that makes me think," Cynthia said, lost in the thrill of detective-time. "If you look at the angle of the gun and the blood-spatter patterns—"

Her jaw dropped open as she looked at the professor. They both grinned.

"I've solved it!" Cynthia said excitedly. "I've solved the mystery! The mother killed her husband and son, and then shot herself! I solved it!"

Professor Gold smiled broadly.

"That's absolutely right, Cynthia."

He turned toward the class. Cynthia returned to her seat.

"The clue is not the thing that tells you who committed the crime," he explained to the class. "The clue is the thing that tells you why YOU were called to solve this particular crime. The question is never: Who did it? There's always one question, and one question only: Who are you, and why are you here?"

Professor Gold looked out toward the class, his green eyes bright and mischievous.

"Here's a question," he said to the class. "How do you know who you are? Or to put it a different way: How do you know you're you?"

Cynthia furrowed her brow, confused.

"Why, I'm Cynthia Silverton," she said. "And I know because—why, because everyone says I am!"

"Now Cynthia," the professor said with a gentle smile. "You know *everyone* has often been wrong before. Remember the time when *everyone* told you there was no such thing as ghosts?"

"That's true," Cynthia said, puzzled. She rolled the professor's question over in her head, and over and over again, and slowly she felt the worst feeling come over her—like she'd stepped off a cliff, and had only just now looked down. She tried to shake off the feeling, but a little of it stuck behind, worrying her in the corners of her mind.

"Now, what if I were to tell you," the professor said, "that 'Cynthia Silverton' is nothing more than a clue to your real identity? Or rather, a set of clues?"

"A clue?!" Cynthia said. "Why, whatever could you mean?"

She had no idea what the professor was talking about, but now that she was on a case, she felt back on sure footing again. She'd never said no to a mystery before, and she wasn't about to start now!

The professor looked at Cynthia seriously, his smile gone.

"Now, Cynthia," he said. "I know you've faced many mysteries before, and you're becoming an excellent detective—one of the best I've seen, to be honest."

Cynthia blushed and murmured a deferment to the professor's compliment. The professor caught her eye and held it.

"But this case," he said, "is like no other mystery you've solved before. In this mystery, you're both the client and the detective. You are the mystery, and the clues are both in you and in the world around you. You can't go back once you know the truth. You can never un-know what you know. Are you sure you want to tackle it?"

Cynthia pursed her lips and considered what the professor had told her. At first she felt scared by the professor's serious face and big words. Maybe some mysteries were best left alone. That was what people were always telling her, at least. Dick sure seemed to think so, and Mrs. McShane would be happy if Cynthia never touched another mystery again! Maybe she was too young. Maybe she should play it safe once in a while.

The long, black, road of a possible life curled out before her in her mind's eye—she would marry Dick, she would have children, they would join the club, maybe get a dog . . .

Or, this.

"I'm in," she told Professor Gold. "Let's solve a mystery!"

But Cynthia's joy was tempered by an odd, sad, look in Professor Gold's eyes. It was almost as if he'd wanted her to say no.

Just what was this mystery, anyway?

"All right, then," the professor said. "Here's your case: Who are you?"

Cynthia started to laugh, thinking Professor Gold was joking. Of course Cynthia knew who she was! She was a teen detective, an orphan, and the best student at Rapid Falls Junior College. She lived with her beloved housekeeper, Mrs. McShane, and had passionate almost-sex with her fiancé, Dick, every Friday night.

But she looked at Professor Gold, and from the look on his face Cynthia could tell he was serious—DEAD serious.

"Who are you?" Professor Gold repeated. "Who are you when you aren't a college student? Who are you when you aren't Dick's girlfriend? Usually we define ourselves by the roles we play in life—daughter, wife, teacher. If we no longer have those roles, what's left?

"Who are you if you aren't pretty anymore? Who are you if you aren't so smart? Who are you when no one's looking? Who are you without the context you've built around yourself? Can those contexts—those connections—serve as a kind of armor to protect from the truth? And if that's the case, what might that truth be? That, Cynthia, is the mystery you have to solve. But you can still say no. Are you sure, Cynthia, this is a case you want to solve?"

Cynthia sat forward in her chair. She felt a flutter of something dark and almost sickening in her stomach.

But underneath her fear, every part of Cynthia yearned for the truth. It was an urge that had been with her as long as consciousness, and maybe before. Like all urges, there was something a little unseemly about it, something embarrassing. But despite—or maybe because of—the ways it made her vulnerable, and sometimes weak, this urge was the strongest, most real thing she'd ever known.

Maybe, she thought, that's who I am—I am a thing that solves mysteries, and is therefore useful. But even as the words formed in her mind, she knew they weren't true enough for her lips. Surely she was more than just a tool to be useful! She had to be something more than that!

Then who was she?

"Yes," she said firmly to Professor Gold, even though the words were thick and frightening in her mouth. "I want to know."

Professor Gold gave her a look that was a little wry, maybe even sad, when he said, "I knew you would, Cynthia."

———

At home that afternoon, Cynthia's happy Irish housekeeper, cook, and surrogate parent, Mrs. McShane, fixed Cynthia her favorite fig-and-yogurt bowl for her afternoon snack. Cynthia sat at the kitchen table, listening to Mrs. McShane prattle on about the neighborhood gossip.

"Mrs. McShane," Cynthia said.

"Yes, m'dear?" the kindly, plump housekeeper replied.

"Who are you?" Cynthia asked.

Mrs. McShane laughed and looked at Cynthia funny.

"Now dear girl," Mrs. McShane said, "you haven't been eating mushrooms from the woods again, have you?"

Cynthia laughed.

"No, not today," she said. She explained her new project to Mrs. McShane: Professor Gold wanted Cynthia to find out who she was.

"I guess I thought if I knew who you really were," Cynthia said, "I could figure out who I am."

Mrs. McShane smiled at her beloved charge, but there was a little wistfulness around her weathered eyes.

"But you already know everything about me you need to know," Mrs. McShane said. "I love you dearly, I promised your ma I'd take care of you, and as long as I'm alive I will."

Tears sprung to Cynthia's eyes. "I love you too," she said, without hesitation. "But who are you when you're not with me? Who were you before I was born?"

"Ah," Mrs. McShane said with a wave of her hand. "That's a long story, and in my eyes, yer still too young to hear it. Lots of blood and lots of death. Ireland wasn't an easy place for a young anarchist with a penchant fer casting spells! But we got enough sadness in this house already. I like leaving mine outside the front door. Now, on to your other question, who are you?" Mrs. McShane said, a twinkle coming back into her eye. "Ah, that'll be quite an adventure for you, girl. You'll find out something the rest of us have tried to hide from you for many years now."

Cynthia felt her stomach drop and her vision start to blur. "What's that?" she asked, fear creeping into her voice.

"That you're a grown woman, and ya don't need any of us anymore!" the housekeeper said with a vivacious laugh.

But that night, Cynthia couldn't sleep. She stood up in the middle of the night in her dark room and took off her white cotton nightgown and her white cotton panties and looked in the mirror. She was too thin, and the outlines of ribs pushed up against her chest. Her hip bones stuck out like corners. Her many scars glowed in the dim moonlight.

She felt like she was looking at a ghost.

Who was she? Who was this woman with this slim, pale, body? With these scars from fights and falls and bad luck? With the small tattoo of the Unspeakable Symbol just above the neat, trimmed line of hair between her stomach and netherlands?

As she looked in the dark mirror, Cynthia had the strangest sensation. As if everything she was or had been could just float away—her body, her house, her beautiful and fashionable wardrobe—it could all just dissolve, and there would be no Cynthia left. Just some small pile of unloved-little-girl, some misplaced little abortion, a puddle of things no one wanted, left behind, a miscarriage not even worth cleaning up . . .

But almost as soon as the sensation hit her, she found it too ugly to bear. She shook it off by reminding herself about the people who loved her: her boyfriend, Dick; her teacher, Professor Gold; her lama; Mrs. McShane; and so many others. She put her nightgown back on as if to protect herself against fate, and went back to bed, telling herself, over and over, that she was real. And as long as she was loved, she could prove that she was real, and would never have to face her own terrifying nothingness again.

The next morning Cynthia overslept, and was late to Professor Gold's class for the first time. Cynthia flew into the classroom like a whirlwind, and all eyes were on her as she tried to take her seat without attracting any more attention.

Professor Gold looked at her sternly.

"Thank you for agreeing to join us today, Miss Silverton," he said dryly. "Perhaps next time you'll even grace us with your presence before class is halfway done."

Mortified, Cynthia stared at her desk and stammered out a response.

"I'm, I'm so sorry, Professor Gold. I was thinking about your question last night and—"

Professor Gold held up one hand to stop her. "It's OK, Miss Silverton. Just be on time next time. Now, speaking of psychic attack, who can tell me how the Violet Flame meditation works?"

Cynthia shot her hand up, ready to answer. She was sure she knew this one.

"Give some of the other students a chance," Professor Gold said, with what seemed like some irritation. "We all know your proficiency with the Violet Flame, Cynthia."

Cynthia blushed to her blond roots. Professor Gold called on Randy Grant instead.

The whole rest of the day seemed to be like that for Cynthia—late and unappreciated everywhere she went! But that night she had an exciting event to look forward to: Cynthia's fiancé, Dick, was throwing a giant gala for his parents' twenty-fifth anniversary at the country club!

After school Cynthia had plenty of time to get ready, so she went for a walk downtown. Maybe Miss Elm, who owned the dress shop, would have something new for Cynthia to wear tonight—a new blouse or a stylish piece of jewelry.

Cynthia was strolling to Miss Elm's, lost in thought, when she nearly tripped! Looking back to see what she'd stumbled on, Cynthia saw it was a long, skinny pair of woman's legs. Following the legs upward, Cynthia saw they were attached to the old lady who lived with her shopping bags in front of Hamburger Hank's.

Everyone just called the woman who lived in front of Hank's the Bag Lady. Looking at her now, Cynthia wondered how the Bag Lady came to be the Bag Lady.

Had she once had a different kind of life? Of course she had, Cynthia chastised herself. No one was born a Bag Lady.

Cynthia had often spoken to the two town heroin addicts who hung around in Hank's, and now they waved at her through the window of the budget-minded hamburger restaurant. Cynthia waved back at Joanne and Yvette. Cynthia was as much a part of the scene at Hamburger Hank's as anyone else—detective work made for interesting and unusual bedfellows!

But she'd never spoken to the Bag Lady. Looking at her now, Cynthia felt a funny little flip in her stomach, like she'd seen a secret she couldn't possibly understand yet—

Cynthia looked at the woman and tried to catch her eye. The Bag Lady ignored her.

"Hi," Cynthia said. "I'm—"

But just as she was thinking about it, she heard a commotion up ahead and ran to the scene—just in time to see Hal Overton running out of the First Bank of Rapid Falls with a bag full of cash!

Without a second thought, Cynthia gave chase to the seasoned criminal. She thought she lost him when he made a swift left on Maple, but Cynthia knew the streets of Rapid Falls better than her own teeth, and she took the alleyways (and cut through Old Mr. Smithee's yard) to meet up with Hal Overton over by the slaughterhouse on Route 3.

Cynthia came out of the maze of alleyways just in time to see Overton heading into the slaughterhouse. Fuck. Cynthia's lungs burned, but there was no time to catch her breath as she followed Overton into the dank, foreboding place.

The smell of blood and shit and the cries of animals hit Cynthia like a tidal wave when the door to the filthy slaughterhouse closed behind her. How often the lama had encouraged her to visit the charnel house to remind her of the brief sweetness of life—and now here she was!

But there was no time to meditate. With quiet stealth, Cynthia weaved through shit and cattle as she looked for Hal Overton. She caught him for a brief second by the pens, but lost him after one quick blow from his fist caused her to slip and fall in a mess of blood. In a moment she was up on her feet again and back on the chase.

She followed Overton back outside, through a horrible labyrinth of caged animals screaming for freedom, and out to the docks beyond.

Stumbling with exhaustion and shock, mind numb and past fear, Cynthia finally had Hal Overton cornered—at the end of the longest pier in Rapid Falls.

The two nemeses stood at the edge of the pier as the sun went down over the Great Unfathomable Lake. Both the detective and the criminal, wet with sweat and blood, smell of death and shit clinging to them, panted and looked at each other.

"Hal Overton," the charming young detective said, regaining her spunk. "I see that Sheriff Brown has let you out on a technicality again."

"Sure. And I hear you're on a big case, kid," the villain said, making a smirk with his horrible, swarthy, lips.

Cynthia wondered how Hal Overton could have found out about her big new assignment. But she didn't dare ask, for fear of giving the criminal any advantage.

"No bigger than the dozens I've cracked before," Cynthia replied, perhaps a bit haughtily.

But a curious smile overcame Hal's lips.

"Sure kid," he said. "But don't forget. I owe you for getting me arrested again. And I've got my new ray gun to help me get my revenge!"

Suddenly Hal reached into his pants pocket and pulled out what looked like a miniature machine gun with a curiously ovoid barrel.

Cynthia wasn't scared, though. She'd been training in

Tibetan martial arts since she was a toddler! Thank Freya she wore her slacks today! With one swift kick she knocked the ray gun out of Hal Overton's spindly, spidery hands.

The villain lost his weapon but not his will, and he threw a punch at the junior sleuth that connected on her left shoulder. Fighting back tears, Cynthia replied with a powerful jab, this one right to Hal Overton's windpipe. The cruel man lost his wind and fell to the ground, gasping for air. Finally, before Hal could recompose himself, Sheriff Brown came running over to help.

"Cynthia," Sheriff Brown said with a somewhat embarrassed smile, vodka on his breath. "You've saved the day again. I sure wish this guy didn't have such good lawyers."

Cynthia agreed. The legal system in Rapid Falls had a lot of technicalities, and Hal Overton and his team knew every one.

But instead of joy, Cynthia felt a curious and unpleasant feeling as she watched the sheriff arrest the criminal. Like she was stuck in a movie, with the same silly scene playing over and over, until it became grotesque and lifeless.

Why, Cynthia thought, it's almost like we're insects—all part of some kind of horrible, unconscious swarm! Cynthia didn't like that thought at all. No wonder Professor Gold had warned her off this case!

Cynthia supervised Sheriff Brown to make sure Brown remembered to read Overton his rights and put him in the police car without injuring him. Then she went back to the police station to make sure the paperwork was properly filled out. Sheriff Brown was a bad alcoholic, which didn't help matters one bit. Ever since the Case of the Broken Wheel, he just couldn't stop drinking, and Cynthia was pretty sure he'd stopped trying.

Cynthia was just checking the locks on the holding cells

when she remembered—Dick's parents and their party at the country club! She was already late! Cynthia rushed to the country club without changing. Surely, she thought, it would be better to make an appearance, even not looking her best, than it would be to miss it altogether.

But as soon as she walked into the gala affair, Cynthia saw she'd been horribly wrong. Everyone else was wearing their best cocktail attire, some of the older folks were in formal wear, and everyone stared at Cynthia when she walked through the door in filthy dungarees.

Dick came rushing over to Cynthia before she even got to congratulate his parents, and pulled her right back out the door.

"What the heck?" the handsome young pre-med student said, eyes flashing. "How dare you show up to my big night like this?"

"I'm so sorry!" Cynthia said. "Just let me explain!"

"I don't even know who you are anymore," Dick said, disgust curling round the corners of his lips.

Cynthia Silverton felt tears spring to her eyes.

"But Dick," she said softly. "I thought you loved me for me."

Dick looked at her with disgust on his face.

"I did," he said. "I loved the old Cynthia. The one who made such special fruit punch! Now you're like a different person. Showing up at my parents' big party in trousers—and with a tooth missing!"

Cynthia poked around in her mouth with her tongue—he was right, of course. Sure enough, tooth number 5, upper right, was gone and forgotten.

"I can explain," Cynthia rushed to explain. "I was fighting Hal Overton, and Sheriff Brown had been drinking again and—"

Dick gave her another withering look. Cynthia felt like she was shrinking under his eyes. Just last night she'd felt so big and strong—now she felt like a speck of dirt.

"I think we need to admit this is over, Cynthia. If this is the best you can do—"

"I can do better," Cynthia whispered. But her words sounded pathetic to her as soon as they came out of her mouth, and she knew she would regret them for the rest of her life.

"And, Cynthia," Dick leaned in to whisper, as if to a child, as if she didn't know, as if it hadn't happened in the course of saving this town's sorry ass one more time, "you smell like shit."

Dick turned and walked back into the party. Cynthia fell to the cold, wet, sweet-smelling earth of the country club.

She felt like half of her had just been burned away.

I thought I'd always have Dick, Cynthia thought as tears fell from her eyes to the impeccably cut grass. First a feeling of rejection overcame her, then shame, and finally fear.

Without Dick, Cynthia thought again, who am I?

———

That night Cynthia went home alone. The house was dark and quiet. It was Mrs. McShane's night off and Cynthia had the house to herself. The junior detective was acutely aware of Mrs. McShane's absence. Cynthia wondered where the kindly housekeeper was.

It fell on her, as it sometimes did at unpleasant moments, that the person she was closest to on this earth was someone she paid.

The emptiness of the house felt frightening to Cynthia,

and she was tempted to take one of the pills the doctor had prescribed her for nights like this. If she took the pill she knew exactly how she would feel: first tense; then hungry; then, after an odd and unhealthy snack, relaxed and drunkenly content. Then she'd fall asleep, probably within arm's reach of a bowl of ice cream and the TV, playing trashy crime dramas or romances.

But Cynthia wasn't so scared of being scared. Not yet. Life had not yet taught her just how fearful fear can be.

For now, Cynthia skipped her pill. Instead, without washing up or even fixing her hair, she took off her clothes and looked in her full-length mirror again, as she had the night before.

Her face was smeared with dirt, made worse by humiliating tearstains. Her eyes were red and puffy. When she forced a smile, she saw blood on her gums. A fresh set of bruises bloomed around her left breast, arm, and shoulder where Overton had attacked her.

A shiver went up Cynthia's spine as she realized how much she now looked like the Bag Lady. How easy it could be to end up living in front of Hamburger Hank's.

Even worse, she saw how little there was to anchor her to this world, and what a worthless world it was.

So who was she now?

Cynthia shook the question off, put on a clean nightgown, and went to bed.

——

The next day Cynthia sat desultorily through her school day, barely raising her hand once, even in Professor Gold's criminology class. She could tell she was getting on his nerves lately. When she finally did blurt out an answer to a simple question on forensics, Professor Gold practically bristled, and after class made an unkind remark—

"Cynthia, if I were you, I'd be working on my assignment rather than showing off my knowledge of Bullets 101."

Well fuck you too, Cynthia thought about the attractive tenured professor. Fuck you too, Professor Gold.

———

After school Cynthia had her monthly appointment to speak with the lama about her spiritual training. As she drove up to the monastery in the high redwood-studded mountains she had to admit she was thinking less about how to dedicate her merit and more about all the personal problems she wanted to talk about with her illustrious and blessed master.

Cynthia had expected the lama to be sympathetic to her trials with Dick and the professor. Instead, after she told him all about her horrible week, he seemed just as mad at her as Dick was.

"Too old," the lama growled, shaking his head. "I'm done playing with foolish children. No romantic problems. Go write Dear Suzy."

Cynthia's face fell. "I-I'm sorry," she stammered. "I know how valuable your time is—"

"And I have too little left of it," the lama said. "Go. If these are your serious problems in life, we're done."

Cynthia stared at him.

The lama stared back. And he didn't ask her to leave again.

Instead, he stood up, and left the room himself.

———

That night Cynthia understood fear a little better than she ever had before.

She didn't want to know it any better.

She took the pill.

She soon found herself in the familiar television/ice-cream haze. But instead of the slightly intoxicated contentment she was expecting, she felt lonely and confused. She tried eating more ice cream, but the stylish junior college student still felt like the witch in a fairy tale who shows up uninvited, and ruins everyone's life.

Like everyone would be happy if she left, and no one would miss her if she were gone.

————

The next day Cynthia woke up determined to shake off all this new, silly negativity she'd acquired over the last few rotten days! She took a long hot bath with Florida Water, styled her hair flawlessly, and made an appointment with the town dentist, Lou Frost, for a new tooth. She remembered to ask after Dr. Frost's disabled son and felt good when he told her the long story of trying to get little Herb in special education. She could tell he really needed a good listener, and she was happy she could be that listener for him.

One benefit of being an A-plus student was that Cynthia had rarely missed a day of school, and could afford to skip a day now. Instead of rushing to campus, she had a long, leisurely breakfast of Mrs. McShane's wonderful poached eggs, and insisted that Mrs. McShane join her for coffee and poppy-seed cake afterward. They had a nice chat and after breakfast Cynthia dressed in casual dungarees and a button-down blouse, topped it off with her mother's pearl amulet necklace, and went for a walk through town.

As she stopped at the bookstore to pick up some titles she'd ordered on astral projection, Cynthia was starting to feel like her old self again. So what if she didn't have Dick anymore? A man wasn't everything! And Professor Gold and the lama would come around and if not, well, who needed them?!

I know who I am, Cynthia thought, confident and in her element at the bookstore, enmeshed in cultural signifiers and paperbacks. I'm Cynthia Silverton, teen— But she stopped herself. In a mere few months, she wouldn't be a teen anymore, but a young lady of twenty.

She wouldn't be Cynthia Silverton, teen detective, anymore.

Cynthia shook off her temporary let-down and bought her books after chatting with the bookstore owner, Mrs. Washington, for a few minutes about advances in alien technology and the government's hidden programs of reverse engineering. But when she left the bookstore, and stood in the hot sun, blinking, on the paper-thin edge of a good mood and abysmal sorrow, deciding what to do next, the Bag Lady across the street caught her eye.

Again, Cynthia couldn't stop her bright and nimble mind from studying the ragged older lady. Was the Bag Lady blond like Cynthia? Had she grown up in Rapid Falls? Had the Bag Lady once had a boyfriend like Dick? Had she, too, once been a junior college student?

With trepidation, Cynthia crossed the street and approached the older woman, nestled in her usual spot in front of the hamburger restaurant among her many bags of garbage.

The Bag Lady didn't look up.

"Hi," Cynthia said. She crouched down to speak to the woman at eye level.

The Bag Lady still didn't say anything.

"Can I grab you a burger?" Cynthia asked. "Maybe some fries?"

Now that she was close, Cynthia saw that the woman was indeed blond like her. But her face was so weathered and brown and wrinkled she looked about a million years old. And yet, to Cynthia's surprise, she didn't look unhappy. If anything, there was something in her eyes that almost made Cynthia forget her problems altogether—

But before the older woman could respond, or Cynthia could collect her thoughts, Cynthia heard a piercing scream!

"Sorry!" Cynthia called out to the lady, and ran toward the scream. It seemed to be coming from around the corner, toward First Street. Cynthia always felt good on a case, and this time was no exception. Her blood was pumping and her lungs were full of oxygen as she ran. I know who I am, she thought again as she ran—

Then why do I keep telling myself that? she immediately thought next.

But her insight was cut short when she heard another scream, this one from even farther away!

Cynthia ran down to Third Street, didn't see anything, and kept running. But she couldn't find the source of the scream. She looked down alleys and side streets and poked into doorways, but found nothing unusual.

Finally she stopped running and stood in the middle of the block, panting.

She looked around. No one was around.

No one was around at all.

"Shit," said the teen detective. "This is not fucking good."

Cynthia felt Hal Overton before she saw him—felt his aura as he pulled up beside her in his late-model Creamsicle-orange Cadillac.

Everything seemed to slow down and speed up at the same time Cynthia turned and started to run back to town. But before she got twenty feet she heard the bang of a pistol and a bullet sparked the concrete next to her spotless tennis shoes.

She stopped running.

Overton came up behind Cynthia and pushed his .357 Magnum into her back.

"Look who's the fucking clever one now," he said.

That was the last thing Cynthia remembered before Overton held his handkerchief, soaked in chloroform, over her nose and—

———

There was a green field. It seemed to go on forever; Cynthia was sure she could see the curve of the earth at the edge of it. And at the end of the field were Cynthia's mother and father. They were alive! Oh, she'd always known it. Always known that they wouldn't leave her like that. They reached out to her, and Cynthia's heart overflowed—

———

"Wake up, you meddling little cunt."

Hal Overton's uncouth words woke Cynthia from her chloroform high.

She sat up and looked around.

They weren't in a lush green field, as Cynthia had dreamed. Instead they were out in a wide expanse of dry, green-brown scrub, surrounded by woods thick with pine, eucalyptus, and live oak. Cynthia made a quick calculation based on the sun, the moss, and the plants around her— and saw that they were in the middle of nowhere! They were miles and miles away from a city, a town, electricity, or running water. Cynthia knew this area—it was one of the least-developed spots in the country, and due to the thick woods, one of the hardest to search.

She was stuck.

Cynthia and Hal Overton stood and looked at each other.

Cynthia bit her lip nervously. She'd been in plenty of jams before, but this was the worst.

"It's finally curtains for you, you meddling teen detective," Hal Overton said with a grin. "Now strip."

Cynthia took off her clothes as slowly as she could. When she was naked, the criminal grinned. Cynthia felt his eyes take in her cold and goose-fleshed hips, her bruised thighs, lingering on the tattoo on her lower abdomen.

"And now hand over that expensive jewelry your parents left for you," he said with pleasure.

"No," Cynthia said, through tears. She'd given up on solving her case, or winning her battle with Overton. But this—this was too much. She felt something twist inside of her. She was drowning, drowning from the inside out, and it was like nothing she'd ever felt before: naked, with nothing to protect her.

"Not the pearl amulet Mother left me," Cynthia said quietly. "It's all I have left of her. I promise, promise on my mother's grave, I'll deactivate its sphere of protection! I'll do it right now! But please. Let me keep the pearl. Mother wore it every day, and it's all I have of her."

Overton laughed cruelly and pointed his gun at her. "Hand it over."

Crying, Cynthia unclasped the pearl necklace and threw it at Overton's feet.

"Keep going," he growled.

As tears fell from her eyes Cynthia took off her gold earrings, the lapis bracelet Professor Gold had given her, and the engagement ring from Dick she still wore. She tossed them all at Overton's feet.

But as awful as it was, and as frightened as she was, there was some very tiny part of Cynthia that seemed lighter with each item she tossed over.

Cynthia had always excelled. Always won. But underneath it all, she now saw, there had always been an undercurrent of fear. Fear of failure, fear of exposure—and worse, fear of her own darker self rising up and taking over. Now she saw how much that fear had stained her consciousness, cut into her potential for joy.

Well. There was nothing to be scared of anymore.

Overton laughed at Cynthia.

"Good luck finding your way home, kid."

Cynthia looked around, horrified.

Overton jumped into his car, and sped away.

———

Naked and alone, Cynthia stumbled toward the forest, crying and cursing her fate. Soon her feet and legs were cut and bleeding, and then her hands and forearms. She was filthy.

What had she done to deserve this? How did she end up here? She did everything right and somehow she still ended up in this accursed place, alone not just in body but in spirit.

She was entirely alone in the world. She knew no one would find her here.

No one but Mrs. McShane would miss her. No one, it seemed, was willing to do the job of loving Cynthia for free.

She shivered from the cold.

After the first two days she was too miserable to feel hunger, but her body shook from lack of food.

There was nowhere to go. Cynthia knew her science well enough—naked and starving and dehydrated, she could easily die from exposure before anyone found her. She was at least a hundred miles away from a paved road.

After three days she knew she wasn't going in any direction that made sense.

She wondered if death would come soon.

"So this is how it ends," Cynthia said to herself. "After all my adventures fighting crime, my great dates, my perfect outfits, and my 4.0 average at the junior college. I thought I was so special and now look—turns out I'm just another victim of the evil Hal Overton. Just another dead girl in the woods."

But as horrible as it was, there was something freeing about the thought. Never again would she struggle to impress the lama or Professor Gold. In death she would never have to worry about letting anyone down again.

And then, just as everything was starting to fade to red and black around the edges, just as the ground was starting to feel indistinguishable from the air, a miracle happened: she found a stream of clear running water. She drank on all fours, like a dog. Water had never tasted so good. Nothing had ever been so enormously wet before.

She hadn't eaten anything since Overton had abandoned her. After gorging herself on water, she rested by the stream for a little bit. Her blood was thinned and her mind was cooled, and she could think a little more clearly. After a little more water, she remembered the obvious. Fish live in water, and this water was clean and running strong.

Cynthia doubted her ability to catch fish with her hands. But there were plenty of bushes and trees around, and it was easy enough to fashion a kind of spear out of a long twig.

She watched the cold water, squatting on the bank of the stream. She failed on her first try, and her second, and her twentieth, and her thirtieth.

But on her thirty-second try, she caught a fish. Once it was caught, she didn't know what to do with it. It flapped around on the stick, iridescent scales glimmering wet, trying to live.

Cynthia decided she would live instead.

She set the fish on the shore and let it die, and then she used the sharpened stick to widen the gash she'd made in it and held it in the water, hoping the blood would flow out. Some did. When it was as clean as she could make it, she scraped off the scales, picked off some of the skin, and ate it raw.

At first it was hard to swallow. She'd lost her taste for food, and her mouth puckered up at the first bite. But after a few bites her mouth began to water and her stomach growled and she ate most of the small fish at once.

Maybe, she thought, I will not die today.

With that thought the world around her took on a quality she'd never seen before—a kind of sharp reality that she knew must have always been there, but she'd never seen before.

Had green always been so beautiful? Had water always tasted so good?

So this is my life! she thought. This is life now!

———

Cynthia ate fish for three days, then found a blackberry bush nearby and ate what the birds had left. After a few more days she trusted herself enough to recognize dandelions and purslane to eat. She had no books, but she had years of study and her own intuition. A few times over the next few weeks she made herself sick eating the wrong plants, but she recovered.

Cynthia had always taken her esoteric upbringing for granted before, but now she saw how truly lucky she'd been. She knew so much, she now saw—the doctrine of signatures, plant communication, the phases of the moon.

She missed her parents.

Every day was a miracle.

———

From far away she heard animals—maybe wolves, maybe coyotes, maybe feral dogs. But she never saw them. She did spend time with birds of all kinds, though, who seemed not to know enough to be scared of her. She knew it was ridiculous and arbitrary, but she could only bring herself to kill the fish for food, never the birds. How ridiculous life is, she thought, that you have to kill in order to live! But that was what it was for Cynthia, at least right now.

At first she tossed her fish bones back in the stream. Then one day she noticed a hawk, just a few feet away from her, picking at the head. She'd never seen a hawk so close before. She was so lonely she ached, and had to hold herself back from embracing him. From then on, she always left her fish heads out on the river bank, and the hawk started visiting more often. Cynthia came to think of the hawk as her friend.

At first, the silence in the woods terrified her. It bore down on her, made her throat burn from silence. She tried talking to herself, but that made her feel like reality was slipping away, like she was moving into a tilted, confused world. When she wanted to use her voice she chanted or sang instead, and that made her feel sane.

Soon the silence came to be a comfort and a friend.

———

Days passed, then weeks. Cynthia thought that once she got her strength back, she would look for a road out again. But as the weeks passed, a road out started to seem like the plan of a silly child. Where would she go? What difference would it make? She would be in her locked room wherever she went. There was no big mystery in walking across a room. This was as good a place to enjoy the room as any.

The days got shorter, and colder. Cynthia couldn't figure out how to make any clothes, but she did make a kind of blanket for herself out of moss and dried leaves. As the days got colder, she began to worry. But then something incredible happened. She'd gotten in the habit of going on long walks every day, to look for food and moss and just to walk. And then there it was, like an answer to her prayers: a dead coyote, not too badly mauled, coat almost intact. It took weeks to skin it and clean it, but Cynthia had a very warm, dry, fur to wear through the winter.

———

In spring Cynthia made I Ching sticks from wild yarrow stalks in the special method Professor Gold had taught her. When she threw them she got hexagram 186: the lotus in the mud.

Image: Lotus seeds can only be planted in the mud. Filth is a superior food.

Meaning: All life must come to an end; but your day is not today. Tomorrow isn't looking so good either. You have one precious human life, and you're stuck with this one: use it wisely, and try not to fuck it up.

Cynthia thought about all the locked-room mysteries she'd solved over the years as a teen detective. But life as herself, inhabiting her own body and mind, which had also seemed so mysterious and elusive, was nothing but another locked room. There was no way in or out. Even if you could escape, you'd be in another locked room: this fucked-up world, which you could get out of easily enough, but never get back into (as far as she knew) once you left.

But this locked room was all that she had—all anyone ever had, or ever would. Everything you could look for, it was here, in this room—in these woods, in this life. There was nothing else. Here we all were, Cynthia figured, locked each in our room, in this house together, and the best we could come up with was ways to murder each other.

But you could find everything you wanted in the locked room, if you looked hard enough. The most interesting things weren't right there on the surface. They hid in the corners, under the carpet, behind the potted plants. Always getting a little farther until you stopped looking. And then somehow, mysteriously, if you proved to the interesting things that you would really listen, that you would really see them, they would come to you.

The less space you carved out for yourself in this house we shared, she now saw, the more space you left for everything else—things that were so much more interesting and important than she could ever have dreamed. And a coyote skin and a fish bone could tell you everything you needed to know, if you listened when they spoke.

———

At first Cynthia missed her old life in the city. But as time went on, she thought about it less and less. And as her hair turned gray and she felt her breasts sag and her face grow soft she came to appreciate her life in the woods more and more. Here she had everything she needed. Here she was really alive in a way she'd never been around other people. Here each moment was real in a way she'd never known was possible.

More and more when she looked back on her old life in Rapid Falls, her life with fancy clothes and a big house and restaurants and hospitals, she felt like she was thinking about someone else. Some overwound girl who worried all the time about things that didn't matter at all. And while she loved that girl, she also felt a little sorry for her. Too busy with her mysteries and meditations and bills to pay and movies to see that life was passing her by before she even knew what she was missing.

Maybe, here in the woods, she'd found a way out of the locked room, she thought sometimes. Or maybe she'd just really, for the first time ever, found a way in.

———

One day Cynthia went back to her camp after collecting dandelions and found an envelope on her favorite rock. Across the front it said, in crooked familiar handwriting:

Cynthia

Cynthia opened the envelope. It was thick paper, maybe silk—how much she had forgotten over the years!—with a string-and-tie seal. Inside was a plain card. Written on the card was:

Cynthia,
A+.
Mystery solved.

PS: I miss you. I love you. You are my friend.

Sincerely,
Professor Gold

CHAPTER 19

THE CASE OF THE INFINITE BLACKTOP

Las Vegas, 2011

R*emember, remember.*

I was tumbling in the ocean, in and out of the waves, gasping for breath—

Remember, remember.

The waves were suffocating me and I was fighting. Fighting and losing—

Remember, remember—

I inhaled. The sharp, antiseptic smell of a hospital.

My eyes tried to open. They wanted to stay shut as much as they wanted to open. A warm net of opiates was holding me together from the inside.

Hospital.

Las Vegas.

Jay Gleason.

I slipped into a warm place close to consciousness, but not entirely there. I tried my eyes again. With a little willpower they opened. There was a feeling across the surface of my eyes that would have been pain if it weren't for the opiates. Across the top of my left shoulder was another, much deeper, nearly sickening, kind of abstract pain.

I sat up and looked around. I was connected to all kinds of machines and IVs.

I was alive.

Everything I'd learned over the past few days fell into my head, bit by bit, block by block. My thoughts were still thick and messy, but the pieces were starting to come together. A picture was becoming clear—a picture of the past few days and a picture of the last forty years.

There are things that bind people forever. Hate. Love. Certain kinds of sex. Mysteries. And violence.

I felt him. Jay Gleason. He was here. In the hospital.

I sat up all the way. I wasn't entirely sure I was awake. It was night and the hospital was quiet. I started taking tubes out of my arm.

I was wearing a hospital gown and hospital socks. I wrapped the gown tight around myself, twice, and tied the ties. It felt like I had stepped outside of time; I could have woken up an hour ago or a minute.

I still wasn't sure I was entirely awake. There was a nagging, haunting echo of a thought in my head that maybe I wasn't who I thought I was at all.

But something else was guiding me, not my normal waking self but some other part, stronger and smarter, that felt the gold thread connecting me to Jay Gleason.

I sat up. Maybe an hour really had passed by now.

Next I stood up. It took a couple of tries but I did it. I was in a private room. It took me a few minutes to find the bathroom and then get the sink on. My mouth and throat were sticky and dry. I drank and drank. I felt a little more real after the water, but not much.

Think, think.

Maybe I was under arrest. The door to my room was partway open and I looked out in the hall. It was empty. The nurses' station was far at the other end of the corridor and whoever was doing the rounds taking vitals was nowhere nearby.

No cops.

I let the golden thread pull me to the man who wanted me dead.

Hospitals are liminal places, at least for the patients, like hotels or resorts or shelters—places where ordinary laws don't apply, and where new laws would be found and applied as they demanded.

I let myself be pulled around the floor, down a flight of stairs, into another wing, avoiding hospital staff, still unsure what, if any of this, was real.

And then I felt him. He was in room 108. There was a cop, a kid in a uniform, sitting outside the door to room 108 with his phone in his hands, fingers flying away at a text or a game or whatever people like him did. Boring people.

I went back around the corner.

Was this real? Was I real? Were any of us, ever, real at all?

Either way, game or real, whatever the prize was: I was going to win.

I went through some corridors, pulled by the gold thread, until I was around another corner where I could keep a good watch on room 108 but the cop wouldn't see me unless he was looking.

It was less than an hour before he left to go to the men's room down another hall.

I stepped into the room. Like mine, it was private. The door shut behind me. There was a chair next to the man's bed and I sat in it, just in time, because I wasn't going to be able to stand much longer.

There he was. Jay Gleason. Not that different than I remembered from when I pulled a gun on him seventeen years ago. At something like fifty-eight Jay had a face that didn't age much and likely never would. His skin was still taut, cheekbones still high, hairline just where it was. As he aged he would just get narrower and narrower until he was a little scrap of wire, and then he would die.

He was beat up bad. I was happy to see that. My bullet had gone through his upper right chest and out his back. My gun had cracked his handsome nose nearly in two. He'd live. So would I. So far neither of us had won. A draw. Or a stalemate.

I looked around the room until I found something useful—a clear plastic ballpoint pen. I took the pen and broke it in half. Ink spilled out in an interesting pattern on the floor, like a cloud in a blue sky. I took the jagged half of the pen and sat in the seat by Jay's bed. I pinched the IV tube going into his arm between two fingers. Then I poked him with the jagged edge of the ballpoint pen. I scratched at his arm a little.

"Good morning," I said.

Jay said nothing. Maybe he was unconscious or maybe he was sleeping or maybe he was pretending.

I took the jagged plastic pen and pushed it gently against his neck. Black ink smeared across his sunburned and stubbled skin.

"Why?" I said. "Was it worth dying for?"

I pricked his skin with the sharp edge of the broken pen. He started to bleed from his carotid artery. Just one drop. Then another.

"If you're not going to tell me," I said, "I guess we're through," and I started to push deeper and his eyes flew open.

But Jay surprised me by sending his hands flying up faster than I could understand and putting them on my chest and pushing me off him, hard. Blood flew out of his neck. I fell back in my chair but adrenaline forced me back up on my feet. Jay jumped up, made it to me in a few fluid strides, and in a second we were both on the floor.

I'd lost the pen. I had nothing. I got a hand free and scratched Jay's face.

But Jay, even at close to twenty years older, was stronger. In a minute I was on the ground, and fighting to keep his hands from my neck.

"What did you do to her?" I said.

"Stop," he said. "Give it up. You know I won't miss again."

I'd never heard his voice before; it was surprisingly rich, grainy, like an actor who smoked.

"You won't have the chance," I said.

But I wasn't sure.

So far I was successful in keeping his hands away from my neck but he was still trying, and I felt my last bit of strength draining out of me.

"Where is she?"

He didn't answer.

I saw now that I'd made a very, very bad mistake leaving my hospital room and coming to Jay's.

"Why?" I said, panting, feeling myself slow down.

He got his left hand to my neck. Fuck. One hand alone wasn't wide enough to choke me. But it was close. He squeezed tight. I tried to fight back. My hands felt like they were floating up and touching nothing. I realized my eyes were closed.

"Why?" I said again, or thought I said.

I felt myself starting to float up above the floor. I heard someone coughing. I tried to breathe, but my lungs were out of space, flattened out. It burned and then it hurt and then it stopped hurting and I started to feel light—

"What the hell is going on in here?"

"Is she OK?"

I felt big soft paws on my face and shoulders. I fell back to earth.

I pulled in air with a horrible sound. Red pain tore through my lungs.

I opened my eyes. I was lying on the floor with an assortment of cops, doctors, and undefined people in scrubs standing over me.

Jay was off me. The cop in uniform, the one I'd worked so hard to avoid in the hallway, had just saved my life. The cop had Jay in a kind of modified choke hold, an arm against Jay's throat, pushed up against the wall.

I heard myself wheeze a few times as more pain shot through my lungs. I guessed I was breathing. I started to laugh.

One of the doctors smiled at me. He was young, and he'd looked scared a minute ago.

"I think she's OK," he said.

"I think I am," I tried to say. It came out garbled. We both laughed again. Then he was joined by another man. The man was about my age and dressed like a detective. After a quick glance at me the detective went across the room to where the uniformed cop was holding Jay. Together they got Jay handcuffed. Back-up came, in the form of two young female officers in uniform. Together the three uniformed officers got Jay out of the room. I didn't know where to.

The detective took me by the arm and led me back to my own room. He knew where it was. He knew more than I wanted him to.

We went back to my room and I crawled back into bed, exhausted. A nurse hooked me back up to my various tubes. I asked the nurse to cut out the opiate and she did. A first for me. But I needed one kind of thought more than another right now, and as the drugs faded off I was more and more sure that we were all real. For now.

"This isn't exactly your first encounter with the law," the detective said, once I was settled in and the nurse was gone. He sat in the armchair next to the bed.

The detective's name was Thule. He had dark hair and looked like all the other homicide detectives—strangely attractive, sad eyes—except his suit was lighter gray and a lighter-weight fabric. It wasn't linen and it wasn't synthetic but I was pretty sure it wasn't wool. Later

I would find out that Thule literally wrote the book—he was just about to have his own textbook published on homicide investigations. It would come out in a few weeks and it wasn't bad.

I did not ask what his suit was made out of. I did ask if he was in the Thule Society. Thule was not amused. He was about my age but looked a hundred years older. I guessed he did things like pay his taxes on time and go to the dentist even if he hadn't lost a tooth. Those things take their toll on people.

He asked if I was hungry. I said no at first but then a minute later I realized I was and changed my answer. Thule sent another cop out to get us sandwiches and juice and coffee and dessert at the cafeteria. It was 4:00 a.m. She came back with ham and cheese sandwiches and little cups of rice pudding and orange juice. We ate it all.

I told Thule a version of the story that wasn't very far from true. I hadn't broken too many laws in Nevada and there was no reason to lie about most of it. Self-defense buys you a lot in most places. More in Nevada. The man had come after me with a gun in front of about two hundred people.

"Here's what I don't get," Thule said. "At the first scene, back in Oakland, why'd you run?"

"Because I was scared," I said. I didn't say that I wasn't sure which I was scared of more: dying or losing.

Thule looked at me with an eyebrow raised.

"Yeah," he said. "You look terrified. So why didn't you talk to the Oakland PD?"

"What would you do?" I said to Thule. "You'd wait for a cop? Or you'd do it yourself?"

He made a face because he knew I was right. I'd broken the law by running but that was Oakland's problem, not his, and we both knew that Oakland, with one of the highest murder rates in the country, had bigger problems to solve.

Thule asked if I knew why Jay Gleason wanted to kill me. I said I had no idea.

I was lying.

I had ideas. I couldn't prove any of them yet, not even to myself, but I had them.

Of course I did.

I'm the best detective in the world.

CHAPTER 20

THE CASE OF THE INFINITE BLACKTOP

Las Vegas, 2011

After Thule left I fell asleep and woke up twenty hours later, in the morning of the next day. A doctor came in to examine me.

"Look who's up," she said brightly when she came in the room. She was blond and thin and looked like a dermatologist. She was a trauma surgeon and, I'd find out later, one of the best in the world, which was why, in a few months, my arm and shoulder would be fully functional again.

The bullet had skimmed the top of my left shoulder. And there were the injuries from the car crash and dehydration and minor infections and scratches on my corneas and et cetera. It wasn't good. I could move my arm and use my hand enough to use a key or pick up a cup of coffee, but my arm was in a sling. My left leg was badly bruised and beat up and needed some stitches but was just shy of an actual fracture. I was told to lay off it, but no cast. A swarm of butterfly bandages attached themselves to the rest of me at irregular intervals.

But for now, I was alive.

I'd won.

Jay Gleason was transferred to another hospital. No one would tell me where.

I felt the usually little self-satisfied thrill of solving a case. But this time I knew it wouldn't even last as long as Carl's broken arm.

I called Claude. He'd been worried, but held it together. I was impressed. I told him to get all my insurance straightened out with the hospital and then to drive out here and bring me home as soon as they said I could leave. While we were on the phone I gave Claude all the facts: everything I knew about the case so far; everything I knew about why Jay wanted me dead, or at least terrified; everything I knew about the bookmobile and the comics and the real author of the *Cynthia Silverton Mystery Digest.*

"So am I supposed to put that all together?" Claude asked. "Am I supposed to solve it?"

"No," I said. "Because I haven't solved it yet. Not completely. See what you can come up with."

"Is this a test?" Claude asked.

"Yes," I said. "If you pass, I buy dim sum on Sunday. If not, you're paying."

I didn't pay Claude much, so making him pick up the bill was always hypothetical. He was keeping a running tab of his debts. We went to cheap places, and so after six years it was still at only eight hundred and forty-seven bucks, even though he rarely won.

Silette wrote: "Unsolved mysteries bring more joy than solved mysteries. Possibilities enthrall us. Seduction is entirely a process of presenting questions, never answers. Once the truth is known, all of the other possibilities are murdered, massacred. But most unpleasantly we are left alone, naked, face to face with both our own wild imaginations, and our own stupid blind spots.

"Life is always sweeter when the dice are still in the air."

————

Four days later, most of it spent sleeping, they let me out. I texted Claude to drive out and meet me at Nero's. While the hospital was doing all the things they needed to do to discharge me, Thule came to see me again.

"Jay Gleason is gone," he said. "We had two men watching him. Now they're both patients."

Thule seemed embarrassed. I commiserated appropriately.

"So why did this guy try to kill you?" he asked again.

"No idea," I lied again.

Thule looked at me. He wasn't dumb. He knew I was lying. I could hardly blame him for not guessing the whole story. It had taken me over thirty years to piece it together.

"Right," Thule said. "You better leave me all your information again. Just in case we find anything."

"Sure," I said. And I did.

————

My shirt had been soaked in blood, and they'd had to cut it off me to get to my shoulder, so they gave me a large mustard-colored sweatshirt that I figured a dead man had left behind to wear with my same filthy and blood-splattered jeans, which looked like they'd lived through an art project or a horror movie.

I signed some papers and was given instructions and bought some sunglasses in the gift shop and walked out of the hospital.

Outside I was surprised to see it was the middle of the day. Life goes on. Your crisis is someone else's mediocre day. All around me millions of people were doing perfectly ordinary things, working and eating and flirting.

Across the street two women, both thin and African American, were leaning against a car in the parking lot of a convenience store. One was smoking.

I crossed the street to them.

"Sorry," I said. "You have an extra cigarette?"

They looked at me oddly. I was limping and squinting, and although I'd given myself a kind of sponge-bath wipe-down with the chemical cleaning foam in the hospital, I hadn't taken a shower, and my hair was slicked back with sweat and dirt and bodily fluids and, maybe, some of the viscera of the man who'd tried to kill me.

Without saying anything one of the women shook a cigarette out of her pack and held it out to me.

"Thank you," I said, and took it without touching her. She handed me a book of matches.

"You can keep that," she said, the unspoken coda being *please go away now*.

So I did.

——

Back at Nero's Inferno I threw out my clothes again and took a shower and scrubbed myself with a washcloth and soap and washed my hair twice and put on my last clean new outfit. Then I ate a bowl of noodles with pork and seaweed at an expensive noodle place off the casino floor. When I was done with that I got a very large eleven-dollar cappuccino with almond milk and an extra shot of espresso. I'd been texting with Claude all day but I was still surprised when I got back to my room and there was Claude, waiting by the door.

I knew that someday Claude would hate me. That was inevitable. For now, he was my best friend.

We sat in my room and I smoked the joint Claude had brought me, unasked. It seemed like a miracle right now that any two people could know each other so well and still enjoy each other's company.

I lay on the bed. Claude sat at the desk chair and spun back and forth. I knew he liked fancy office chairs. I decided to buy him one for his bonus that year.

"So," I said to Claude. "Did you figure it out?"

He made an equivocal face and spun. Claude rarely smoked, but he put out his hand. I handed him the joint and he had a tiny hit and gave it back.

Then he looked at me.

"So," Claude said. "Is she alive?"

———

In 1973, Belle Silette was stolen from her parents. As far as I knew, none of us had ever found a hint, not a clue, not a whisper. She was just gone.

I was wrong. Jay Gleason found something: a clue, or a hint, or a whisper; I didn't know what it was, but he'd found something. Something to make him believe Belle was not only alive, but had been stolen, and placed with a family in a small, unattractive corner of Brooklyn.

Maybe he always knew it was Tracy. Maybe he just knew it was one of us.

But I believed it was Tracy. Who else? Who else was perfect enough, brave enough, smart enough? Not me. Not Kelly or anyone else.

Had Jay known all along? Had he been watching us? Had he studied us, like fruit flies in a jar? Maybe. I didn't know. I did know this: Jay had somehow left the copy of *Détection* in my parents' attic. He'd arranged for the bookmobile to show up on our corner. And he'd written the Cynthia Silverton books, and written them just for us. And he'd done it with the goal of finding Belle, and getting her to respond to that ad. Tracy had answered the ad. I'd seen the reply in her mail.

Either Jay found Tracy and killed her and tried to kill me so no one would find out.

Or, Jay had found Tracy, not killed her, taken her away and given her a decent life, and then tried to kill me so no one would find out.

So either she was alive, or she was dead. When you put it like that, I didn't know much more than I did last week. But somehow, everything was different.

———

Before I could answer there was a knock on the door and then someone came in without waiting for an answer. It was a man in a suit. I figured he was hotel security.

"Hotel security," the man said. "This is a no smoking room. And we have a no-drug policy. But that's not why I'm here."

Claude and I looked at him like we'd been caught smoking in the bathroom.

"Markson sent me," the man said. "He's left town for a few days. He said to tell you that your tenure here is no longer, um . . ."

"Allowed?" I suggested.

"Welcome?" Claude guessed.

"Tolerated," the security man clarified, with a pleased look at his vocabulary skills. He'd earned it. "Your checkout time is midnight tonight. He said to tell you that after that police will be involved."

He looked at us, we nodded, and he left. It was time to go home.

CHAPTER 21

THE MYSTERY OF THE CBSIS

Los Angeles, 1999

I left the Richter office and drove back to San Francisco, my knuckles bloody and bruised. My old hotel room was free and I checked back in. I didn't know what I was going to do. I figured I'd have to move. There was nowhere in particular I wanted to go, but I couldn't work here anymore. I figured I'd get in my car and drive and see what happened. I'd done it plenty of times before. It wasn't so bad.

I just didn't think I'd be doing it again.

I didn't have anyone in San Francisco to tell I was back except Nick Chang, who didn't really care. Not yet. We would become close with time, but that time was in the future. The only person happy about my return was Flea, the cat.

Two nights later I was lying on the bed with Flea smoking a cigarette when there was a knock on the door. It was the guy who ran the hotel, Billy Zheng. Billy was a thief, as I'd found out when I caught him looking for something to steal in my room one night—there was nothing—and a good guy, as I found out when, after the cops knocked me around, he went out and got me a big bowl of congee and a box of Yunnan Paiyao capsules. He'd been taking care of Flea while I was gone.

"Hey," I said.

"Letter," Billy said. "Letter came for you. Messenger delivered last night."

He put an envelope in my hand and stood there in the doorway as I opened it.

"Looked important," Billy said.

I stood in my room with the envelope in my hands. It was a nine-by-twelve envelope with a string-and-tab closure. But the paper was heavy and felt like silk. My name was hand-written on the front in curvy script.

My hands shook as I opened it.

Inside the envelope was a note on a white note card in unfamiliar script.

> *The path is often lonely and frightening, but many are on*
> *your side. Welcome, and know that even in the darkest hour,*
> *you are never forgotten.*
>
> *We're rooting for you, Claire.*

In the envelope with the note was a license for private investigation issued to Claire DeWitt from the California Bureau of Security and Investigative Services.

Expiration date: never.

"Good news?" Billy said.

"Yes," I said, shivering. "Good news."

———

That night I couldn't sleep and as the night tilted toward the next day I walked out to Fisherman's Wharf. I stopped at the only crab stand that was open. I asked the man working there if I could see some crabs in a barrel. He was a big fat man who spoke with a Portuguese accent. He looked pretty happy. Fishmongers in general seemed to be pretty happy. I made a mental note to look into the suicide rate among fishermen and fishmongers. Maybe it was all an act.

I had to repeat it a few times before he understood, but finally he led me around to the back of the market to have a look. There was a big oil-drum-type barrel half-full of crabs. It looked like one of Ann's Beehives.

I watched the crabs for a long time. All together like that they looked a bit like insects, something sordid, with a hive mind. But that's what most things look like if there's too many of them in one place, people included. We're all better with a little breathing room and a pretense of some individuality, fake and prideful as it may be. Or maybe there was something better to find, something you could only find naked and alone.

Just as Linda Hill had described, if one crab tried to escape, the others would grab it with their little claws and pull it back in. Maybe, like Linda said, the ones doing the pulling knew something the other crab didn't. Or maybe it was just what living things were like. Scared of the unknown. Scared of dying and scared of living. And when we loved something, we were scared for them, and would pull them back in to that tiny little part of the world we understood, for no reason better than that we could understand it.

But sometimes, a crab did get out. Change was possible. At least for crabs. Maybe for me. I saw one escape from the barrel, sidle all the way across the pier, clicking his claws on the wood all the way, and jump back into the giant, dark, mysterious ocean, where life was harder, but the rewards, on some dim foggy mornings, at least for a few minutes, at least sometimes, were worth it.

The Mystery of the CBSIS was solved.

CHAPTER 22

THE CASE OF THE INFINITE BLACKTOP

Las Vegas, 2011

We were driving back to San Francisco in Claude's Toyota. It was night. Claude was silent. The quiet felt good, like a balm. Life felt tangible, material, as it always did when you came close to losing it. It would pass.

It was pitch-black out. The road back to California was unfathomable, and seemingly infinite.

What if Jay killed Tracy that night in 1986, and she'd been dead all these years, and all our searching had been for nothing?

What if Jay had saved Tracy that night in 1986, taken her away from her alcoholic father, given her a good life, and she'd been alive this whole time? What if all our searching was for nothing because she was never missing at all, just didn't want us anymore?

But the biggest question of all was how, for forty years, I had ignored the clues right in front of my face.

"The client already knows the solution to his mystery," Jacques Silette wrote. "But he doesn't want to know. He doesn't hire a detective to solve his mystery. He hires a detective to prove that his mystery can't be solved.

"This applies equally, of course, to the detective herself."

"So what are we calling it?" Claude asked.

"Calling what?" I asked.

"The case," Claude said.

Silette also wrote, "The road to the truth is crooked and disreputable. But the detective's devotion must be absolutely plumb straight, as sure and fast as an American highway."

I looked out the window. The long black road looked like it would go on forever, any destination always out of reach, the moment at hand always wasted, happiness always further down the road, never now. But for a quick moment that wasn't true: the sharp smell of the desert air and the light on the blacktop and Claude beside me and knowing Billy and Nick would be waiting for me at home and feeling like I'd saved my own life and knowing I'd done a good job of it and knowing that the solution to the biggest mystery I'd ever had was coming toward me—I could feel the solution and almost taste it, reaching to me across the ether like a bullet or an evil eye, as close as my own heartbeat—and it all fell into place and now happiness wasn't there, at the end of the road. It was here, on the blacktop, right now. I knew it wouldn't be long before I chased it away, but for the moment I felt light, and like maybe beauty was possible, even—especially—under the bright light of the truth.

"We're calling it," I said, "the Case of the Infinite Blacktop."

"Good," Claude said, and we drove down the long dark road toward home.

Sara Gran is a novelist, screenwriter, and occasional essayist who lives in Los Angeles, California. She is the author of five previous novels, including *Claire DeWitt and the City of the Dead* and *Claire DeWitt and the Bohemian Highway*.